FALLS

THE

SHADOW

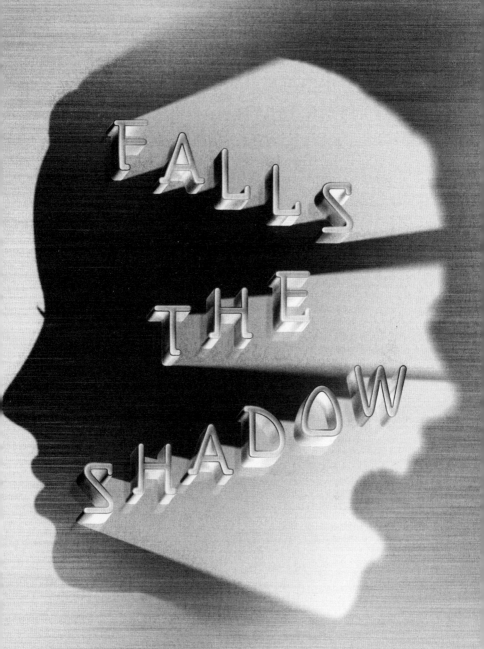

FALLS THE SHADOW

STEFANIE GAITHER

SIMON & SCHUSTER BFYR

New York   London   Toronto   Sydney   New Delhi

SIMON & SCHUSTER BFYR

An imprint of Simon & Schuster Children's Publishing Division
1230 Avenue of the Americas, New York, New York 10020

For information about special discounts for bulk purchases,
please contact Simon & Schuster Special Sales
at 1-866-506-1949 or business@simonandschuster.com.
The Simon & Schuster Speakers Bureau can bring authors to your live event.
For more information or to book an event, contact the Simon & Schuster Speakers
Bureau at 1-866-248-3049 or visit our website at www.simonspeakers.com.
Also available in a SIMON & SCHUSTER BFYR hardcover edition
Book design by Laurent Linn
The text for this book is set in Arrus.
Manufactured in the United States of America
First SIMON & SCHUSTER BFYR paperback edition November 2015
2 4 6 8 10 9 7 5 3 1
The Library of Congress has cataloged the hardcover edition as follows:
Gaither, Stefanie.
Falls the shadow / Stefanie Gaither.—First edition.
pages cm
Summary: When her sister Violet dies, Cate's wealthy family
brings home Violet's clone who fits in perfectly until Cate
uncovers something sinister about the cloning movement.
ISBN 978-1-4424-9753-5 (hardcover)
ISBN 978-1-4424-9754-2 (pbk)
ISBN 978-1-4424-9755-9 (eBook)
[1. Cloning—Fiction. 2. Sisters—Fiction.
3. Science fiction.] I. Title.
PZ7.G1293Fal 2014
[Fic]—dc23
2013035560

*For Mom, because you told me so,
and for Grant, who steadies me through the shadows*

ACKNOWLEDGMENTS

To Sara Megibow, who I'm convinced is not entirely human, but some sort of super-creature made of boundless enthusiasm and ninja agenting skills. To my editor, Navah Wolfe, who saw everything this book could be and then helped it become exactly that.

To all of the teachers I've had along the way, who encouraged me and my writing in some way or another. The English department and visiting writing professors at Lenoir-Rhyne, for starters. A special mention is also in order, I think, for Mrs. Kim Walden, for not only encouraging, but also reading all of my ridiculously long and detailed essay responses and not threatening to steal all my pens if I wrote another word she had to grade; and to Mrs. Carol Johnson, who is the reason I graduated high school, because she believed in me during a time when I'd forgotten how to believe in myself. I never properly thanked Mrs. Johnson for that, so I'd like to think that this book is at least partly proof that I was listening when she told me to keep going.

To Leah Rae Miller, because JHFP, this book wouldn't exist without her, and neither would "author Stefanie," because I would have curled up in a corner and rocked myself into an insane asylum long ago if I hadn't had her to routinely bedazzle my life. Also, BAP BAP.

To my friends and family, blood and otherwise: my brothers, who taught me all about sibling love (and loathing); Erin Gaither and Rachel Miranda, who have been my cheerleaders for as long as I've known them; Karla Davis, for convincing me to show my writing to people other than my mother; Vanessa Robinson, Katelyn Canonica Nardone, Kristin Kelly, and everyone else who read that first really awful book and convinced me I should keep writing anyway; to both of my mothers, for not letting us starve as we became artists; to grandparents, aunts and uncles and cousins, most of whom have been telling people that I was an author since long before I ever signed any contracts. To all of the fantastic writers I've met along the way—Abigail DeWitt, Rhett Trull, Kelsey Sutton, my fellow Secret Lifers, the fabulous girls of the Class of 2k14, and to so many others whose names I could fill pages with—I am continuously humbled by all of your talent and eternally grateful for your support.

And finally, to my husband, always and always. Thank you for still loving me even on the horrible, ugly, no-good very bad writing days, and also during the good ones where I'm so into the words that I inevitably forget about that whole dinner and laundry and cleaning the house thing.

FALLS THE THE SHADOW

Between the conception
And the creation
Between the emotion
And the response
Falls the Shadow

—T. S. Eliot, "The Hollow Men"

PROLOGUE

The Replacement

I took some of the flowers from my sister's funeral, because I thought her replacement might like them as a welcome-to-the-family present.

An hour's drive later, most of the velvety petals had little tears and creases in them, because I couldn't seem to get my fingers to hold still. Mother had already fussed at me for dragging my nails through the leather seats (*you'll leave scratches!*), and for drawing pictures on the foggy windows (*those were just cleaned!*), and when I absently sent yet another piece of petal fluttering to the floorboard, her hand snapped out and wrapped around my wrist like a whip.

"Honestly, Catelyn, I wish you would stop fidgeting. There will be nothing left of those flowers by the time we reach Huxley."

I sank farther down into the seat. The seat belt cut into my neck, but I ignored the burning and focused instead on the wobbly, watery world outside my window. Any second, the towering gray buildings of the Huxley Laboratory Compound would be coming into view. Father was already there. He probably already had the paperwork filled out. New-Violet was probably already waiting by his side.

Not New-Violet, my mother's voice scolded my thoughts. *Our Violet. The same, the one and only Violet.*

She was right, of course. The girl we were picking up couldn't have *been* any more identical to the big sister I'd always known. She was her perfect genetic copy. And thanks to Huxley's advancements in mind-linking and uploading technologies, this Violet had all of the old one's memories, too. She would fit right in. It would be like my sister never left.

I was still nervous.

We reached the lab, and our driver pulled around to the front entrance, parked, and went to Mother's door with an umbrella. Before he could come around to mine, I was already unbuckled and halfway outside. I landed bright-yellow boots first in a huge puddle, splashing bits of dirty water up my legs and onto the ruffled hem of my dress. Mother glanced at me and plastered on a smile. Her grip on her leather handbag tightened, but I knew she wouldn't scold me just then.

Not in front of the paparazzi.

And they were everywhere that day, in spite of the rain. For security reasons, they couldn't follow us inside the gates, but they were still clinging to the metal bars, watching us, zooming in on our lives with their shiny black cameras.

"Animals," my mother said under her breath, her perfect smile twitching just slightly. I hoped and prayed no one caught it on camera. Because I could imagine the headline that would go with her almost-grimace:

Wife of Mayor Benson Regrets
Controversial Cloning of Daughter.

And then yet another article underneath, detailing the evils of cloning and of the entire Huxley corporation. More scathing words to accuse my father of crooked morals, our family of setting a poor precedent and dragging the entire city of Haven down with us. I used to think—to hope—people would get tired of reading about us. Gawking at us. That there were enough problems in our world that surely everyone would eventually find something else to distract themselves with. Some other family to point their fingers at.

A naive hope, maybe, but I held on to it all the same.

We had supporters, too, obviously—my father wouldn't have been elected to his third consecutive term without them—but they weren't usually as vocal as the protestors were. Especially not on days like this. I guess because it was easier to shout hate than understanding, since you don't have to think about hate as hard. If I had been on the outside looking in, then maybe I wouldn't have known what to say to us either. Maybe something like *I'm sorry your daughter is dead, but congratulations on the new addition to the family?* I didn't think they made cards for this sort of thing.

So that day it was just us and a handful of bodyguards, alone with all of those people outside the gates shouting, calling us monsters and heathens and other names that would have gotten me grounded if I'd dared to repeat them.

My mother walked on as if they weren't even there, because she treated everyone the same, whether they loved us or hated us. *You don't want to give anyone the illusion*, she always told me, *that anything they do can affect you. You can't give them that control, because there's no telling what they'd do with it.* So she always walked with her head held high. Made sure her smile was brighter than all the camera flashes put together.

Because after all, people were easy enough to fool, if you knew how to do it.

I didn't yet. Not as well as she did, at least; I tried, but I'd never been able to carry myself the way Mother did. She was a stone-faced, walking statue that words and rain and mud hit and just slid off of.

As for me? I wanted to shrink away from it all, to somehow make myself tiny and insignificant enough to slip out of sight without anyone noticing. But my mother just took my hand in her stiff grip and pulled me under the umbrella. And without so much as a backward glance, we started what felt like an incredibly long walk to the entrance, to the future on the other side of those tall glass doors.

I tried my best to smile.

Smiling was easier. Easier than trying to explain our lives to anyone. To explain why my parents made the decision to have me and my sister cloned at birth, to have our genetic twins raised in a safe, controlled environment. To have them there as replacements. Just in case.

And just-in-casers was what my parents were, anyway; they weren't like some fanatics of the cloning movement who'd made dozens of copies of their children, who'd given everything they owned to achieve some sort of immortality for their sons and daughters. No. My parents weren't crazy. They only wanted a backup copy in place, because sometimes the unthinkable happened. Even now that the war that had desecrated their childhood had been confined to history books, to horror stories that no one liked to tell, accidents still happened all the time. Sometimes it felt like the world was just one big accident. Just a week before, a boy from my class had slipped, hit his head, and drowned in the creek outside town. Now his parents were childless. A year ago, the house down the street from us burned to the ground. Mr. and Mrs. Adams made it out without a scratch. Their children didn't.

No one expected things like that.

And no one expected Violet to get sick.

But she did.

Now she was back, though, like she never left.

Lucky us.

I squeezed Mother's hand a little tighter, wishing she would squeeze it back. I wasn't surprised when she didn't.

Her walk became more brisk, and I had to move in hops and leaps so my short legs could keep up. We reached the front steps just as the double doors opened and a tall man in a Huxley lab coat stepped out.

"Mrs. Benson," he greeted my mother, tilting his head forward in a polite nod.

Inside, the bright fluorescent lights stung. It was like walking into heaven. A very cold, very sterile sort of heaven that smelled like rubbing alcohol and made my eyes burn and water. I pulled my hand from Mother's and used both of my palms to try and rub away the tears. By the time I finished and reached for her again, her arms were already folded across her chest. My hands dropped back to my sides and I fell in line behind her, followed her and the Huxley man along the hallways that seemed to twist and turn endlessly, up and down and left and right and folding back into themselves. It made me dizzy, but at least it was safer in here. Quieter. We'd left our bodyguards at the door, and the people we passed in here all smiled at us, or at least nodded in pleasant recognition.

I wasn't a monster to them.

We reached a small room that smelled more like coffee than rubbing alcohol. The man instructed us to have a seat, and then he disappeared through a set of metal doors. Mother sat in one of the stripe-patterned chairs and crossed her feet at the ankles. She pulled her compact mirror from her purse, flipped it open, and started slicking back the stray frizzies that had escaped from her bun. Her hair was the same rusty-brown shade as mine, and when she let it down—which was almost never—it fell in pretty waves all the way to her elbows.

"How are your flowers?" she asked, shutting the mirror with a sudden *snap!* that made me jump.

"Dying," I answered, holding them up so she could see how they drooped.

She frowned. "You shouldn't hold them so tightly." She got up, took the flowers, and went over to the water fountain in the corner of the room, then grabbed one of the little paper cups beside it. "Maybe we can get them to perk up before your sister gets here?" she suggested. This was the only way my mother ever showed affection—by taking all of my broken things and fixing them.

I watched as she filled the cup with water, arranged the flowers in a sad-looking bouquet of purple and white before moving silently back to her seat. Looking at the flowers made me think about Old-Violet, which made my eyes start to water again.

I forced myself to find something else to focus on.

There was a clock above my mother. A bright red disruption in the otherwise solid white wall, ticking the seconds loudly away. After a few minutes, I started to imagine a symphony to go with it, where the steady ticktock kept rhythm with the lights humming overhead, with the tapping of my mother's foot and the occasional gurgle of air bubbles in the water fountain. In my head I wrote lyrics to go with the music, though I knew better than to sing them out loud; my voice may have been a gift—at least according to my teachers—but using it was just showing off. And my mother didn't approve of showing off. It only attracted unnecessary attention.

So I started counting the gray-speckled ceiling tiles instead. I'd just made it to twenty-seven when I heard the heavy *whoosh* of a door opening, and I looked down and met my father's gaze. He was wearing that new, cautious smile of his. The one that never quite made it to his eyes the way the old one—the one he'd had before Violet got sick—did. And without a word to me or Mother, he stepped to the side and pulled my sister's replacement into the room.

It was like seeing a ghost. My heart skipped wildly, all the way up into my throat. I swallowed several times, trying to get it back down to where it belonged, trying to clear a path for words.

As if I really knew what to say.

What should you say to someone you'd known your whole life but were just now meeting for the first time? Was I just supposed to pick up where we left off? That was what my parents wanted, I knew. That was how this worked. And it was what Mother was doing now, fluttering all over New-Violet and asking a million pointless questions, saying a million pointless things. I hadn't seen her this animated in a long time.

But then, first impressions were important. So of course she was making the extra effort.

I thought about following her example—I should have followed her example, maybe—but I couldn't bring myself to do it. I was still too numb. Confused. She seemed to have forgotten about me, anyways, and after I purposely avoided my father's gaze, he left me alone too. I clasped my hands behind me, leaned back against the smooth wall, and just studied my new family.

Before she got sick, Violet had always been beautiful. Like a thunderstorm was beautiful in its chaos, in black clouds billowing and lightning dancing across the dry earth. It was the kind of beautiful our grandma said would get you into trouble if you weren't careful.

It didn't seem possible or fair, but somehow this Violet was even more beautiful; her skin was like porcelain, flawless and perfect. Her cheeks were rosy. Those dark, dark eyes sparkled underneath her long lashes. This definitely wasn't the sick Violet I'd gotten used to over the past months; the circles and tired creases that sank her skin were gone. Her hair wasn't dull and coarse anymore, but black and shiny as polished obsidian. And when she moved that tall, willowy figure, it was with grace and purpose—like she'd choreographed every step.

Mother said the old and the new were the same.

I reserved judgment.

"Catelyn," Father said suddenly. "Are you just going to stand there? Come say hello to your sister."

My sister.

Sister, sister, sister. They called her that so easily. Cautiously, reluctantly, I pushed away from the safety of the wall. My father's words were heavy with expectation, and I didn't want to disappoint him.

New-Violet's eyes followed me as I stepped toward her, a smile forced onto my face. *Do I look like Mother now?* I wondered. *Am I a statue? Am I doing it right? I'm not going to disappoint them, am I?*

"Hi," I said. My gaze didn't quite meet hers; instead I stared at the faded painting of wildflowers on the wall behind her. "I'm—"

"Catelyn," she interrupted with a small smile. "But you prefer Cate. And you're twelve, and you're in seventh grade—an honors student. You love singing and horses and strawberry ice cream, and your favorite color is green." She laughed; a quiet, twinkling sound. "You don't have to tell me anything."

"I—"

"I know all about you," she said.

And in that moment, I loved her and I hated her all at once.

I wanted to make it go away, but the smile seemed determined to stay on my face. Apparently, if you faked it long enough, things like that could get stuck. Mother's smile was stuck too. And Father's. We were all stuck, but somehow still moving through the room, talking and laughing as we collected our things and headed for the door as one big, happy family. Complete again.

On the way out, I grabbed the flowers from their makeshift vase, spilling water over the counter in the process. Then I handed them to Violet, blushing and apologizing for the way they'd started to brown around the edges.

CHAPTER ONE

Masks

Present day; four years later

I never much cared for Samantha Voss.

Nobody did, to be honest. Or, at least, nobody *really* did; but the girl had money, and her parents owned half of the city of Haven, so of course she always had a date to socials and an entourage wherever she walked.

Once upon a time, I was even part of that entourage.

Sort of.

Thing was, my parents were always trying to arrange dinner or tea or some other boring affair with the Vosses. Looking back now, I know that it was mostly a smart political maneuver on my father's part, an attempt to win over one of the richest families in Haven. But at the time I could only think about how much I detested it, the way they were always dragging me along with them to these dinners, all the while gushing about just what a lovely, positively *splendid* child that oldest Voss daughter was. How she would be such a good influence on me, and why didn't I have more friends like her? Violet and Samantha had always gotten along well enough, so what was my problem?

Of course, the get-togethers stopped soon after we brought my sister home. Or my sister's *replacement*, as the Vosses loved to point out—while at the same time forbidding their daughter to have anything to do with this new Violet—because they've always been among the most vocal members of Haven's anti-cloning community, despite my father's best efforts to win them over.

I wonder if they regret that, now that Samantha's dead?

They told us in second period. Some of the girls in the front row started to cry. One of them had to leave the room. Jordan Parks asked if this meant we could have the rest of the day off, because he is a stupid, inconsiderate little twit like that. Most of the class—myself included—just sat in stunned silence while the police officer told us how they'd found her body down by the abandoned railroad tracks, and about how they were still investigating what had happened. The officer was a younger guy, clean shaven and with a crew cut that meant business, and in his super-official-sounding voice he told us what a serious investigation this was. Then he gave us a number to call if we knew anything that might help. The call would be confidential, he promised, and though he never came right out with it, we all knew that meant they were looking for clues.

That there was a very good chance Samantha's death wasn't an accident.

That announcement's been hanging over the school ever since. By the time the bell rings for fourth period, everyone's still speaking in hushed voices. They go straight to class, like death is something contagious. Like it might catch them if they linger too long beside their lockers.

That uneasy stillness, at least, is contagious; I keep my eyes straight ahead as I walk toward the auditorium for Theatre II, and my step is even quicker than usual. I'm trying not to think about it, but I still can't help but remember how I'd normally pass Samantha on the way to this class. I think she was on her way to Biology then. We'd always nod to each other. Just a nod, but somehow I still miss it.

So what if I didn't like her? Doesn't mean I wanted her dead.

And it doesn't mean I'm looking forward to telling my sister about this, if she hasn't already heard. Violet isn't at school today, and maybe that's for the best—because there's no telling how she'll react to this news. Not well, I'm guessing. Samantha was one of the few people besides me that she was actually close to. And it seems strange, since Violet has technically already died once herself, but I suppose this is really the first time she's going to have to deal with *actual* death. The complete and final kind, the kind that the person she cared about isn't coming back from.

What would that be like, I wonder? When it happened to me, at least I had a replacement to take my mind off the funeral. And after four years, I don't even think of her as a replacement. Not most of the time, anyway. Most of the time she is just my sister, for better or worse, and she at least makes it easier to pretend I never had to watch the first Violet die.

And I've gotten very good at pretending. About lots of things. It's taken most of those four years she's been here, but now I can look at this Violet and I can almost force myself to forget that her life didn't begin like mine. I can pretend she's just like me: soft skin, fragile bones, a brain that makes perfectly messy thoughts instead of supercomputer calculations. On a good day, I can convince myself—and anyone else who needs convincing—that this is the same girl who held my hand and walked me into school on my first day of kindergarten. The same sister who managed to convince me to eat a worm when I was three by telling me it was candy. Because this Violet knows all of these things happened, doesn't she? They're all safe and secure, the memories uploaded into that computer brain.

And so on a good day, it's like Violet Benson never died.

Not the way Samantha Voss and everything that went with her did.

I reach the auditorium, go straight to the storage room behind the stage, and grab the things I'll need for the scene we're dress rehearsing today. Opening night for our production of Shakespeare's *Much Ado About Nothing* is in less than a week, and we're still trying to get act two just right; Mrs. Heller is insisting on going all out for the masked-ball scene, which means a completely choreographed traditional dance with everyone up on that tiny stage. It wouldn't be that bad if all the girls weren't wearing huge dresses, and if we weren't all wearing these masks that bring our peripheral vision down to about zero.

I'm taking my own mask out of my locker when some more of the class trickles in—a group of girls, flocking and giggling around Seth Lancaster. Yes, Seth Lancaster himself—with his tan skin and dreadlocks that I somehow find both incredibly hot and incredibly disgusting at the same time. The girls hanging all over him are part of a familiar sight, and I ignore them all while I smooth out the feathers glued to the corner of my mask. They ignore me, too. Nothing new there, either. If all the world's a stage, then this scene could represent my entire existence at Haven High School.

See, people like Seth, and all those girls—they aren't mean to me. Unlike my big sister, I don't get picked on. I don't get bullied or called out. I just get overlooked. I'm like a piece of furniture that's just *there*, upholstered in some boring shade of brown that blends in perfectly with the walls.

And I've worked hard to keep it that way. For months after my sister's replacement joined our family, people kept trying to drag me away from the walls, out into the open so they could attack me with their words and threats and insults. Calling me a freak of nature. A clonie. The paparazzi were worse than ever, following me to school, waiting outside to ambush me when the day was over.

Weathering the storm, Mother called it. That's what we did that first year. Or it's what I did, anyway; and as the months passed, I slowly, slowly managed to become like her—skin thickening, hardening until I was finally that statue nothing could crack. That didn't have to fight back or shout back or have anything to do with anybody. Who cared what they said? Who cared what they thought? I only needed me.

I only need me.

Not that I'd have anybody else if I wanted them, anyway. Because even though it's not like I'm the only one at this school with a replacement hibernating over at Huxley's labs, I might as well be. Because my father's third term isn't quite over yet. So he's still Mayor Benson, which means Violet and I are still the poster children for cloning in the city of Haven—for better or worse. And at school, it's usually for worse. Even the other kids like me, other *origins*, don't want much to do with me anymore, and I can hardly blame them. Not when there's a spotlight following my every movement.

I'd stay away from me too if I could.

It all stung at first—the hastily averted glances, the whispers behind my back—because I've spent my entire life in this city. I grew up with most of these kids. I went to their birthday parties, rode bikes with them, endured ten years of questionable-looking cafeteria lunches with them. And when we were younger, nobody cared who people's parents were, or about who was an origin or who was a clone. We *knew* about these things of course, because ten years ago the city legislators passed an ordinance that made it mandatory for all of Haven's five hundred and something Huxley families to be registered in a publicly available database. It was supposed to create peace of mind, the proponents of the new law claimed. To show people that their neighbors, that kid they hired to mow their lawn, the teenager checking them out at the supermarket—all of these people could be clones, and they could assimilate naturally and peacefully into society. That was the intention.

But mostly, I think, it just gave the anti-cloning community clearer targets to aim for.

I'm not sure when it happened, exactly, when the people I used to call friends started aiming for me and my sister. And I have no clue who decided that growing up meant we had to divide ourselves into these tidy little cliques, to absorb the political agendas of our parents—all I know is that it happened. Sometimes I wonder what the city would be like if that law had never passed, or how things would be different if my father wasn't the mayor.

But then I remember what my mother says—that wondering is a frightful waste of time—and then I stop and I go back to blending in with the scenery.

I head to the back room and change. The dress is heavy, with its layers and layers of tulle and faux silk, and it smells faintly of the mothball-filled trunk it was stored in. Its stiff collar makes the back of my neck itch. But it does make me look like I've got some sort of figure—the way it cinches in my waist and pushes up my barely there boobs—so that's kind of nice. I would never wear anything that did that outside this class, of course. But then, I do a lot of things in this class that I wouldn't do anywhere else. It's different here. Outside, I may play the same role over and over—statue-girl, the unbreakable—but in this auditorium, I can try on other lives. I can be whoever I want to be, as long as I can memorize her lines.

And for the next hour, I'm not living Catelyn Benson's life. This time, I'm coming alive as Shakespeare's sharp-tongued, quick-witted heroine Beatrice. And she can look people in the eyes. She doesn't have to fade into the background or hide from camera flashes or pretend she's got somewhere else to be when people try to talk to her.

I take a moment to admire this other self in the mirror. Admiration turns quickly to loathing, though, when I think about how much better the whole ensemble would look if I could pull my hair up instead. This dress needs some sort of braided bun or something—not my scraggly, shoulder-length waves just hanging limply above it. An updo isn't an option, though, because it would leave the back of my neck visible. And even though everyone knows I have it, I don't like showing off the scar that Huxley's chip left when they embedded it underneath the skin there. The scar, or the identification number tattooed over it: 1001. It's just something else to provoke people. Another ugly reminder of things I don't want to think about if I can help it.

It's a necessary part of the process, though. The neurochip implant is what links origins like me to our clones, initiating a new transfer of thoughts and memories once every twenty-four hours or so. And it's continuously relaying more simple information from the motor cortex, too. So when I walk, my possible-replacement unconsciously walks with me—only, in place, and from within her developmental cell over at the lab. As I'm standing here, going through the motions to prepare for my part in *Much Ado About Nothing,* so is she. Creepy as hell, yes; but this way, we not only have the same thoughts and memories, but my clone and I will develop physically along similar lines.

At least as far as appearances are concerned. Because while our bones and muscles take on the same shape and size, Huxley's genetic modifications make certain that the clones who replace us don't suffer the same weaknesses that their origins did. So frames that look essentially the same are actually made up of stronger bones and more supple joints, all of it protecting organs more resistant to disease and deterioration. And that's the part that I don't like thinking about: knowing that there's a stronger, physically superior version of me just waiting around for me to die.

It's unsettling.

Now that I'm thinking about it, though, I can't stop, and my hand reaches automatically for that scar underneath my hair.

Don't make such a fuss over it, Catelyn. That's what my mother would say if she caught me. *It isn't as though it's going away anytime soon, so you may as well embrace it.*

But I know she only says things like that because she's self-conscious about her own scars, even if she'd never admit to it. Not scars like mine, but ugly purplish marks all over both her arms. They aren't fading away, either. If anything, they're getting darker. Which is why she always, always wears long sleeves—even when it's pushing one hundred degrees outside: so she can act like those scars don't exist. But I've seen her studying them in the mirror when she thought I wasn't looking.

My hair looks fine down, I decide.

I slide the mask on next. I made it myself, and it's easily my favorite part of this costume; maybe because it actually turned out halfway-decent looking. Which is a big deal for me, considering I'm the only person I know who failed at making macaroni art in kindergarten.

I'm always one of the first to class, so I've got a few minutes left to run lines with my reflection before I have to join everyone else onstage. A few minutes. That's all I need to slip the rest of the way out of this skin and into my character's. I close my eyes and imagine the rest of the cast around me, hear them saying their lines, hear myself answering, see us all dancing gracefully over the—

"Hey Benson."

Seth. Probably calling me by my last name because he doesn't actually remember my first. I open my eyes and see his reflection right next to mine, both hands in his pockets, head tilted just slightly to the side.

"Question," he says.

"What?" I ask, trying to sound casual.

"Where's your sister been the past few days?"

Violet. Of course. Why else would he be talking to me? He's only trying to pry into my family's business, just like everyone else.

"Who wants to know?" I ask, surprising myself with my own audacity. Must be the Beatrice in me.

He grins lazily. "The person asking," he says. "She's my lab partner, and we've got a project due Monday. It's not doing itself, and I'm sure as hell not doing it, so—"

"She's sick." The lie comes easily, quickly. It's not the first one I've told for her. The truth is, she was suspended—again—this time for skipping class and then refusing to tell the principal what the heck she was doing running around in the woods behind school. Sometimes I think this Violet doesn't know the meaning of "weathering the storm"—not like the rest of the family. She's a pro at creating them, though. And I'm usually the one who gets to pick up the debris that her lightning and raging winds leave behind.

Most of the time, I try to convince myself that if the first Violet had lived, she would have turned out to be the same wild, tabloid-fueling girl that this one has become. That the spotlight would have stayed on our family all the same.

But other times I wonder.

Although right now, I really don't have time to wonder, because Lacey Cartwright just appeared in the corner of the mirror.

"Sick?" she repeats in a singsong voice while absently twirling a curl of her chestnut hair. "That's not what I heard."

"Maybe you should double-check your sources, then," I say, and my voice doesn't shake, even as the rest of her group joins us in the already-crowded hallway. They're cornering me against the mirror, but they don't scare me. I've had to defend Violet enough times that this is just another role I can slip into and perform. All I need now is a little bit of concentration and a few deep breaths. It doesn't hurt that I'm still wearing this mask either. *Beatrice could take on every single person here*, I remind myself. *She could probably do it with one hand tied behind her back.*

"I heard she got caught in the woods," Lacey drawls on, "With Parker Maples."

The girl next to her looks up from pretending to study her nails and gives Lacey a serious look. Like we're discussing politics or something, and not a bunch of stupid made-up drama. "I heard it was Alex Camden," she says.

Lacey shrugs. "Probably both of them," she says, which earns her a chorus of exaggerated giggles from the rest of the girls. I'm probably imagining it, but I think I see Seth rolling his eyes. The possibility of that calms me down a little; at least I'm not the only one who thinks Lacey Cartwright is a complete waste of time and space.

"So who is your sister officially with now, Cate?" she asks in a mockingly interested voice.

My cheeks burn, but I try to ignore her. She doesn't seem like she's in a particularly venomous mood today, just bored more like. Maybe she'll drop it if I ignore her. I turn back to the mirror and work on straightening out the collar of my dress.

"I know it's hard to keep up," she presses.

This collar is really annoying.

"I mean, the girl's a bit like a revolving door, isn't she?"

I'm probably going to have to take it home and iron it.

"Apparently, when they manufactured her in that lab,

they forgot to give her any sort of common-decency genes or—"

"So what's your excuse, then?" I snap. "And why are you so worried about it, anyway? Are you afraid my sister might challenge your reign as resident whore of Haven High?"

Someone gasps. Seth laughs. And all I can think is, *Crap. Did I just say that out loud?* Maybe this mask is making me a little too brave.

Lacey gives me a look that could get her accused of attempted murder. She takes a step toward me, and I'm suddenly very painfully aware of how much bigger than me she is; I'm not exactly small and delicate, but she's cocaptain of the volleyball team and apparently takes her weight-training requirement very seriously. Plus, she's about half a foot taller than I am. And those bright-red nails look like they could easily claw open a person's throat.

I probably should've stuck to my role as furniture. Furniture rarely gets the crap beat out of it.

"What did you call me?" Lacey's smile is disgustingly sweet.

It's too late to back down now. So, in a voice that sounds a lot more confident than I feel, I say, "You heard me."

"Oh, yeah, I heard you. I was just giving you a chance to take it back before I did *this.*"

Her hand flies at my face. I twist away instinctively, but she still catches the corner of my mask. It rips off, the rough edge of it leaving a long scratch across my jawline. I stumble, tripping over the too-long hem of my dress, and my elbow slams into the mirror. A long crack splits up the center of the glass, and so instead of one Lacey diving after me, I see three split images of her. I don't aim at any of them. I just spin around and swing. My fist barely grazes her shoulder—just enough to piss her off more, if that's possible.

The others are converging now, some of them shouting at us to stop, but most of them jeering and egging us on. The blood is pounding in my ears, and when Lacey runs at me this time, I'm ready. I throw my fist at her face as hard as I can.

Seth steps between us at the last possible second.

And I punch the most popular boy in school right in the nose, just as Mrs. Heller storms into the hallway.

"What is—*Miss Benson!*"

I freeze. My fist is still hovering just inches from Seth's head, and he's holding a hand over his face, trying to contain the blood that's gushing from his nose.

I really wish I was furniture right now.

CHAPTER TWO

Hypothetically Speaking

Suspended. For the first time in my life. My parents are definitely not going to be happy about this. I'm not supposed to get suspended. I'm not supposed to be the problem child. That's Violet's job. Mother's going to have a heart attack when she finds out that *both* her children aren't allowed to set foot on Haven City Schools' property for the next two weeks.

And what if the press gets hold of this? They're going to find the most unflattering picture they have of me in their archives (and, god, they have plenty) and splash it across the home page of every tabloid that will pay for it. Probably pair it with some story about how I'm turning into a wild child just like my sister. And the CCA—Clone Control Advocacy—members? They are definitely going to use this as evidence against the movement. Because they're always after this sort of evidence. Anything to make Huxley look bad, to sway public opinion toward their own personal beliefs about cloning and genetic engineering.

Forget that Huxley has provided the public with plenty of documentation about the benefits of cloning, and that the clones themselves prove over and over—in almost every kind of study imaginable—that they're smarter, stronger, and healthier than the originals they came from. They don't care about any of that. The CCA and its supporters are always trying to claim that clones and their origins, and any people involved with cloning, have a tendency toward instability and violence, a greater chance of developing serious mental-health issues, and a bunch of other crap that they rarely have the facts and figures to back up.

But that bloody nose I just gave Seth Lancaster is a fact. Which means I'm going to be news. Maybe even bigger news than Violet, since at this point I think some of the paparazzi are getting tired of her everyday exploits. But wait until they tell the public what the younger Benson sister has been up to. Wait until the press reveals how unstable Huxley's experiments have made *her*.

The office smells like cleaning chemicals and a stomach-turning mixture of whatever food they've been heating up in the secretaries' break room. I'm alone in the little hallway outside the principal's office, waiting for Miss Davis to get off the phone. I'm not allowed to go back to class, so I'm going to have to call home and have someone come get me. Not looking forward to that conversation. Miss Davis can stay on the phone for the rest of the afternoon for all I care. Though I am getting tired of drawing circles in the faded blue armrest of this chair.

My mind follows the circular pattern my finger is making, and I've started to zone out when someone sits down on the bench next to me and clears his throat. I don't look up. I've done enough interacting for one day. Plus, I don't want to have to explain why I'm sitting here dressed like I'm about to go to a masquerade ball.

Or why my costume has blood on the sleeve.

"Did you at least win?"

I still don't want to look up. I shouldn't look up. But I know that voice. His accent has a soft lilt to it, like most of the people from the Southside section of Haven have; a lot of the ones who originally built up that part of town—the area the Neuse River winds through—were refugees from the war-torn ports of coastal Georgia. His family used to have an estate in a city called Savannah, which I know thanks to the projects we had to present in a contemporary-history class I took last spring. We had to chart population migration to and from cities, as affected by the war. I was bored out of my mind while most people were presenting, and spent the majority of that class period trying to find a way to hack through the school's Network blocks so I could play games instead.

But I paid attention to his presentation.

Because the truth is, I've always been a little bit in love with that voice, and with the person it belongs to. Which is why I can't help myself now. I tilt my head toward the bench. And sure enough, Jaxon Cross is sitting less than two feet away from me. And like it's done during every one of our grand total of about five interactions, my mind goes completely blank. Perfect. So now I can check "humiliate self in front of crush" off my list of things to do to make this supremely awful day complete.

What the heck is he doing here?

I know the answer as soon as I ask myself, though: He's an office assistant during fourth period. Something about the way his credits worked out; they won't let students with empty spaces on their schedule just skip a class, so they usually make them fill the time doing busywork around the school.

I don't know how much work Jaxon actually does, though. I don't think a day goes by that I don't see him wandering up and down the halls outside the auditorium, and there's been more than one occasion when he's played an impromptu audience member for our rehearsals.

Not that I'm keeping an eye out for him or anything.

"Well?" he presses with a friendly smile. It's a permanent accessory to his face, that smile—so you'd think I'd be used to it. Especially since this isn't the first time it's been directed at me either. Because while most of the student body of Haven High is perfectly content with me being furniture, Jaxon always makes a point to remind me that I exist, even when I'm trying desperately to fade into the background. He always waves to me. Always smiles at me. Sure, he does that to most people—but that's the point. I'm just like most people to him. It's like he's completely oblivious to who my family is. Like he doesn't know me at all, but at the same time he's somehow closer to me than anyone else in school. I find that both terrifying and exhilarating.

Mostly terrifying.

"I . . . What do you mean?" I ask, my fingers tracing the eyeholes of the torn mask in my lap.

"That scratch on your face," he explains. "It looks like it hurt. So I'm hoping you at least won that fight."

"That fight . . ." My stomach sinks. Does he already know about that? Does the whole school already know?

"News travels fast," he says, holding up his phone.

Seth must have messaged him, I realize suddenly. The two of them are always hanging out, even though they seem like complete opposites to me. Because unlike Seth, Jaxon isn't a complete ass.

I manage a few calm breaths. So what if he knows? That doesn't mean the whole school does. It's just Jaxon. And the entire Theater class. And whoever they've told, which means the whole volleyball team probably knows, and so does every teacher Mrs. Heller's gotten a chance to talk to. And Seth's got a bigger mouth than all of them put together—so on second thought, I'm kind of surprised paparazzi and CCA members aren't breaking down the office door this very second.

Jaxon's looking at me expectantly now, waiting for me to say something. So I laugh nervously. "This?" I say, motioning toward the scratch. The breeze my hand creates makes the raw skin sting. "It's nothing. It doesn't hurt or anything."

"Well, that's good," he says, running a hand through his hair. It's longer than I've ever seen it, but it's still got that messy-but-styled look to it. It's not as dark as mine, but it's close. Or maybe it just looks darker next to his fair skin. This is the first time I've really looked at him, I guess. I mean *really* looked at him, and studied him; when you're trying to blend in to the scenery yourself, you can't stare too long at anyone. I'm usually ducking around corners or tripping over things in my herculean efforts to avoid eye contact with him—and I guess that makes it hard to notice little things like the square outline of someone's jaw or the way his eyebrows lift a little when he smiles or the way his nose is just the tiniest bit crooked.

I could probably study that face all day, now that I've started; but silence is threatening us, so I smooth out some of the wrinkles from the front of my dress and say, "Um, I'm guessing Seth told you what happened?"

His smile widens. "Yeah. He sent me a picture, actually. One of the girls in your theater class managed to snap it—it's a great action shot."

Oh no.

"A picture . . . ?"

He nods, then holds up his phone again. And there I am, in all of my mortified glory, fist still raised, mouth open and gaping. Seth is just to my right with his hand clutched over his face. Barely in the frame, but it's more than enough to incriminate me.

"Great." I stop messing with my dress and try to smile back. Maybe I can joke this off. Jaxon, at least, seems to find it amusing. "So, um, yeah. I didn't exactly win, as I guess you saw. In fact, I didn't even hit the right person."

"I dunno," he says with a shrug. "I feel like Seth needs to be punched every now and then. It's good for him—keeps him in line."

My smile becomes a little more genuine, a little less

nervous. Because all of a sudden I realize: I am having an actual conversation with Jaxon Cross. And he thinks it's funny that I punched one of his best friends in the face.

At what point did I step into this alternate reality, exactly?

"Still," I say, "can you, like . . . message him and tell him I'm sorry or something?"

"Consider it done." He starts messing with his phone, and I don't even realize I'm watching him until he glances up at me a minute later. My heart thumps right up into my ears, and the back of my neck starts to burn. It should be illegal to have eyes as blue as his. "So what happens now?" he asks. "They going to haul you off to jail, or what?"

"I wish," I say, frowning. "It's worse, though—I have to go home. And I'll be there for the next two weeks. I was waiting for Miss Davis to get off the phone so I could call our . . . so I can call someone to come get me." I almost said "our driver." And though it's no secret how rich my parents are, I still hate calling attention to it. It's just one more way that I'm different from most people.

"I could take you home," he says.

My mind threatens to go blank again. "I can't . . . I mean, you don't have to do that," I mumble.

"It's nothing. I'm bored anyway—they've run out of stuff for me to do, and I slip out of here early all the time." He casts a glance toward the secretary, and even though she looks completely oblivious to our conversation, he leans in closer to me before quietly adding, "I just tell Davis that I'm going to the middle school to help tutor the kids in math. I've done it for real enough times that she doesn't question me about it anymore."

"I—"

"And this way you can put off explaining things to your parents for a little longer," he says, hopping to his feet.

I try, but I can't seem to come up with a decent argument. I mean, it's an incredibly tempting offer. Not only would I not have to call home, but I'd also be sharing a car ride with Jaxon Cross. It's . . . almost too good to be true.

Maybe that's why I feel nervous again. Why is he being so forward all of a sudden? He's always been nice, yeah, but he's never been *this* nice. I don't want to wonder why, because it deflates the warm bit of hope that's been ballooning in my chest. But I can't help it. Being followed around by cameras your whole life, and having half of what you say misquoted by reporters all over the state can make a girl paranoid. And Jaxon already has a picture of what I did to Seth. Maybe now he's just looking for content to go with the story he plans on selling to the highest bidder:

Catelyn Benson's Wild Rampage.

Yeah. He could make a small fortune off a story like that, if he's got any sort of negotiating skills. Which he's already proven he does. He's persuasive enough to make furniture talk, at least.

But that's stopping right now.

"No thanks." I know it's the right thing to say, but I can't help the disappointment that washes over me. Just once, it would be nice to forget about who I am, and who my family is, and about what we've done and whether it's right or wrong or something in between. To just jump in a car and go.

"Come on," Jaxon insists. "You live over toward the Forsyth Park district, don't you? Same neighborhood as Samantha did—I've seen you around. I go right past there on my way home."

"I was . . . I was actually thinking I might take the ETS home," I lie. The Electronic Transport Shuttle coils around Haven like a giant, silver-scaled snake; you can't go anywhere in the city without being able to look up and see it.

"Do you even have an S-Pass?" Jaxon asks, raising an eyebrow.

I find a coffee-colored stain on the worn carpet and try desperately to focus on it.

"Have you ever even *been* on the ETS?" His voice still has that gentle, friendly cadence about it; but the words irritate me anyway. Because I know why he's asking. Most people who take the shuttle do it because they can't afford the steep fees that come with owning a car these days.

We have the war to thank for those fees, since the hostilities that led to it made energy conservation one of the government's highest priorities in the thirty years that have followed it. After the treaties were signed and the smoke had cleared, they went a little crazy slapping environmental regulations and restrictions onto everything—some of which made it near impossible to own a personal car. It was one way to keep people from complaining when billions of scarce taxpayer dollars were slotted to build energy-efficient transportation services. Most designated Restoration Cities like Haven are now served by ETS systems or something similar; it's all Mr. Ballard talked about in my Political Science class last spring. The crazy government and its crazy regulations, and about how things are even worse now than they were when practically half the world was using our country for target practice.

Except, of course, his choice of words was always much more colorful.

"I have been on it, thank you very much," I tell Jaxon. So what if it was only once and it was ten years ago now? It had been an emergency then; my father sent Violet and me away from a campaign meet-and-greet that had been violently crashed by his opponents, trusting one of his secretaries to get us home as discreetly as possible. No one expected the mayor's children to take the ETS, and the paparazzi were busy hounding my parents. So for a little while at least, we were just two normal children, blending in with all the other normal children. It was terrifying at first, but my sister always had a way of making even the most frightening things into a game we could laugh about. So by the time we reached the stop near our house, we'd become secret agents on a mission to infiltrate the mayor's home—and there was no room for fear when we had such an important job to do.

I don't have Violet or our silly make-believe games now, maybe, but I can still handle public transportation. Just because I'm rich doesn't mean I'm completely helpless.

He's right about one thing, though: I don't have a pass. And in a fantastic twist of irony, I'm pretty sure I don't have any money on me either.

"You know," he says innocently, "people get mugged and stuff on the ETS. Happens all the time."

"So if anybody tries to mug me, I'll punch them in the face. Giving people a bloody nose can become my signature move."

He laughs. I wish he would stop doing that, because I'm falling in love with the sound of it; it's so pure, and so tantalizingly real. It makes me second-guess myself even more. Maybe I'm being too paranoid after all? Maybe he honestly just wants to help? There has to be some honesty in the world, right?

"That's it, then?" he asks with a good-natured sigh. "There's no convincing you?"

Before I can answer, Miss Davis calls my name, tells me the comcenter's free if I'm ready to call home. Which I'm not. I don't know that I ever would be. I don't know that I'm ready to trust Jaxon, either, but I have to admit those deep blue eyes plead a good case for him. And in my head, I'm already practicing the lines I'm going to give Miss Davis about how there's no one to pick me up. How I'm just going to go to the middle school with Jaxon, do a little community service and help him with tutoring, and then catch a ride home.

"I . . . I'll be there in a second," I tell her. She answers with an uninterested nod, then spins her chair around and starts tapping away at her computer. When I turn back to Jaxon, he already has my bag in his hand.

I had a clean record before today, and that, combined with Jaxon's charming smile, is enough to persuade Miss Davis to let us go without much fuss.

Outside, it's a typical hot, humid day. I did take the time to change out of my costume, though, so at least I'm in jeans and a modest tank top instead of a five-hundred-pound dress.

His car is beautiful. It's a pearly blue color, and the paint literally sparkles in the sun, as do the polished chrome wheels and bumpers. The windows are tinted. It doesn't have an aerodynamic, rounded body like most of the cars you get today; it's all fierce corners and angles, and the front end alone is as big as most of those newer cars. When we first walk up to it, I'm sure we must be at the wrong parking spot; his family isn't very well off, I don't think, so I have no idea how he could afford this thing—especially since it looks like an antique. I doubt it meets regulations; the ownership fees alone have to be staggering.

"Took me four summers of working my ass off and saving every cent to buy it from my uncle," he says, answering the questions I don't dare ask out loud.

"What kind of car is this?"

"2005 Camaro," he answers. "A classic."

"It runs on gasoline?"

"It's modded so it can use gas and electric. Gas when I

can find it, and when I've got extra money. And when my fuel permit's clear. Usually." He grins. "Though I might have driven it a time or two when it wasn't cleared."

"Aren't there huge fines for that?" I ask as he opens the passenger door for me.

"Only if you get caught," he says, ducking inside and dropping my bag behind the seat. His shoulder brushes mine, and he lingers just long enough for me to breathe in a hint of some sort of spicy-scented cologne. While he walks to the driver's side, I close my eyes and hold my breath. Absorbing that scent, that moment. Part of me wishes I could bottle this all up somehow, keep it for later—a little piece of real that I could unleash whenever I get tired of hiding behind my mask, or whenever this stone casing I'm in starts to suffocate.

That's stupid, though. You can't bottle moments any more than you can stop them from happening. And I'm still not convinced he's completely real, anyway. Who says he's not hiding behind a mask of his own?

I don't say much on the way home. The car doesn't have any sort of autodrive—which isn't surprising, given how old it is—and so Jaxon has to keep his eyes on the road and his hands on the wheel the whole time. It's a little nerve-wracking to watch, and even though he seems comfortable with it, I don't want to do anything that might break his concentration. I can't imagine what it was like when everybody was *manually* driving cars like this around, especially since there were probably five times as many of them on the roads back then. Our car has a manual-control mode, yes, but I could count on one hand the number of times our driver has actually used it; mostly he just inputs the navigation commands, and the car's computer does the rest. It even parks itself. One of my father's favorite things to complain about is how having a driver—as pleasant as he is—is really a waste of money. But Mother likes the appearance he gives, and at this point, she probably doesn't even remember how to open a door for herself. So his job is secure for now.

We're about halfway to my house when the comcenter in the middle of the dashboard lights up and starts to beep. Jaxon glances down at the ID flashing on the screen, and the smile in his eyes disappears for a split second. But it's back so fast, I wonder if I didn't imagine it.

"Deny," he tells the computer, and the car goes silent again.

Something else has joined our silence, though— something uncomfortable and uncertain. It's shedding off him, twisting into an almost tangible thing that sits on the armrest between us.

The comcenter lights up again a minute later.

"Deny," he repeats firmly, without even glancing at the screen this time.

I stare out the window, at glass building after glass building gleaming in the sunlight as we blur past. Some of the light refracts off the sunglasses in my hand, throwing a rainbow of colors across the dash. I move my hand in circles, up and down, forward and back, to create my own personal kaleidoscope. The curiosity is burning inside me, along with the uneasiness from earlier. Who is he avoiding? And why? Is it because I'm here, and he doesn't want to talk to them in front of me? Should I ask him who was calling? It would just be making conversation, right?

"Sorry about that," he says before I can get up the courage to speak. And just like earlier, he answers the questions I haven't even asked. "It's my mom. She can be a little . . . overbearing. This car has a tracer on it, so she's probably noticed I'm not at school anymore and is wondering if I'm heading straight home."

I don't miss the way his fingers clench a little more tightly around the steering wheel as he speaks, or the subtle change in his voice. He sounds less confident. He sounds like he's lying.

Or maybe you're just being paranoid again?

Probably.

"You should meet *my* mother," I say drily, thinking I might be able to shake off this paranoia if I can focus on making conversation. "Talk about overbearing."

He glances over at me with a mischievous smile. "Are you inviting me to meet your parents?"

"I—"

"Shouldn't we go on a date or something first? It feels like we're moving too fast."

I'm blushing again. I can feel it. The heat doesn't stay on my cheeks this time either; it spreads all over my body, rushes down my neck, tingles the tips of my toes and fingers. "I didn't mean it like that," I say. Then I apparently go crazy, because in a voice that doesn't even sound like mine I ask, "But are you asking me on a date?"

"Maybe," he says, almost coyly. "It all depends."

"On?"

"On whether or not you'd say yes. Hypothetically speaking, of course."

"I see." My head is on the verge of spinning again. "So, you're only asking if I'm going to say yes."

He shrugs. "I don't handle rejection well." And I laugh, because the thought of anybody rejecting a date with Jaxon Cross seems really absurd to me.

And yet the thought of agreeing to it myself somehow petrifies me straight to the bone. I have to say something, though. I can't stop now. That seems to be happening a lot today; it's like throwing that punch earlier swung my whole life into motion, and now I just keep stumbling forward. "Well, hypothetically speaking," I say, my eyes still on the blurs of shape and color outside, "I would probably say yes."

"Probably?" he repeats. "I don't know if I like those odds . . ."

"Okay *yes,*" I say, laughing again in spite of myself. "Yes, I would go out with you." I can't believe I just agreed to that. I can't believe he even asked me—well, sort of asked me—in the first place.

"It's a date, then," he says, and I officially give my head permission to start spinning. "We can . . ."

I don't have to ask why he trailed off. Because just then I turn and look out the front window, where I know my house will be looming straight ahead at the distant end of the street. And there it is, with its old-fashioned bricks and tall white columns and its perfectly landscaped yard that's always been my father's pride and joy.

He's not going to be happy about all the vehicles parked on the grass.

Reporters. Everywhere. And at least a half-dozen police cars too. Even worse—far, far worse—are the gray trucks with the CCA logo on the side. What are they all doing here? Surely this isn't about what happened at school. It wasn't that big of a deal, was it? And how can they already know? How can they already be waiting for me?

"You probably don't want to get too close," I mutter to Jaxon. "If they get a picture of us together, then your face is going to end up on the pages right next to mine. They'll probably call you my accomplice or something. Invent some ridiculous personality for you, give you a tragic back-story and everything."

He ignores my warning and pulls right up to the curb, as close as he can; our driveway's blocked by a line of camera crews that the police are trying to force back into the street. Before the car rolls completely to a stop, my door's already open. Jaxon catches me by the sleeve when I try to jump out. I twist back around. His mouth opens, then closes soundlessly. I don't have time to wait for him to find words.

"Thank you for the ride," I say, jerking free. I see my parents on our front porch, surrounded by officers trying to form some sort of barrier between them and the deluge of people pushing in, shouting questions. I don't look back.

I just run.

CHAPTER THREE

The Storm

When I reach the porch, all attention shifts to me. A man with stringy brown hair and a computer in his hand grabs my arm and tries to pull me back down the steps. My father intervenes, shoves the man so hard that he tumbles back onto the lawn. His computer goes flying; it lands upside down, and I catch a glimpse of the CCA logo on it before I turn back to my father.

"What's going on?" I demand.

Before he can answer, someone thrusts a small silver recorder in front of my face. "Catelyn, can you tell us the last time you actually saw your sister? Actually talked to her?"

"My sister . . . ?"

So this isn't about me. It's about Violet.

She just has to out-storm me, doesn't she?

"What happened?" I ask my father, ignoring the reporter. "What did she do this time?"

"Nothing. There was an accident with the oldest Voss girl—" my father tries to say under his breath.

They still hear him.

"An accident, he says! No proof yet, Mayor Benson, but are you saying you know something that we don't about the young Miss Voss's tragic death? Something that might suggest it *was*, in fact, only an accident?"

"My understanding is that there is no proof either way," my father says. His eyes are locked straight ahead, his shoulders stiff. He's in press conference mode.

"We have eyewitness accounts stating your daughter ran from the police who arrived on the scene."

My father says nothing.

"And she was down by the old railroad station late last night, correct? You can confirm this much?"

Violet? They think *Violet* had something to do with Samantha's death? Is that seriously what's going on here?

And why do their questions sound so much like accusations?

Samantha was her *friend*. She had been, for as long as I can remember. And when Violet's replacement happened, Samantha was one of the few "normal humans" who didn't join the crowd and turn against my sister's clone. And though Samantha and I never got along fantastically, I'd always given her credit for that—even while so many others detested her for the exact same thing. Others including her parents. Violet's clone had always been like a weed to them, I think, a bad influence they were constantly, unsuccessfully trying to pull from their daughter's life. I say unsuccessfully because for the past two years, Samantha had been sneaking out at night and on the weekends, playing the role of loyal accomplice whenever my sister wanted to stir up trouble.

Most people don't know all that, though, since they

basically ignored each other at school and anywhere else they deemed too public to be seen together. The only reason *I* know they were still close is that Violet usually tried to get me to go along with their exploits. Or to help cover them up, at least.

Maybe I should tell all of these people that. Tell them they've got it all wrong. If Violet is nowhere to be found, it's probably only because she's out looking for whoever *really* hurt Samantha. If she ran from the cops like that supposed witness claims, then the most obvious explanation is that she doesn't trust them to figure out the truth.

Right?

I can think of a million reasons why my sister is innocent.

So why can't I find the voice to say a single one?

I grab my father's arm to steady myself as the shouting around us gets louder and louder, the voices all garbling together into one giant wall of noise. Between that and the heat and all of the bodies pressing in around us, I start to feel faint. The world blurs. In the distance I see a smudge of blue—Jaxon's car, still parked along the curb. And he's more clear than anything, standing beside it, watching me. There are so many people between us now that I couldn't fight my way back to him if I tried.

"I will not confirm or deny anything at the moment," my father is saying as I move behind him, trying to hide from Jaxon and everyone else. But one of the reporters sees me trying to shrink out of sight, and for some reason he decides that means I have something to say.

"Cate, don't you have anything to—"

"Don't speak to them, Catelyn. Don't even look at them. Come here. . . ." My father puts an arm around me, blocking my face from the flashing cameras, and shepherds me toward the front door. "We were trying to get this over with before you got home," he says under his breath. Then to the crowd behind us he announces, "This conference is over. Any other questions you have may be directed to my secretary and staff, who I believe most of you are intimately acquainted with. Natalie!"

My mother turns at the sound of her name, and the three of us retreat silently into the sanctuary of our house.

Hours and hours of police questioning later, Mother is still attempting to act like everything is fine.

She's cooked a full dinner, turned the television off, shut the blinds, and set four places at the table. She moves with an unyielding precision that reminds me of the fancy pocket watch my grandfather showed me once, gears turning, hands ticktocking from one place setting to the next without hesitation.

Time never stops, and neither does my mother. At least not until she starts to scoop vegetables onto the plate in front of Violet's empty chair, and then my father reaches out and stops her himself. He guides her to her own seat and makes her sit down, while I stare at my plate and divide my mixed vegetables into little piles that I count silently to myself. Seven carrots. Eight pieces of broccoli. A bunch of green beans—I've gotten tired of counting by the time I get to those. And then I get tired of looking at the piles, so I swirl my fork through and mix them up again.

I've never been less hungry in my life.

"You had better not waste that food," my mother says, as if I'd just thought that out loud. "You know how expensive fresh vegetables are these days."

I stab at a particularly leafy-looking piece of broccoli and glance up at my father for help. But he just mirrors my mother's stern look.

Once upon a time, my father was the one who would always come to my rescue. Even long after my mother had perfected the art of smiling for the cameras, of holding her head up high, of turning to granite at a moment's notice—even for years after that, my father stayed soft. When the reporters weren't looking, he kept laughing. When my mother wasn't around to stop us with disapproving glances, we made up ridiculous songs and danced silly dances, and whatever was going on in the world outside, whatever people were saying about us, it didn't matter.

Not to me.

But I suppose it must have mattered more to him than I realized, because eventually Mother managed to convince him that it was easier not to feel, not to show any sort weakness that the press could get hold of and twist. There's nothing soft left in his eyes now. I'm not even sure I remember what his laughter sounds like.

"Catelyn." She hasn't touched her food either, but my mother is still glancing from me to my plate, expectant.

"I'm not hungry."

From the look on her face, you'd think I'd just cursed her name and threatened her life all in the same sentence. She doesn't say anything, though. Not at first. At least a full minute passes before her expression twists into something I don't recognize, and then to my amazement she says, "You don't have to eat, then."

And that's the moment, I think, that I realize how serious this all is.

So serious that even my mother doesn't know how to handle it. And if she can't handle it, then what are the rest of us supposed to do? It doesn't feel like the normal weathering the storm anymore. Nothing makes sense now. My thoughts are all twisted up, darting around, quick and impossible to keep track of. Which is maybe why I can't stop the question that rises to my lips, that cuts its way out through the heavy air before I can swallow it.

"What if Violet had died and never come back?"

I know instantly that I've said the wrong thing. The most terrible, most impossibly wrong thing. My father's expression turns from stern to disappointed instead.

God, I *hate it* when he looks at me like that.

My mother doesn't look at me. She just does what she usually does when I start asking questions about all of this and she isn't in the mood to scold me for it herself: She goes into the living room, creaks open the cabinet in the corner, and takes the video disc from it. Then she comes back, grabs my father's work tablet that's on the nearby counter, and situates it in front of me.

If I were more like my sister, maybe I would have the guts to do what she always does when Mother tries to punish her with this: simply get up and walk away. Maybe laugh on my way out the door. Because I've seen the awful video that's loading now more times than I care to count, and I hate it more with every viewing.

But I'm not my sister. So I just sink farther into my chair and try to become the polished oak until this is over with.

Even if I don't listen, though, and even if I let my eyes glaze over, I can still picture what's playing perfectly in my mind on the tablet's screen. It's a video produced by Huxley. It starts with a brief history of the war, of the overpopulation and climate change that led up to a crisis of resources and then to tension, tension, and more tension until some countries grew weary of searching for solutions and instead started searching for someone to blame. And then it talks about how much of the Western world—particularly the United States, with its massive population and less-than-conservative lifestyles—was a natural target.

There were no explosions. That's why, while the rest of the world usually refers to it as the States War, most of the ones who lived it—like my parents—refer to it as the Silent War. Silent and deadly, with no flashy show of weapons or outward flexing of military muscles for Huxley's video to re-create. Instead, the screen shows dramatic reenactments of a sickness slowly overtaking the population, of streets growing less and less crowded, of poisoned water supplies and infected, withering crops.

The drone of a man's voice follows, reading out death

and destruction statistics. Almost one hundred million dead. those who were exposed to infected water or food but who still managed to survive ended up developing the strange marks on their bodies like the ones on my mother's arms.

Aside from those marks and occasional odd stomach pains, though, she's healthy enough. And my father was even luckier. He waited out the worst of the hostilities overseas, spending several years living with my great-grandparents in Germany. When they came back to the rural North Carolina town he was born in, they found it more or less untouched.

But others weren't so fortunate, and the video doesn't spare any details about all of the horrible, lingering effects most of the country has faced; the war summary ends with a series of graphs and maps and charts, depicting new political and economic divides and the instability of what was once supposedly one of the greatest countries on earth. They talk about the infected, like my mother. About the way they were treated almost like lepers in the immediate postwar world, when people weren't sure what they were dealing with, or whether they were contagious or not. No one could be sure.

And that brings Huxley to the point they're making, as the sharply dressed scientist in the video tells me now: *You never know what the future holds, or how quickly things can change. But with cloning you can enjoy the peace of mind that comes with knowing that at least something you love is not as irreplaceable as it used to be.*

My mother has left the table now; I hear her pacing back and forth on the tile floor in the foyer. Probably tugging the sleeves of her cardigan down a little more with each step, absently trying to cover the marks that are already out of sight to everyone but her. Guilt gnaws at the back of my mind as I think of her face, and I wish, again, that I'd just eaten my vegetables and kept my mouth shut. Haven't my parents been through enough already?

They were just kids when everything in that video happened—which means they've had practically an entire lifetime to live with the fear of it happening again. Now add the fear of something happening to me, or of us losing Violet all over again, and suddenly everything that scientist is saying makes perfect sense. I understand.

I still don't want to listen to him anymore.

Mother's been gone long enough that I assume she's waiting for me to leave before she comes back. The video is still rambling on about the benefits of cloning when my father clears his throat, gets to his feet, and starts to gather our mostly untouched plates. He piles his napkin and silverware onto mine and then just hovers awkwardly beside me for a moment, like he's an understudy who has no idea how he ended up onstage.

He eventually remembers his lines, though. "You should get to sleep early tonight if you can," he says. "We likely have a long couple of days ahead of us." Then he plants a quick, hesitant kiss on the top of my head and disappears into the kitchen without another word.

I don't get to sleep early.

Instead, I lie awake listening to my parents arguing. My

father's calm, unyielding tone. Mother's clipped words and occasional shouting. I have my sheets drawn up over me like a tent, but through them I can still see the bright green display of the clock that tells me it's well after midnight. In just a few hours, I'm going to have to face the world outside the safety of these walls. Which is going to be even more complicated now that I can't even take refuge at school. I've managed to keep the whole suspension thing from my parents for now, but what, exactly, am I going to do come tomorrow morning?

I sit up. While my mind chases questions and possibilities, I let my gaze wander toward the figures outside my window. Earlier, I set the glass to a dark tint—like I always do to block out the setting sun—so I can't make out distinct people. They're all the same, though. They all blur together to me. The anxious camera crews. The CCA members standing on our street, lecturing about the evils of cloning in loud, booming voices. The police officers there to keep a riot from starting—and waiting to question Violet themselves, when she finally comes home. Everyone wants to be the first to see her, to catch her, to demand answers from her.

I'd like to demand some myself.

I'm not going to be able to sleep in my bed tonight, it looks like. This isn't the first time reporters have camped out on our lawn, though. So I'm already prepared for this. I've got places to hide.

Our house is one of the oldest in Haven. The rooms are laid out strangely, and they're not uniform in size or shape. It's all so haphazard and uneven, full of nooks and crannies that Violet and I spent an entire childhood discovering. It's almost as if the builders were simply making things up as they went along. Just one more reminder of how different my parents used to be; they're really too practical, too no-nonsense for this house now. Which may be why Mother talks all the time about moving. She always comes up with a reason to stay, though. *Too much work. Too many memories.* And her favorite: *Too many people speculating about what ran us off.*

In my room, there's a random tiny space within my closet that I discovered when I was little; the door to it blends in so seamlessly with the wall that it's almost impossible to see. To pry it open, I have to slide a thin butter knife, which I keep in a shoe box under the bed, beneath the tiny crack between the door and the floor.

I already have spare pillows and blankets in here, and I bring my computer tablet and the digital picture frame from beside my bed to give me some sort of light. I make myself comfortable and set the frame down beside me. It sifts dutifully through its pictures, oblivious to the world outside the memories it holds; black-and-white, artsy photos of me and Violet playing dress-up, of our whole family at the beach, of the last time our grandmother visited us.

If you were only judging by the pictures in this frame, the logical conclusion would be that we are a normal, happy family. If you were an outsider just glancing in, you wouldn't be able to tell that the pictures of my sister are of two different people.

But I can tell.

Most of the time I don't want to, but I still can.

What will I do when Violet comes back, I wonder? Maybe I'll scream at her. Hit her. Pick up this frame and throw it at her feet, hard enough to shatter it into a hundred tiny pieces. And then maybe I'll grab her by the shoulders and shake her. Ask her, *why? Why do you keep making things worse? What is wrong with you? You're the big sister. You're supposed to watch out for me, to set an example, to give me someone to look up to. Don't you know that? Didn't they program that into that stupid brain of yours? You should know that that's how this is supposed to work.*

Maybe that's how it would have worked too, if the first Violet was still here. If the first Violet was still here, maybe I wouldn't keep finding myself in this same place, hiding and doing everything I can to avoid the wake of destruction this one leaves in her path. And maybe I wouldn't have to sit across from an empty chair at the dinner table, and we'd have normal conversations there, instead of ones about war and politics and paparazzi.

Instead it would be *How was school today, Cate?* or *Tell me about that boy who drove you home, Cate.*

If only she was still here.

I glance over at that frame. The display's stuck on a picture of the two of us, Violet with her arms wrapped in a playful headlock around me. It's recent. Definitely New-Violet. I think about flipping the picture over on its face so I won't have to look at it anymore. I think about taking it and burying it in the darkest corner of my closest too, or maybe going back to my window and throwing it outside, right into the crowd of all those people who are waiting for her. *There she is*, I'd shout at them. *Take her. I don't care. I'm tired of looking at her.*

Suddenly I feel a crawling in my skin—a disgust with myself for thinking these things. I wrap my blanket tighter around myself and curl closer to the corner, like I could somehow sink into the walls, the floorboards. Away from myself. I don't like having these dark, terrible thoughts about Violet. But sometimes they're just there, and sometimes I just can't get away from them.

I hear the old house creaking through the walls. My parents climbing the stairs to their bedroom, probably. I wonder if they'll sleep tonight, or if they'll lie awake like me, having terrible thoughts of their own.

Or worrying.

Because there's no denying that the spaces in my thoughts—the ones that aren't filled with anger—are filled with a gut-twisting anxiety for Violet. In the end, I know I'm only fooling myself by thinking I could stand to never see her smiling face again. I don't even know if I could yell at her or hit her or do any of those things. She is my sister, after all. Or what's left of her.

And right now I just want—need—to know she's safe.

But I have a bad feeling about that.

Thirty more minutes have somehow slid by, according to the tablet's display. It's going to be morning before I know it, and I still have no idea what I'm going to do. All I know is that I can't tell my parents. One delinquent daughter is plenty for them to have to deal with. My problem, as usual, is silly compared with the ones surrounding Violet; mentioning it would just be an extra irritation they don't need.

My options are limited, though. Faking sick is out; Mother's only let me stay home from school one time—and that's only because I passed out on the front porch after she insisted I get up and get ready. You have to show up, she always says, or people will start talking.

As if they didn't do that already.

I don't have a license to drive, and our driver would tell my parents if I tried to skip school. And I don't think my parents would approve of me taking the ETS—especially with everything that's happened today. They'd be right to disapprove too, because I'd probably get jumped by more crazies like the ones outside.

There's only one other option I can think of: I grab the phone from my sweatpants pocket and start to flip through my contacts. It's a short list, so it doesn't take long. It also doesn't take long for me to realize that I wouldn't feel comfortable calling any of these people and asking them to pick me up in the morning. How sad is that? After sixteen years of living here, it seems like there should be somebody I could call.

And then it occurs to me: *Jaxon.*

His face, his voice, his laugh—it all drops into my head and sets it spinning again. I don't have his contact information, but I should be able to find it easy enough; he doesn't seem like the type who would try to keep that sort of thing off the Network.

I pick up my computer tablet. Or me and Violet's computer tablet, rather—because we share most things like this. I think my mother believes that forcing us to share will equal obligatory closeness. When this Violet first came to live with us, my mother even tried to force me to share my room with her. Just until she felt "at home." That wasn't happening. It was one of the only times I actually managed to stand up to my parents with any sort of success.

But me and Violet still share the same computer, the same clothes, the same everything else. We even shared the same phone for a while, as impractical as that was. And when things like the computer are taken away from one of us (usually Violet), it's taken away from the other, because when you're family, you don't get to pick and choose what losses you suffer alongside each other. My sister's pain is my pain, and her punishment is my punishment.

So I'm not supposed to be using the computer now. Because three weeks ago, Violet got detention for the third time this year and had her computer privileges revoked. My father even went so far as to install a program to lock the whole thing down, preventing any sort of access to the Network.

That's not fair, though. Which is why I figured out a long time ago how to get around stuff like this. I rebel in little ways—it helps me keep my sanity. And it's made me really good with computers, at least.

Now if I could just focus on what I need to find.

The thought of talking to Jaxon again doesn't make

that especially easy, though. I run my nervous fingers over the virtual keyboard, swipe through the images on the monitor until I come to one of him. Smiling. Of course. Is he ever *not* smiling?

I hesitate. What if he thinks I'm needy or clingy or just plain annoying for doing this? We haven't even gone on a date, and I'm already asking for favors. Maybe there's someone else I could call? Or maybe I should just suck it up and tell my parents?

Except, just then, I hear my father raise his voice. They're still arguing. And I know it's gotten serious, because he almost never yells.

There's no way I can give them something else to fight about.

So I take a deep breath and dial the number on the screen.

CHAPTER FOUR

Charades

At precisely seven o'clock the next morning, Jaxon knocks on the front door. Twenty minutes later, we're outside, and I'm still trying to figure out if this is really happening, or if I just haven't woken up yet.

Then the camera flashes start.

And then I know I'm awake, because even pinching myself as hard as I can doesn't make this nightmare go away.

"What are you doing?" Jaxon laughs, glancing down at the red mark I pinched into my skin.

"Nothing." I rub my arm furiously. "And I'm sorry about this," I add, motioning to the small crowd that's following us. "I thought more of them would be gone by now." I also half expected my parents to have bodyguards assigned to escort me to school. But I guess I shouldn't be surprised that I slipped their minds, since I don't think either of them got much sleep last night.

At least it will be easier to skip school without extra people following us.

Jaxon shrugs, looks back at the crowd, and flashes them a smile. I grab his shoulder and jerk him back around. "You really shouldn't do that," I say, voice perfectly deadpan. "At least make them work for the shot."

He keeps making charming faces and posing for the cameras, while I focus on getting to his car as quickly as possible. His car that is a different color today, I notice. Now it's a shiny black that clearly reflects everything against its surface—both Jaxon and me and the crowd of camera-faced people behind us.

"I liked the blue better," I say conversationally.

"Really? I'm sort of partial to the black myself. Feels more manly."

"Tint adjustor?"

He nods. "It has an opacity adjustor, too."

"Isn't that illegal?"

Before he can answer, one of the paparazzi gets brave and falls into step right beside us, his recorder lifted shamelessly into Jaxon's face. He must have heard me say "illegal." The press loves buzzwords like that.

Jaxon patiently grabs the man's wrist and shoves the recorder away. Then his hand finds the small of my back and he urges me a little faster, until we've put enough space between us and the recorder man that he can tilt his head close and safely whisper, "Almost as illegal as driving without a cleared gas permit."

I can't help but laugh, shaking my head at him.

"What?" he asks with a grin.

"You just don't strike me as someone who would break a law. Any law."

"I break all kinds of laws," he says matter-of-factly. "I drink and smoke, and I run with a tough crowd when I'm not at school. I'd tell you about all our nefarious deeds, but I don't want to scare you away."

I raise an eyebrow. Did he just say "nefarious"? Who uses that word in a conversation?

He sighs. "Okay," he says. "Maybe those last few things weren't true. I'm not that cool. Sorry." He flashes me another grin, and at least for the moment, I forget all about those people behind us. "But I'll try to be cooler," he adds, opening the door for me as we reach the car.

"Please do. I can only handle so much lameness."

"Point taken." He closes the door, and I watch him move to the driver's side. It's not really on purpose; my eyes just sort of follow him. Naturally. This all feels a lot more natural than I was expecting it to. At least until he drops down into his seat and looks over to find me still staring at him. Our eyes meet, and we both look away, embarrassed.

"What is it?" he asks.

"Nothing. I was just thinking."

"About?"

"This is . . . You just seemed a lot different from a distance, I guess."

"Doesn't everybody?"

"I guess so," I say.

He hesitates. "Different in a bad way?"

"No." Definitely no.

He looks like he's about to say something else, but just then a reporter appears next to my window, camera raised and ready. I grab a notebook lying on the floorboard and press it against the glass, hiding as much of my face as I can.

"I bet that gets old," Jaxon says offhandedly as he digs the car keys out of his pocket. I still can't get over the fact that they're actual, honest-to-god metal keys. What if they get lost or stolen? Our driver starts our cars with just a touch of his hand against the bioignition panel; that just seems a lot more practical to me.

"Having to hide like that, I mean," Jaxon goes on.

"I don't normally bother to hide from them like this. I just pretend I'm invisible or something. But today I just—" My eyes fall back to the keys. The shiny brass flashes in the sunlight flitting through the car as we drive; it reminds me of a tiny fire flickering to life.

Today I just what? Why do I feel so different today?

I never really fell asleep last night. Instead, I lay awake thinking, thinking about how wonderful it would be if I really could hide. Not forever, necessarily. Just long enough for everyone to forget about Catelyn Benson, and then I could reemerge, reinvent myself as someone else. Someone who didn't have to try to sleep while people whispered outside her window. Someone who didn't have to push and shove her way through those people just to get to the car.

Someone who didn't belong to my family.

"Have they heard anything from your sister?"

Speak of the devil.

I don't answer right away, and Jaxon tightens his grip on the steering wheel and clears his throat uncomfortably. "You don't have to answer that," he says.

"I haven't heard anything," I tell him. Not a word.

I have ideas about where she could be, of course—because it's not like this is the first time she's disappeared on us. It *is* the first time she's left without telling me where she was going, though. Normally when she decides to run away, I'm the person she tells about it. I don't know why. Maybe because she wants someone to know where she went, just in case—and because she knows I won't tell on her. She goes to a handful of the same places every time, stays in one of them just long enough to cause a scene. Then she always comes back.

I'm not sure what I would do if she didn't.

"Seth told me why you punched him," Jaxon says. He's trying really hard to keep the conversation going; I get the impression he's not as content with silence as I am.

"I didn't mean to punch him, exactly," I remind him.

"Well, he told me what happened with Lacey. What she said about your sister."

I shrug, trying to roll away the anxiety that's tensing up my shoulders. I don't really want to relive yesterday any more than I have to.

Jaxon mimics my motion. "I just think that's really cool, what you did."

"What, punching people?"

He laughs. "No. Standing up for your sister like that. I feel like you do that a lot, don't you?"

Now I think I know where he's really going with this: back to four years ago, right after the new Violet first started school. Or *descended* on the school more like, in a swoop of gale-force winds striking through the halls, drawing stares the way a tornado draws debris and dust. She wasn't the first clone to assimilate into Haven High School, no. There were dozens who came before her, and dozens more after, but she easily made the loudest entrance. Most slipped quietly, gently into their life, seamlessly carrying on the one they had replaced. And Violet started out doing that too. True, there had always been that quiet, smoldering chaos surrounding the first Violet—our grandmother had warned my parents about it—but just as the first Violet had always done, for the most part her clone kept it perfectly in check. There was something wild there, you could tell; but you could only see it in certain lighting, or maybe in quick glimpses out of the corner of your eye.

By the end of that first summer, though, I feel like something must have short-circuited in her brain. Whatever code or file she had that reminded her she was supposed to control that wild part got rewritten somehow, and she's spent practically every day since transforming into someone I recognize a little less every day.

Maybe because of all that, it took less than a month for Lacey and her minions to start bullying her. Because Violet wasn't just a clone. She was a *weird* clone. Different. Unstable. She was unpredictable, and she didn't care what others thought about anything she said or did. She didn't care about acting like the one she'd replaced. If she had been born a natural human, then maybe people would have just called it a phase. Maybe they would have just called her weird—like they do that senior girl who dyes her hair a different neon color every week—and left it at that. People change. They do strange things, but so what?

But I never heard anyone, except maybe my mother, suggest Violet was going through a phase. Mostly they repeated the things Lacey said, claiming in frightened whispers that my sister was a prime example of a Huxley experiment gone wrong. And then they stood back, or looked the other way, when she was bullied—even when Lacey and her friends used to take Violet's food at lunch, claiming that she wasn't a real person, or even a proper copy of a person, so she didn't need to eat, did she?

But of course, I stood up for her back then, too. Which resulted in them bullying me and taking my food instead, because if I starved to death, I could just be replaced—and then I could become a freak just like her. One big happy family of freaks.

Jaxon knows all about these incidents, because he's the one who ended up getting them to finally leave me alone. He even tried to give me his lunch on a few of those days when mine ended up getting "accidentally" knocked on the floor. I was too embarrassed to take it.

And I'm embarrassed now, just thinking about it.

"You and your sister are close?" Jaxon asks. Except it sounds more like a statement than a question. And I don't know why, but for some reason that bugs me a little.

"We're sisters," I answer, voice calm and calculated. "Family. Which is why I had to stand up for her."

He considers my words for a second. "Had to? Or wanted to?"

What the hell kind of a question is that?

"Why does it matter?" I ask with a frown. "Can we just drop it? Talk about something normal? Like school or sports or philosophy, or—"

"Philosophy?" He cuts me a sidelong glance.

"Okay, maybe not philosophy. But something else. Anything." *Except Violet.*

"Okay, okay. Sorry. Just curious."

I sink back against the seat and close my eyes for a second. "Yeah, you and the rest of the world," I mutter.

"Well, let's focus on where we're going, then. And maybe on what we're going to do about those guys."

"What guys?" My eyes flash open, and I follow Jaxon's gaze to the rearview mirror. There are three trucks behind us. The one in front is close enough that I can see the tiny silver torch—one of the many symbols the CCA proudly uses—swinging above the dash. I curse under my breath.

I wonder how long it will be before one of them reports that I'm not at school?

How suspicious will they decide that makes me? They're going to accuse me of trying to hide, and my hands start to shake at the thought of being caught, of being dragged in for more police questioning. I grab the corner of the seat, trying to steady them, while my lips silently recite lines from *Much Ado About Nothing*; it's a nervous habit I've developed, performing plays and songs in my mind when I want to slip away from the moment I've found myself in. It normally calms me down. Today it doesn't seem to be working, though, and I've made it through almost all of act five, scene two, before Jaxon interrupts.

"Geez. Are they always this persistent?"

"Some days it's worse than others."

He's quiet for a minute. Then, "All right. They are entirely too close to my car, and it's stressing me out." His fingers fly across the buttons on the side of the steering column. "I'm going to lose them."

"What? How?"

"You wearing your seat belt?"

"Yeah, but—"

"Good."

There's a high-pitched *ding*, and all the display screens across the dash glow blue for a second. Jaxon's hand falls to the gearshift between us. He jerks it back, over, and up, and a split second later the car rockets forward. The momentum throws me back and all but takes my breath away.

"Holy crap," I manage to gasp.

"Sorry about that," he says. "I should have warned you; the gasoline engine has a lot more get-up than anything electric. Which is why they're never going to catch us." I can hear the smile in his voice. I'm not looking at it, though, because there is no way I'm taking my eyes off the road. He's going to hit something, weaving in and out of lanes like this. A car. A person. A building. And whatever it ends up being, I don't want it to catch me by surprise.

He manages to surprise me anyway, though, when he reaches over and lays his hand over mine. My heart skips several beats, and when it picks up again it's pounding even faster than before.

"You okay?" he asks. "You . . . um, you look a little pale."

My eyes leave the road for a fraction of a second. "Why are you looking at me?" I breathe. "*The road* . . . Watch the road. . . ."

"I am—" He swerves wildly, just barely missing a car that starts to pull out in front of us. "See?"

"You're going to get us killed."

"Not today." He takes a sharp left, cutting off a woman on a mach bike as he turns into a huge concrete parking garage. He twists and turns through the garage, still going entirely too fast until we reach the lowest level, where he parks in the farthest, darkest corner.

He could have parked anywhere, really, because there are almost no other cars in here. I'm not even sure what building the garage is attached to, but the fact that it's concrete instead of steel—and the fact that it has parking spaces for so many cars—tells me that it's old.

"What are we doing in here?" I ask.

He cuts the engine. "The car stands out too much, and everyone's seen you get in and out of it now. I think it'd be better if we made the rest of our escape on foot."

"You're coming with me?" I ask.

He's already halfway out the door, and he ducks back under the frame to answer. "Hey, if you get to skip school, then I do too."

"I'm not actually skipping school, you know. I sort of

don't have a choice." I'd go if I could, just to keep people from talking.

"Besides," he continues as if I haven't spoken, "you owe me a date."

Once we're outside, this corner seems even darker. In the distance I can see stretches of sky through the rows of parking decks; it looks like it's clouding over. The only light we really have comes from the white safety lamps lining the ceiling—and half of those are burnt out or flickering halfheartedly.

I hug my arms tightly against myself and try to keep my focus straight ahead. It's useless, though, because I can feel Jaxon watching me. Refusing to ignore me, just like he always has. I would find it annoying, maybe, except for the way his eyes light up whenever our gazes catch; it's as though he's seeing me for the first time, every time, and that somehow makes my heart race and leaves me feeling completely at ease all at once. He just has that effect on me in general, actually; it's like I know I *should* feel anxious, like I should keep blocking him out. And with anybody else, that's exactly what I would do. It would be safer that way. Easier. There's something about Jaxon that won't let me be nervous, though—or at least not as nervous as I normally am.

I think I actually want to trust him.

Problem is, I'm so used to not trusting people that I don't really know how to do it. I slow for a few steps without meaning to, while my mind tries to make sense of this strange new sensation settling over me. Jaxon glances back and gives me a look that's half-amused, half-concerned.

"You all right?"

Then suddenly I'm moving, one foot in front of the other. And I think, *Maybe that's how you do it.* Maybe you just keep walking and hope that the stone casing you're in cracks—and that something more trusting, something more brave, works its way free.

I catch up to Jaxon, and we walk in silence for a few steps before I find the courage to speak. "I can see why you chose this spot for our date," I say. "It's incredibly romantic."

"Isn't it? I really think that damp, mildew scent adds to the ambience of this place."

"Definitely. The flickering lamps remind me of candlelight."

"I knew you were the romantic type." He darts over to a nearby concrete column; there are weeds sprouting up through the cracks at its base, and he swipes a handful of them, jogs back and offers them to me. "Which is why I got you flowers," he says.

"Oh, you shouldn't have." I take the bunch from him and arrange it into a makeshift bouquet. Among the green clover are two puffy white flowers with reddish pink centers. I pick at their tiny petals, pulling out the ones that have started to brown. I'm surprised anything—even just weeds—has managed to grow this far down, with nothing but the dim artificial light. Life can be persistent when it wants to be, I guess.

I look up from my bouquet just in time to see a gray truck hurtle around the corner.

I don't think twice. I just grab Jaxon's arm and jerk him behind the nearest column. "Those CCA guys . . . ," I whisper.

"No way they saw us come in here. . . . I was a mile ahead of them," Jaxon says. "Maybe they're just looking around. Maybe they don't know we're here."

"They'll see your car," I say, "And you're right—they're going to know it's the one I left in. This is going to be all over the news. . . . I should have just told my parents what happened. I should have—"

"Elevator," he says suddenly, nodding to the right. "It's just around the corner up there; we can take it to the street level and lose them, but we'll have to be fast. As soon as they turn into the next row . . . and . . . now!"

I've never run so fast in my life. My hair whips in my face. My feet pound against the sloped ground. I fly around the corner, so close behind Jaxon that it's a miracle we don't end up tripping over each other.

And there are the elevators, just like he said.

We reach them and he slams his hand against the access panel. The doors slide open almost instantaneously, and we half run, half tumble inside.

I lean against the far wall while Jaxon swipes his fingers over the control screen.

"Close, close, *close*," he chants at the doors. They finally do, and I tilt my head back, shut my eyes in relief, and try to get my breathing back to normal. My body continues to thrum with nervous excitement, though, and suddenly I find myself fighting the strange urge to laugh. At me, at him, at this elevator, this moment—it just all seems so surreal.

And then I look at Jaxon, who's still messing with the controls, and I stop fighting. I just laugh at the craziness of it all. He turns at the sound of it, watching me with a bemused smile until I start laughing so hard that my balance actually sways a little; he catches me, steadies me with his hands around my waist.

"You okay?" he asks, almost laughing himself now.

"I'm sorry. I just . . . this is crazy. And god, I am *so* dead. When my parents find out about this, when this ends up in the news . . ."

"Maybe it won't."

"I admire your optimism, but . . ." I look up so he can see the sarcasm in my smile, and it's then that I notice exactly how close he is to me. My giggling fit ends abruptly. "But I, um, I'm just . . ."

He's so close that he's making it difficult for me to form any sort of rational thoughts. He must realize it too; because he makes what looks like a concentrated effort to take a step back from me, and to pull his fingertips away from where they'd settled against my hips.

"But I'm glad you knew this elevator was here," I say, filling the silence with words before it has a chance to become any more awkward. "So at least we didn't have to deal with those guys right now."

"Yeah."

There's something off about the tone of his voice. Without saying anything else, he moves back to the control panels near the door and starts inputting commands. He's quiet for a long time, until I can't help but ask, "Is something wrong?"

"I'm just trying to figure out how this works."

"Need some help?" I offer. "I'm pretty good with computers and stuff."

"No," he says, too quickly. Then in a calmer voice he says, "No. I mean, I think I've got it now."

I shrug and lean back against the metal wall, which is cool and refreshing against my heat-flushed skin. The elevator shifts into motion a few seconds later. It's a lot jerkier than most of the ones in newer buildings around the city, and it makes my stomach flip uncomfortable. I stare at a bright red button on the wall next to Jaxon, try to concentrate on its stillness, to pretend we aren't moving and that I'm not about to be sick. My gaze is torn from it, though, when Jaxon finally turns back around to face me.

He looks . . . strange. His smile is gone. If I didn't know better, looking at him now I'd believe he'd never smiled a day in his life. An edgy, tingling feeling creeps up the back of my neck and over my scalp.

"Are you sure nothing's wrong?" I ask, straightening up again. He nods. The elevator shudders to a stop. I hear voices outside, and the breath I managed to catch gets away from me again. I keep listening, hoping to hear the hum of traffic, too, or at least the sound of footsteps hurrying past, or of birds calling or dogs barking. Sounds of the city. I've never wanted that barrage of noise so badly as I want it now.

Something isn't right.

The doors open.

There's no city. There's no sunlight. There's only a giant room lined with computers and desks and swarming with people. And everything—from those computers to the clothing the people wear to the information boards across the wall—all have the same three letters blazing across them: CCA.

CHAPTER FIVE

Truth

This can't be right.

Jaxon can't be CCA.

He was it. The. Only. One. The only one who's never looked at me like I had some sort of disease. The only person who's ever stood up for me. How could he have been pretending all these years?

"Okay—I can explain this." Jaxon's eyes are pleading with mine, but I only meet them for a fraction of second before we're interrupted. Two men and a woman file into the elevator between us; the woman taps away at a silver palm computer while one of the men grabs me by the arm. My gaze darts to the close door button, and then to the one labeled G, which I assume stands for garage level. And for one desperate moment, I think about diving for those buttons. But even if I could somehow fight everyone off and make it back to the parking deck, then what would I do? Walk home? Straight through who knows how many more CCA and news trucks that are probably nearby, looking for me?

Cooperating may be an even worse idea, but before I can make up my mind either way, the man holding my arm gives me a rough shove. The other two crowd closer to me, and I'm marched from the elevator without a word from any of them.

"Guys, come on," I hear Jaxon say. "I can take her myself. This isn't necessary."

My heels dig instinctively into the floor. Take me *where*, exactly? What are they planning on doing with me?

"Vice President Voss's orders," says the computer woman. I'm so stunned that it takes a second for the name to register in my brain. *Voss?* As in Samantha Voss? She has relatives who are CCA?

It shouldn't come as much of a shock, I guess. Like I said, the Vosses I know have never been especially shy when it comes to voicing their opinions about the cloning movement—or my sister.

Still, though . . . vice president? They never seemed *that* passionate about it. Of course, maybe they just didn't want their cover blown. It's not as if I've ever known any other CCA members to flaunt their titles in public; I didn't even know they had titles—and I never would have expected anything like this base, filled with what looks like a ridiculous amount of people and technology for what I always just assumed was another protest group. A more organized, more persistently annoying than most protest group, yes.

But this is different.

And the deeper it all sinks in, the more I wish I'd put up a better fight in the elevator.

Our footsteps echo throughout the dome-shaped room as we walk farther inside, a metallic *ting ting ting* against the grate flooring. The blinding fluorescent lighting and the sterile recycled air reminds me of the last place I want to think about right now: Huxley. The memory of the day we brought my sister's replacement home crowds its way into my mind, and it feels like I'm walking through those winding halls all over again. It's sort of ironic, these two places filled with people who hate each other and their beliefs so much—but all I can think about is how they're the same. And I wonder: Am I here because of Violet again?

Did they bring me to this place because of what people are saying she did? Because they want information about her that I don't even *have*?

Almost everyone stops what they're doing and glances up at us as we pass. I'm used to stares, though, and to whispers and poor attempts at trying to look subtle. I keep my head up and walk on, telling myself that this is just like at school—that there's no difference between people like Lacey Cartwright and the people in here. Last spring, I played the lead role in the school's production of *The Scarlet Letter*, and that's who I try to imagine myself as now: Hester Prynne, with that bright, ostracizing letter sewn onto her clothes, surrounded by hypocrites whose favorite pastime is judging her.

That role would be easier to slip into, though, if the grip on my arm wasn't getting tighter with every step. At school I may be a shunned villager, but right now I feel a lot more like a criminal being dragged in for sentencing.

A few hallways later, we come to a set of tall, imposing steel doors. The woman steps from my side, places her hand on the panel outside them, and announces our arrival. A computer voice grants us access, the doors slide open, and we step into a dark room. Dozens of pictures in antique wooden frames wrap around the walls. The floor actually has carpet instead of metal grating—a shaggy off-white carpet that matches perfectly with the throw pillows on the leather couch that's taking up most of the right wall. The whole room has an old, traditional feeling to it, and it reminds me of pictures I've seen of my grandparents' old house. I never went to that house, but I can imagine it smelling similar to this: a mixture of cedar and old paper books with a faint overlay of dust.

My escorts all stop at the door, arranging themselves so the exit is blocked, and Jaxon pushes his way past them and to my side. I force myself not to look at him. Or slap him.

Because I am seriously considering slapping him.

How could I ever have trusted that jerk?

There's a huge desk in the corner opposite the couch, and Samantha's father—Atticus Voss himself—is sitting at it, staring at a computer that seems too new to belong in this room. My pulse jumps and my knees go weak at the sight of him, at the thought of all the nasty things he's said about my family since my sister's replacement. And it's one thing to hear those nasty things he had to say secondhand, or to read them in the political editorials he's written about my father, or to have to endure his nasty remarks and glares at social events—but to be face to face with him like this? Alone, without any of our hired bodyguards?

I would rather tell my parents I'd been suspended from school. For life.

He tilts the computer monitor toward him, studies something on the screen for a moment before he says, "Mr. Cross, your presence is no longer needed."

"Right," Jaxon says, "but I just wanted to tell you—"

"I sincerely appreciate your help." Voss's tone is louder but still perfectly calm. Eerily calm, almost. "But you can go now. I will be handling things from here."

Jaxon still doesn't move. Voss rises from his chair and gives him an irritated look, his nostrils flaring slightly and his tiny blue eyes glaring. He's a monster of a man, really, with a thick neck and a hulking, well-muscled frame. I don't remember him being so imposing, or so terrifying to look at; maybe it's the lighting in here. Or maybe it's just because so many of the memories I have of him are from those dinner parties and political outings my parents used to drag me to, where he was much more civil looking, dressed in those fancy suits and ties.

He doesn't say anything else to Jaxon. Instead, he turns to me, and his face lights up like he's just now noticed I'm standing here.

"Hello, Catelyn. It's very nice to see you again," he says, stepping around his desk and crossing to me. His still overly polite tone makes me even more nervous. "And how are your parents? Well I hope?"

"They're fine," I say, frowning. I know he didn't bring me in here just for small talk. "But they might be a little concerned about what's going on here."

He plasters on a smile. "And what, precisely, do you think is going on here?"

I look from Jaxon to the people behind us and then back to Voss. My hands try to shake, but I force them to be still, then clear my throat. "It . . . it looks a lot like a kidnapping," I say. My voice doesn't carry as impressively as his, but at least it doesn't tremble.

Voss laughs. "Don't be ridiculous," he says. "I only want to talk. And I believe you'll agree that the outside world is rather hectic for you right now, isn't it? This just seemed simpler to me. No cameras or reporters or any of that nonsense. Here it's just you, me, and a few of my closest friends." He motions to the people standing guard at the door. One of the men snickers.

"My parents will come looking for me," I say, and this time my voice does shake. Not because I'm afraid of how close he's standing, or of the way his lips curve cold and cruel as he brings his face even nearer to mine. No. What I'm afraid of is how long it's going to be before anybody actually *does* come looking for me. My parents think I'm at school. And maybe they'll notice when I'm late this afternoon, but even then, they're so busy worrying about Violet that who knows how long it will be before they do anything about it?

"Let's hurry this up, then, shall we?" Voss says, his smile abruptly disappearing. "Your sister. She was the last person anyone saw with my daughter. Where has she run off to?"

"I don't know."

It's the truth, but still the wrong answer, apparently. He grabs the collar of my shirt and jerks me toward him. I duck away, and my forehead brushes the unshaven stubble of his throat. "Where. Is. She?"

"*I don't know.*"

"You're *lying.*"

His face is blood red, teeth clenched into the terrible smile of a madman. His calmness is way past gone; now he sounds more like a man who has lost his child, and who's desperately trying to find somebody to blame for her death. I really don't want to be that somebody. And I don't want Violet to be that somebody, either.

Though for a brief, unpleasant moment—as my ears are ringing with the threats he's half shouting directly into my ear—I'll admit I find myself wondering. If I *did* know that Violet had anything to do with it all, would I tell him?

I know all the places she hides when she runs away. I could find her if I had to. If anybody could find her, it would be me. Especially if I had the CCA's help tracking her down.

Would I find her, though? If it meant that all of these people would leave me alone and let me go back to blending into the scenery?

I'd like to say no. But I don't know. My head is spinning, and everything that's happened this morning is crashing in around me, and to tell you the truth I'm not sure of anything anymore. I just want to get back to yesterday. To before I threw that punch. To before I talked to Jaxon and thought that maybe, just maybe, I'd found someone I could trust.

"Get your hands off her, Voss." It's Jaxon speaking, I know, but it's weird to hear him sound so angry, so dangerous—so far from the easygoing person I thought I knew.

Voss spins around, jerking me with him. "This has nothing to do with you anymore—I don't care who your mother is." He keeps his teeth clenched, and little flecks of spit push out with his words and shower the side of my face.

"If the president knew what you were doing, you know she wouldn't approve. She would—"

Suddenly, the door behind us slides open. And for a moment, everything stops. Then Jaxon mutters, "Guess we'll see what she would do," under his breath, and Voss slowly, finger by finger, unclenches the grip he has on my shirt. I push him away as hard as I can and turn around just as the people behind me part respectfully to let a woman step into the room.

My first thought when I see her is of a movie I remember watching as a child: a fairy tale set in ancient times, with castles and royal palaces and balls. I don't remember the story, but I remember the way the queen of the castle carried herself from room to room, because the first Violet and I used to mimic it: chin lifted, steps falling quick and purposefully while her eyes saw everyone but bothered with none of them. This woman is wearing a tailored, dark navy pantsuit, but it's not hard to picture her in a flowing gown, or with a tiara perched on top of her smooth black hair.

"What is going on?" she demands in a brisk, business-like

tone. "Atticus?" Her gaze is leveled at Voss, but it's Jaxon who answers her.

"I did as I was told," he says angrily. "But if I'd known you were going to let this bastard"—he jabs a finger toward Voss—"treat her like this, then I never would have brought her back here."

"One of these days, that mouth of yours is going to push me too far," Voss growls, taking a step toward him.

The room goes very, very quiet.

"Are you threatening my son, Atticus?" The woman's voice, sharp and quick, shatters the silence. Her eyes shine with dark amusement, and her thin lips part, just barely. And I imagine this is the look a queen might get just before she commands someone to be executed.

"Madame President—"

"Oh, I so sincerely *hope* you are not threatening my son in front of me."

"Of course not."

"Good." She turns to Jaxon, and I see the resemblance between them now; they have the same fair skin, the same jewel blue eyes. "However," she says, "I did not raise my son to be so disrespectful. Apologize."

Jaxon's eyes narrow. He opens his mouth and starts to say something, but then he just turns around and leaves, slamming the door on his way out.

"Temperament just like his father's," his mother says wistfully. She looks back at me and gingerly places a hand on my elbow. "We have other things to worry about at the moment, though. If you'll follow me please, Catelyn?"

I think about protesting, but she seems more rational—or at least less crazy—than Voss; so maybe if I cooperate a little, she'll listen to reason and get me out of here.

She steers me toward the door without so much as a backward glance, though she does pause at the door long enough to tell Voss—Dr. Voss, she calls him now—that he should go on home for the day. He doesn't say anything, and I don't turn around, either. But I can feel him staring after us. The back of my neck burns, like the fire in his eyes leapt from them and is now trying to burn its way through my skin.

"You'll forgive him, won't you?" President Cross asks once we're safely outside that room. "He's taking the death of his daughter very hard. I'm afraid it's unhinged him a little."

I nod, thinking of how the news of her death had affected me, even though I barely hung out with her anymore—so I can't imagine what he's going through right now. But I'm willing to bet he's miserable enough that he deserves a few free act-like-a-jerk passes.

"Although to be honest," the president continues, talking more to the air than to me, "his performance over the past year or so has been growing steadily less satisfactory. I had actually been planning on disposing of him soon—by which I mean firing him, of course, so there's no need to widen your eyes like that—but with the death of Samantha . . . well, I'm afraid I may not be able to find the heart. The whole thing is just so tragic, isn't it?" That last part sounds like an actual question, as if she herself hasn't quite decided how she feels about the whole thing yet. I don't know why she's asking me, though; I'm not here to help her sort out her feelings. I'm having a hard enough time with my own.

"I wish there was something I could do to help with that," I say pointedly. "But what I was telling Dr. Voss was the truth. I don't know where my sister is, or why she was with Samantha that night, or if she even *was* with—"

President Cross stops so quickly that I almost step on the back of her shiny beige stilettos. "It wouldn't be in your best interest to lie to me right now, Catelyn." She smiles down at me. It's not the same as Voss's frigid smile, but there's no warmth behind it either. "I just want to make that perfectly clear."

"I . . . I'm not lying. I swear."

"Glad to hear it." She turns and walks on, more quickly now. I almost have to jog to keep up with her long-legged strides. But even as I focus on not losing her, I can't keep my eyes from wandering around the spaces we pass through. There's plenty to take in, from the people typing away on their computers to the others with pensive faces and arms folded across their chests as they watch the monitors mounted on the walls. Various news reports flash across those monitors, and almost all of them are focused on the same story: Samantha's death. Or—more specifically—the persons responsible for it. Because I guess they've decided to stop calling it an accident now; words like "foul play" and "suspected homicide" probably make for better ratings.

The scenes keep jumping back and forth from panoramic shots of the local Huxley laboratory compound to the abandoned railroad tracks where they found Samantha, and then to a roundtable discussion going on between reporters. I'm not close enough to hear exactly what they're saying, but I don't need to be. I know what they're debating. The safety of cloning, the choices of families like mine, the morality of companies like Huxley and the existence of people like my sister.

All of these topics are such *endless* fun, after all.

Scenes from the press conference outside our house flash on one of the nearby monitors. Inset near the bottom right corner is a picture of Samantha, smiling and chillingly unaware, of course, that anyone would ever be discussing her death like this. The picture fades into a close-up of my father, and I slow to a stop, caught up in the tired creases around his eyes and the determined vagueness in his expression. Even though I know that really is what he looks like most of the time now, splashed up there on that screen it seems . . . off, somehow. Like they've got the wrong guy. Because the person up there looks like he's always been like that, but I know better; however worn and worked over the old memories of him are, I still have them.

"Things seem to have gotten a bit out of control for Huxley with this one," President Cross says, stopping and turning around to follow my gaze. "The cloned daughter of a politician doing something like this? This won't be swept under the rug for a while now—chances are it will be brought up at every press conference and town hall meeting that your father attends in the foreseeable future." She gestures toward each of the monitors as she speaks, looking a little too pleased about it all in a way that makes my stomach curl. I feel like I should remind her of the whole *a teenager was just murdered* thing, but she walks on and changes the subject before I can.

"But I didn't bring you here to discuss politics, so—"

"Why *did* you bring me here?"

"A couple of reasons," she says, holding up two fingers, but not stopping again or even glancing back at me. "One, for your own protection. And two, because there's something I want to show you. We'll say it's an olive branch that I'm extending to you. Take it, and I think we may be able to help each other. Or at least come to some sort of understanding."

She halts abruptly then, in front of a wide control panel with a complicated-looking mass of buttons and dials and touch screens. Her fingers rest for a moment on one of those touch screens near the bottom, and then a series of holographic command prompts flicker up into the space directly in front of us. Her hands move over the panel, quickly and expertly shifting through password prompts and navigation options until a series of images take shape in the space instead: four identical 3-D humans suspended in the air.

"This is a model I began working on some years ago," she explains. "And I'm still working on it, to be honest; there is still plenty of research to be done, and there are loose ends to be followed up on, of course—but I'm confident enough in its accuracy that I don't mind sharing it with you. Hopefully it will help you appreciate exactly what we're dealing with."

"What is this a model of, exactly?"

"Of the effects of the mutagens introduced into our food and water supplies by the bioagent weapons used during the war. The ones that caused the marks on your mother, and on so many others? What the government doesn't want people to know is that the long-term effects of said mutagens are going to be considerably more serious than just a few recovered people with some rather nasty-looking scars."

She types in a few more commands, and two of the human figures change from black to a pale, pinkish red color. "The infected," she says, pointing to them. "The infection the bioagent unleashed targeted the chromosomes containing genes crucial to reproduction, causing mutations in most of the people exposed to them."

"Which is why the birthrate has gone down," I say, thinking of that stupid video. "That isn't a secret the government is keeping from anybody."

"Right, because your parent's generation is still producing a fair amount of healthy children—you and your sister are proof of that. So, no need to be alarmed just yet, right? Your mother may have mutated genes, but they aren't completely defective. Just an unfortunate side effect of war that, if the government's pacifying lies are to be believed, we will overcome. It's a nice sentiment, but . . ."

Two diagonal lines strike out from beneath the

pinkish-colored human models and cross, and two more figures appear at the end of each of the lines. They are a much bolder red; the color of blood, almost. And out beside them is a calculation, a percentage labeled HEALTHY RATE OF BIRTH.

Eighty percent.

"See, there was something terrifyingly brilliant about this particular mutagen," President Cross continues. "The mutation, this syndrome that it caused . . . it's not something that is so easily overcome, no matter the amount of nationalistic propaganda pushing us. It's not a disease we can simply outlast as a population. Because not only is it autosomal-dominant, but its effects get stronger with each generation that it's passed down to. A stuttering—or unstable—allelic trait: that would be the proper scientific term for it, if you care to know. And it is a frightening term to apply to something affecting nearly one-third of the remaining population—especially since even that is a low estimate of the number of people who suffered direct exposure."

I watch as the diagram continues to unfold in front of me, the diagonal lines darting out and crossing underneath the figures, which grow darker and darker as the calculations on display beside them show smaller and smaller numbers. Generation after generation, all the way down to almost zero percent.

Funny, Huxley never mentioned this in any of their videos.

"A crippling, drawn-out depopulation: assurance that

this country never rises from the ashes of its defeat," President Cross says, as though I really needed the explanation.

I can feel her eyes on me now, but I'm too horrified by the last of the humans on the screen to say anything right away. My hand lifts on its own and traces through the air, circling that ominous number out beside them.

"How do you know all of this?" I ask quietly.

"Because Huxley was hired by the government to research the long-term effects of all this—and I was one of the head scientists involved in that project."

That snaps my attention back to her. "You worked for Huxley?"

"What seems a very long time ago now, yes. I did. And so did Dr. Voss; he was a little more sound of mind back then, and we were partners." I must still look skeptical, because she adds, "They were a very different organization when I signed on with them twenty years ago. For decades before that, they had been a highly respected research facility, and it was a lot of people's dream to work for them—including mine. And I had the credentials, of course, but I was still shocked when they actually offered me a position. I suppose I made a good impression on Huxley himself in my interview; I ended up reporting directly to him. The two of us became rather close." She pauses and glances around the room, her focus eventually falling on a few of the people filing robotically past us. Her mouth slips into an almost-smirk. "He's taken my whole operation here rather personally, as you might imagine," she adds with a grim laugh. She looks like she's considering saying more on the subject but instead waves a dismissive hand.

"Anyway, much of my work at Huxley was centered around finding ways to increase human longevity, through both gene manipulation and the study and prevention of deadly and infectious diseases. So, when the government was faced with a sickened population after the war, my former employer was the group they turned to for help. We were tasked with trying to find a cure, a way to undo the damage—and we only had so much time to do it, with the threat of every generation becoming sicker than the last hanging over us. Damaged DNA is very difficult to repair, though. Not to mention it was dangerous, working on actual humans without having time to run trials first; so some of the scientists in our group started teaming with members of Huxley's controversial cloning division, growing test specimens and modifying and manipulating their DNA instead, in search of the answers they couldn't find. At some point the focus shifted entirely to those specimens, and then to fully developed clones that were starting to turn out stronger and healthier than even the healthiest natural humans.

"Some of the scientists started to talk about using the clones to supplement the population, to mix them in and gradually grow it back stronger than before. Then talk of *supplementing* turned to plans for more or less *replacing*; the idea being, I suppose, that sometimes it's easier to just start over than it is to try to fix what's broken. If you ask me, I think the cloning division had been waiting for this all along—for an excuse to unleash their creations, to test them out in the world outside the labs. And as soon as I realized that . . . well, that is when we reached a parting of ways, I'm afraid. I left. Voss and a few others came with me, and we've been fighting Huxley ever since."

"But what about what they were trying to do? What about the future?"

"We had very different visions for it, I'm afraid. And still do. However grim things look, I still don't think the answer lies in erasing the human element so completely as Huxley wants to. In the beginning, I think their intentions may have been pure enough—mine certainly were—but then, most of the things that are bad in this world started off as someone's idea of good, didn't they? I don't think their goal now has anything to do with securing our country's future. Securing their *own* future, maybe, but . . ."

She goes back to the computer panel, and I watch as the diagram fades away and a series of folders take its place. She taps the center touch pad a few times, and some of those folders open, spilling pictures and words into the air. After a few seconds, they arrange themselves into profiles, and then there are a half-dozen young, smiling faces looking back at me. And stamped across each of their pictures is the same word: DECEASED.

"This is a small selection of origins known to have died or disappeared under strange circumstances—circumstances we can link back to Huxley agents."

"What do you mean that you can 'link back' to Huxley agents?" I want to laugh at the impossibility of everything she's saying. But there's a heaviness on my chest that's making it hard to breathe, and it takes me a moment to even ask the rest of my question. "You think Huxley is going around killing off all the origins?"

"Not all of them, no. Just as many as they can get away with for now. We believe they're creating a presence, a small army of clones among the general population—because they know it won't take many for them to overpower the normal humans, especially when they already have fear working in their favor. It's only a matter of time before they have everything in place and they've gained enough power and control to start carrying out their plans."

"Which are what, precisely?"

"I told you. President Huxley has no faith in human-kind, in its ability to survive, to keep evolving into a race that will make the most of this planet's future; he sees only the flaws in people, and only the need for someone to *fix* them. And more important, he has convinced himself that he is the one destined to do the mending."

"By replacing the human population with his own man-ufactured, perfected clones." I still can't keep the incredu-lity from my voice, even though I know now that she has a reliable source for at least some of what she's telling me; what else does she know about President Huxley, I won-der? It's still weird to picture them in the same room, hav-ing any sort of civil conversation about all of this stuff—or about anything else, for that matter.

She nods, her gaze drifting back to the diagram. "That's what we believe their plan is, yes."

"But that could never happen."

"It's happening right now."

"The government—"

She laughs again. "Has been in Huxley's hand from practically the beginning," she finishes for me. "Think about it, Catelyn: our losses in the war were humiliating. Our future was uncertain. People were scared and desperate for quick answers. So all it took was a group of Huxley's most brilliant, most persuasive scientists to corrupt the right government officials into believing that cloning was the solution already at hand—that with the right funding they could even develop more streamlined, efficient cloning methods that would allow them to make quick copies of those officials themselves. They promised them immortality. Supremacy over death. Is there anything more tempting than that?"

"But it's not supremacy over death at all if they have to *kill* the origins, is it?"

"Well they don't pitch it that way, do they? The body is just a throwaway instrument to them, one that can be molded, altered, replaced—whatever is needed to ensure that the mind lives on indefinitely. And they're smart enough to have convinced others that this is the most important part; that actual *life* exists solely in thoughts, in memories, and that they can transfer these things to a new body—a physically superior body—over and over again, and thus the person being transferred never has to actually die."

Just like my sister never actually died?

It seems like I should be nothing except horrified by everything she's saying, but I mostly feel only a numbing confusion, a strange buzzing in my brain as it tries to make sense of all this. Can everything she's saying be true? And if it is, then whose side am I supposed to be on? The CCA has always been the enemy. And Huxley . . . Huxley is the reason I still have a sister. It feels almost like a betrayal to her, to start thinking that everything they've done is all wrong. Because what does that make her, then?

The thought makes my knees feel weak.

"It's such a tantalizing possibility, at least on paper," President Cross is saying, "so of course most didn't want to listen to scientists like me. Scientists who tried warning them what a slippery slope cloning and genetic manipulation and such was, even though it had its benefits. And who tried to warn them that there would be a cost. Because there is always a cost." She lifts her eyes back to the projected faces and sighs. "And they're too far gone to listen to me at this point. To most of the higher-ups, the officials with any power to put a stop to all of this, *we're* the crazy ones now."

I follow her gaze, and suddenly my head is spinning, cold sweat shivering up and sliding down the back of my neck. There's no way she can be right.

This is too much. It's too huge, too crazy even to think about. I don't want to think about what her accusations might mean, about the impossible future scenarios she's painting.

It's amazing how you can believe your life is so awful,

but then something worse comes along, and suddenly you'd give anything to just have that normal, awful life back. I want my parents. I want my sister calling me names and breaking things and blaming it on me. I want those stupid people shouting, protesting outside my window all night, and I want that to be my only problem. Wasn't that a big enough problem by itself?

"You said you brought me here for my protection." My voice sounds like it belongs to someone else, someone who's accepted the impossibility of all this while the real me is hiding someplace far away. "Why?" I ask. "Do you think Huxley is planning to kill me too?"

"We actually think they'll be more interested in your sister's clone."

Isn't everyone?

"I'm not an expert on clones or their programming, but it doesn't take a genius to see that something about your sister's replica seems to be off. She's spent most of the time since her activation drawing bad publicity to Huxley, and while we're thankful for it, somehow I doubt her creators are. And this latest deed that she's committed—"

"*Supposedly* committed," I correct automatically.

"—is a bit over the top, don't you think? Huxley is looking for her along with everyone else now, I'm sure. I imagine they're scrambling, trying to figure out where they went wrong with her, and they'll probably see you as a potential link to figuring that out." She hesitates, presses her fingertips to the corner touch screen again. The projections fade into the air, and the computer's control panel makes a soft humming noise as it shuts down. "Jaxon tells me you and Violet are close," she adds. "And that if anybody would know how to find her, it would be you."

Just his name is enough to irritate me all over again. What else has he told her, I wonder?

"Which is why I've confided all of this to you," she says. "I thought if you understood where I was coming from, you might help us do precisely that."

"What do you plan on doing with her if you find her, exactly?"

"You're very protective of her, aren't you?"

"Of course I am. She's my sister."

The president's smile is smug. "Is she, now? You're sure of that?"

Shut up, I think. But my mind is as far as the words get. However much I might want to shout them at her, something stops me. I lower my eyes, pretend to be very interested in a black scuff mark across the metal-grate flooring. I want this conversation to be over. If my father were here, it would be; this is the point in the conversation where he would say, *No more questions—this interview is finished.* In my mind, I can see him clearly: stoic and unyielding, looking straight ahead until the reporters and protestors finally get tired of trying to make him talk, and just move on. At least until next time.

But President Cross doesn't move on.

"We only want to contain her, Catelyn. To keep her from Huxley's scientists, because if she *is* a broken link in their experiments, then we want to do everything we can to stop them from figuring out how to fix it. She would be safer with us than she would be with Huxley, anyway. You have my word on that."

"Which is more or less worthless to me," I say. After all, I took her son's word for things, and look where *that* got me.

"I'm sorry you think so." She pauses thoughtfully, picks a loose thread from the cuff of her jacket and flicks it away. Somehow, she manages to make even that small movement seem oddly menacing. "Because I so wanted us to be on the same side for once," she says.

No more questions. This interview is over. Don't speak to her, Catelyn. Don't even look at her.

She isn't going to listen to anything I have to say anyway, because she already knows what she wants to hear. And I'm not telling her that, for the same reason I didn't tell our mother where Violet was hiding that day my sister painted obnoxious words on the fence around the backyard—just because she was feeling "artsy," she told me later. Mother was almost as menacing then as President Cross is now, and if Violet got in trouble, it wasn't going to be because of me.

It's never going to be because of me.

Secrets make sisters. Every time she asked me to cover for her, that's what this new Violet would say. So I keep her secrets. Because this way, in the moments when she doesn't seem so much like the old Violet, I've at least got some sort of connection to her left. Something that's only ours and that no one can ever take away.

The president is silent. Waiting for me to speak, to blurt out some sort of confession, maybe. But I could endure her incriminating stare all day if I had to. Furniture-girl, remember?

"I will find your sister," she says after another long moment, after I've apparently made it clear enough that I have no plans to talk. "With or without your help, her fate is already determined—all that's left to be decided is yours. And as far as I'm concerned, you are either working for us or you are against us. I've no use for people who insist on staying caught in the middle." She glances at the communicator on her wrist, jabs a few times at one of the buttons on the side. "And do keep in mind, Catelyn," she adds, still messing with that button, "that I'm being exceptionally gracious in giving you the opportunity to be *with* us. Do you know they all laughed at me when I suggested we ask an origin to help us?"

"I'm not going to help you."

She glances up at me with a smile.

"Oh, we'll see about that."

CHAPTER SIX

Deals

Six hours.

That's how long I've been in here. And if I have to spend another six hours in here, I am going to go insane.

I've been passing the time by watching the minutes slide by on my phone's display; it's about all I can do with it, because the solid concrete walls of this prison cell make it impossible to get any sort of signal. That's probably why they didn't bother to take it from me. I couldn't call anybody for help if I wanted to.

Another minute goes by. I toss the useless phone onto the bed in the corner; the mattress is so stiff that the phone bounces several feet in the air after hitting it, then lands on the metal grate flooring with a sharp *clang!* that makes me cringe. I go to pick it up, to check the damage I've done, just as the door behind me slides open.

I turn around, and Jaxon is standing in the frame.

He doesn't say anything at first, but I'm instantly, painfully, aware of how different things are between us now.

Those eyes that used to be one of the brightest parts of my day are guarded now, and all they do is make me angry—because all I can think about as I look into them is how stupid I was to get into that car with him not once but twice.

Twice.

How could I have been so embarrassingly stupid?

"What do you want?" The memory of that embarrassment—along with six hours of this cell—makes my voice a lot edgier than normal.

"I just want to talk," he says.

"I don't have anything to say to you."

"Well, just listen, then."

"You know, I see your lips moving, but all I hear is white noise. It's really weird."

"Cate, please don't be like that."

My glare is so intense that he actually stumbles back a step.

"I didn't know it was going to be like this," he says. "I swear I didn't."

"But you knew your mother was the president of the CCA," I say. "Or did that slip your mind too?" I force myself to unclench the phone from my hand and set it back down on the bed, so I'm not tempted anymore to throw it at him. I don't want to break it for real this time.

"She said she just wanted to talk to you."

"Well they always say that, don't they? And then the talking turns to shouting, and the shouting turns into them throwing bricks through our window, and then—"

"I know this sucks, okay? And I'm sorry about everything the CCA has done to you. I really am. That's why I'm here—to apologize." He steps cautiously toward me. Takes a deep breath. Hesitates, like he hasn't completely decided whether or not he wants to say this next part out loud. "Because just for the record?" he finally continues. "I don't agree with everything that goes on here. I don't agree with a lot of it."

"But you don't agree with people like me, either, right? People like my sister."

"I didn't say that—"

"You think my sister killed Samantha Voss. That's why you brought me here. You think I know what happened and I'm just not telling you."

Another deep breath. In his nose, out his mouth. He doesn't answer me.

"That's what I thought," I say.

"Well," he says, "*do* you know what happened?" His features are perfectly stoic. He's actually asking me that. He actually thinks I might be an accomplice to murder.

Suddenly I'm so angry I can hardly breathe, much less talk; after several attempts, I manage to force two scathing words from my mouth: "Get. Out."

He folds his arms across his chest and leans against the wall, frowning.

"Okay, then *you* stay. I'll leave." I shove past him just as the door slides open again, and Seth Lancaster—of all people—steps inside. Because that's what I get for thinking today couldn't get worse.

"You too?" I mutter under my breath, staring at the huge grin on Seth's face.

"So it's true," he says. "She really is here. Excellent."

My face flames. Of course he'd find it excellent. I'm sure he thinks this is fantastic payback for me punching him yesterday. Although I'm not sure it's a fair trade-off—since his nose seems perfectly fine today. If I'd known he was CCA, I probably would have punched him harder and at least made it worth getting suspended over.

"What are you doing in here?" Jaxon asks. The edge in my voice is in his now too, and Seth seems taken aback by it. He gets over it quickly enough.

"Looking for you, actually," he says, "because I was wondering how things had turned out. But now I see it for myself, of course—and can I just say thanks?"

I'm even more confused than ever, but Jaxon shakes his head and says, "You and Alex have been betting again, haven't you?"

Seth beams at him. "You know that moron bet me a fifty the other day that you wouldn't be able to pull this one off?" he says, pointing at me. Because I'm apparently just a "this" now. "And when you f'ed up yesterday, I talked him into going double or nothing. So you know what that means? It means I'm a hundred bucks richer because *I* kept the faith in you, my friend."

My eyes narrow. "You were placing bets on whether or not Jaxon would manage to kidnap me?" I ask, taking an angry step toward him.

He spins around and does this crazy kung fu pose, his hand up like he's going to karate chop me or something. "Back up, devil woman," he says. "You punch me again and I'm hitting you back this time."

"No. You are not," Jaxon says, grabbing Seth by the sleeve and jerking him back.

"Did you see what she did to my nose yesterday?" Seth protests, shrugging his arm free. "She has a mean right hook. I don't care if she is a girl—it would still be a fair fight."

"Yeah right," Jaxon says. "She would kick your ass, and we both know it." He flashes me a quick smile. I don't return it, as charming as it might be. That charm is what got me into this mess in the first place; I'm not falling for it again.

"That was cold, man," Seth says.

"Get out, Seth," Jaxon says.

"Are you betraying me for the clonie? Because I feel like I'm being betrayed for the clonie."

"Don't call her that."

Seth's grin is unapologetic. "And getting defensive, too? Right . . . I think I get what's going on here. Did I interrupt something? Is that why you both looked so pissed off when I walked in?"

"*Out*, Seth."

"Because, you know, you could have just kept on doing your thing. I could have sat quietly in the corner and waited."

"Kept on doing *what* thing?" I ask.

He cocks an eyebrow. And I clench my fist and draw it back, thinking about hitting him on purpose this time.

"Please don't hit me," he says, throwing his hands in front of his face. "Save your wrath for someone less handsome. The world can't afford to lose a face like this."

"Debatable," Jaxon says.

Seth fakes a crushed expression. "If that isn't betrayal, I don't know what is."

"Can I make up for it by walking you to the door?" Jaxon suggests.

"All right. Okay. I can tell when I'm not wanted."

"Sometimes I wonder about that."

Seth's smile only widens before he turns and walks to the door. "Oh, and by the way," he says, glancing back at Jaxon, "mama-president was looking for you. Said it was urgent."

"You couldn't have told me that five minutes ago?"

He just shrugs and then disappears into the hallway.

"Sorry about that," Jaxon says.

"Why are you apologizing for him?"

"I think it's just a reflex at this point," he answers, trying that smile out on me again.

Still not letting it work.

"Sometimes I don't even listen to what he says," he goes on, "but I still apologize for it, because nine times out of ten *someone* needs to." He laughs, shaking his head. "He doesn't mean half of what he says, though. Especially not the name-calling part. The clones and Huxley and the CCA—I don't think he could care less about any of that."

"But he's CCA, right?"

"Technically, yeah. But mostly he just hangs out around here because he's got nowhere else to go."

"What do you mean?"

"Both his parents are dead, we think. He's never told me how, or when; he doesn't talk about it much. I just know my mom found him wreaking havoc in this park near where we used to live, like ten years ago; he threw a rock at her car, and she chased him down and made him apologize for it. She brought him home when she found out he was alone, 'cause he looked half-starved. Wouldn't even tell us where he'd come from or anything. He's been sort of like a little brother to me ever since he got here; sometimes I think that's why Mom actually brought him home—because I always complained that I didn't have any siblings or anything, and it was boring as hell around the headquarters here by myself. Like how some parents get their kids a dog for company, you know? Well, my mom got me a homeless kid." He raises one shoulder and lets it drop. "Same difference. Except Seth doesn't fetch worth crap, and he's proven impossible to house-break."

So they're family, then. And now I understand why he apologized. I'm guessing it's for the same reason I find myself apologizing for the things Violet says and does—even though there's no way I can control them. Because that's what you're supposed to do for your family, right? Try to protect them from everyone who doesn't understand?

"So he lives with you?" I ask.

He nods, and then there's a long, uncomfortable silence where I think we're both wondering when and how we started conversing civilly again, and whether we're supposed to pick up our argument or just let it fade into the background for now.

I clear my throat purposefully.

"Your mother's probably wondering where you are," I say.

He frowns again but doesn't keep arguing. He does pause on his way out, though, and turn to me one last time. "Just . . . look, if you need anything . . ."

What I *need* is for him to not be such a liar. I need him to be the person I thought he was, who would never leave me alone in this cell to rot. I need for my šister to stop wrecking everything, and for my life to stop being such a mess. But since I don't think he can deliver on any of those things, I settle for asking for something more practical: a computer. He looks at me like I'm crazy for thinking he could get away with slipping something like that into this cell. Then he leaves without another word.

But less than an hour later, he's back. He hands me a thin tablet computer and then leaves again, just as silently. I stare at the door for a long time afterward, trying to make sense of his motives. He said he didn't agree with everything that went on here. But was he telling the truth?

Or is this another trick?

It doesn't matter, I eventually decide. I can't just sit here and see what happens. I have this computer now, for whatever reason—and one way or another, I'm going to use it to get out of here.

Now I just have to decide how to go about that. My first thought—the whole reason I asked for it in the first place—was so I could use it to send a message to my parents, to tell them what's happened and to send help. If I could somehow make sure it wouldn't be intercepted by anyone, that would be the most obvious solution. And home is the most obvious place to go.

But what's waiting for me there?

Jaxon told me there's still no sign of Violet anywhere, which means our house will still be crawling with expectant police and protestors. I don't want to deal with them. I don't want to have to face the press, either, shoving their recorders in my face and demanding to know where I've been, what I've seen, what I know. Especially since *I* don't even know what I know.

Because, as much as I want to deny it, I can't help but wonder: What if everything President Cross said is true? What if everything my parents have ever told me about the cloning movement—about my whole life—really is a lie? What if they don't know what's really going on either?

I'm not sure how I'm supposed to separate the truths from the lies, when they both sound the same to me. But there has to be a way, right? Some way to grab truth at the source, instead of waiting for it to trickle down to me only after it's passed through the filters that my parents and society and everyone else has set up?

The more I think about it, the more I wonder if that source is Violet.

And the more I think that maybe I don't want to go home just yet.

Since last night, I've been running through this list in my head of all the places she might go, and I have it narrowed down to a handful. The most likely location, I decide, is the cemetery about an hour and a half outside the city. It's where the first Violet is buried, and this Violet has always had a strange, secret obsession with visiting it. It's far enough from Haven to keep her out of the city police's immediate radar, and it's the last place anybody would probably think she'd go—so it seems like a good place for me to start looking.

Now I just have to get out of this room.

I wait until half past midnight to put my plan into motion. By then, the intercom hasn't beeped in over an hour, and the chatter of people outside my door has stopped. I still press my ear to the cold steel for a minute—holding my breath and listening for footsteps or voices—before creeping back to the bed and picking up the computer.

Bypassing the login screen for the Network is a simple matter of finding the right password files and decrypting them. Soon I've got full administrator access, and I'm able to configure the connection to use the anonymization proxy server I set up on my parents' computer (unknown to them) a long time ago. So now I've got complete access to wherever I need to go, and anyone who might intercept what I'm doing won't be able to trace me. Easy enough.

I find the president's com-address. I'm signed in as a guest, and the way I have things configured, she should see nothing but an anonymous sender on her end. But now comes the hard part: trying to convince her that the anonymous sender is Violet—and that she's somehow figured out that the CCA is holding me hostage here. If Cross asks about that, I'm going to have to convince her that someone in here is leaking information. Which will mean I'll have to decide who I'd rather blame that on more: Jaxon or Seth. Jaxon, probably. It seems like fair enough payback.

I have the first message already typed: *I want to make a deal.*

I tap send.

I want to make a deal is what Violet would say. She would be straightforward like that. Wouldn't she? I was so sure when I typed it, but now I'm getting nervous. When and if President Cross answers me, what will she say? And how would Violet reply? I should know. We're sisters. No one knows her better than I do. Me and the first Violet even used to pretend to be twins when we were little; we'd switch names and spend the day as each other, and when our mother was in a good mood she'd even play along with us. Sometimes I'd be my sister all day long, and then Mother would tuck me into Violet's bed, and Violet into mine. Just a game, but we took it so seriously sometimes. That was Old-Violet, though. And now I can't help but worry—what if I don't know New-Violet as well as I thought I did?

But maybe what I know isn't that important, anyway. It only matters what I can make other people think.

The monitor blinks. I've got it set to visual notifications only, because I'm still paranoid that there are people waiting outside, listening for any sort of noise.

On the screen is a short message, demanding that I identify myself.

So I do.

This time my name is Violet Benson. And if the president wants me to cooperate, she'll bring my little sister Catelyn to the ETS C-station in Westside. Because I'm the one they want.

Not her.

CHAPTER SEVEN

Truce

The air in Westside always has a metallic, chemical-like scent, thanks to the numerous energy reactors that dominate the skyline. It's a poor, run-down area filled with people who usually didn't end up here by choice. Not the safest part of town, but it's also the place I'm least likely to be recognized (my mother would not be caught dead in this neighborhood), and the station here is the closest one to what's left of Highway 21, which I think I can follow out of the city and north to the cemetery.

Once I get outside the city limits, the details of my brilliant plan get a little . . . fuzzier. I know that the only vehicles that really use the old highway system are trucks from the massive complex of warehouses to the south of Haven. They deliver all up and down the East Coast, and I'm hoping I'll be able to stow away on one of them for most of the trek up to my sister's grave. It wouldn't be impossible to walk if I had to; I'd just rather avoid that if I can. The quicker I find Violet, the better.

"Your sister is late," President Cross says, walking over to me with her arms folded across her chest. It must be after four a.m. by now, but she still has that tense, hawk-like alertness to her face.

I don't say anything. I've managed to fool her this long; now I'm just waiting for the perfect moment to set off the distress disc I had stashed in the pocket of my jacket. My father bought me several of these discs after Violet and I had a particularly nasty run-in with some persistent paparazzi. *Just in case*, he said. I had no idea I'd end up being this thankful that he always nagged me about keeping one with me at all times.

"It seems she doesn't care very much about you after all, does she?"

I try my best to look disappointed. Like I was really expecting Violet to show up and rescue me. President Cross looks convinced; her smile is brisk as she whips a phone out of the bag at her side, then walks over and disappears into the shadows of the looming ETS tracks above us. Three of the men she brought along follow her at a distance, leaving only two more that I have to outrun.

I take one last look behind me. It's a straight shot to a narrow street that looks like it forks both directions at the end. Not much to trip over; I can run it with my eyes closed.

I slide my hand into my pocket and find the grooved button on the side of the disc. A high-pitched whine starts, gets louder and louder; I shut my eyes tightly and toss the disc just as the sound is becoming unbearable. Even through my eyelids I see the explosion of light it releases, and I hear the shouts of agony from the CCA members. I turn and leap into a mad dash. Someone gets a hand on my arm, but I blindly twist free and keep running— hopefully still facing the right direction.

Once I feel like I've made it at least twenty feet away, I open my eyes just enough to see the street beneath me. So I notice the massive crack in the pavement ahead. Just not in enough time to avoid tripping over it. I roll over the ground, scrape my arm and shoulder badly enough that warm blood starts to bubble up on my skin, but I don't even come to a complete stop before leaping back to my feet. After a few wobbly steps, I regain my balance and decide that it's probably safe to open my eyes completely now.

So I do, and I find myself approaching a concrete wall that has to be at least twenty feet high.

Crap.

How did I get so turned around?

I barely have time to curse before I hear more shouts. They still sound disoriented, but it won't be long until that wears off. To my right is a building that looks abandoned. Half of its windows are missing, boarded up, or broken and glistening in the moonlight. The window closest to me is covered in a thick layer of grime, but still intact; I grab a chunk of broken concrete nearby and fling it at the glass.

Inside, it's almost pitch black, and it smells like dust and what has to be years' worth of rat droppings and whatever trash the rodents have brought in here to build nests with. I hold my breath and feel my way along a narrow hallway, jumping at every noise and sincerely hoping one of those rats doesn't decide to run over my feet.

I make it to a large, open room; there's a huge skylight overhead that's nearly opaque from filth, but it still lets in enough moonlight to illuminate stacks of metal pallets that have rusted to varying degrees. Between some of the pallets are piles of dirty blankets and pillows and the charred remains of little fires; the air in here smells more like alcohol than dust, and the bottles and beer cans scattered over the floor make me almost as uneasy as the possibility of any CCA members catching up with me. I don't want to have to fight off any drunken homeless people either.

I take a deep breath and start down the next set of hallways, then up a staircase that's missing its railing. I reach the top step, and less than ten feet away I see what's left of a set of double doors leading out into the street. The glass is gone from these, too, and most of the frame is missing from the one on the left. I creep toward them, listening intently to the distant murmur of city traffic, and for any possible sign of people outside.

I'm about to make a run for it when I hear footsteps echoing off the cinderblock walls in every direction.

I break into a sprint. Less than two feet from the door, someone grabs my arm and jerks me back, clamping a cold hand over my mouth. I kick the person as hard as I can in the ankle, but the hold just gets tighter and I keep getting dragged backward. It's not until I bite the hand covering my mouth that a familiar voice hisses in my ear, "Catelyn, it's me."

And I'm so stunned to hear Jaxon's voice that for a moment I can't do anything *except* calm down and let him pull me farther back into the darkness. But after about ten more feet, I get over that, and I kick his ankle even harder this time. He finally lets me go then, but he moves around to block my way back to the exit.

"Calm down," he says. In the darkness I can't see his face, but I can hear the sharp note of anxiety in his voice.

"What are you doing here? If you came to try to talk me into cooperating, you can forget it—I'm not going back." I try to fight my way past him, but in the dim light I end up running straight into his chest instead. He wraps his arms around me, refuses to let go even when I get my fingernails up under his shirt and dig them as deep as I can into the skin of his stomach. I keep digging and twisting and kicking, but he's a lot stronger than I would have guessed from just looking at his skinny frame.

"I don't want you to go back." His voice is a quick, rough whisper now. "I want you to be quiet before my mom and her guys hear us and we *both* end up in a lot of trouble."

I stop fighting as the meaning behind his words sinks in. "Your mother doesn't know you're here, does she?"

"She will if you keep making all that noise."

Blood thumps in my ears. Is he telling the truth? What am I supposed to do? I can't trust him. I could probably outrun him if I could get away, but I don't know if I'm strong enough to fight him off.

"Let go of me," I say. "Let go of me and I'll stop being loud."

"And you won't run?"

"No."

"Or kick me again?"

"I'm not making any promises about that."

He hesitates. Then his hands slide slowly, cautiously, from my waist. But the very tips of his fingers still linger, a ghostlike touch against my skin, anticipating movement. And he's right to anticipate it. Because my first thought is to bolt, despite my promise. I'm not sure why I don't. Still too shocked, maybe.

"Why are you here," I ask, "if you don't want to take me back to your mother?"

"Where are you planning on going?" he asks instead of answering me.

"That's none of your business."

"I could help you."

"The same way you helped me yesterday? Yeah, thanks but no thanks."

"You never really let me explain that."

"Is there anything to explain? You *lied* to me. I trusted you, and you betrayed me before we even—"

"I didn't lie."

"What?"

"I never said I *wasn't* going to bring you to the CCA."

"You . . . you are unbelievable, you know that?"

"And if I hadn't taken you there, somebody else would have," he presses. "Because I've never seen my mom so desperate to track down a clone as she is with your sister. She isn't going to let Huxley get to Violet first. And my mom's convinced you're the best key to finding her—so there's no telling what they would have done to get you back there if I hadn't volunteered to do it myself."

"So am I supposed to thank you, then?"

"No." We hear footsteps, far in the distance, and he leans in a little closer and lowers his voice. "But you could give me a little more credit. Maybe I'm not as horrible as you think I am."

"Or maybe you're a liar."

"Or maybe I'm just trying to figure things out, and you're making that incredibly difficult for me." I can hear the frustration building in his voice.

"Me? What have *I* done? And what do you have to figure out, anyway? All you have to do is follow orders. The CCA has its mission statement, right? If you get confused, just repeat it to yourself a couple times and that should sort things out."

He takes a step back. "You really don't get it, do you?"

I'd started trying to shove my way around him again, but something in his tone makes me hesitate. I attempt to keep going anyway but only make it a few steps before he says, "You're thinking about leaving the city, aren't you?"

I stop and tilt my face back toward him even though I can't see anything in the darkness. "How do you—"

"Why else would you tell them to take you to that particular ETS station?" he says drily. "I know you didn't come to Westside for the scenery. Or the gigantic mutated rats."

"Those are an urban legend."

"We hope, don't we?"

I suppress a shiver as I turn around. "Fine. Yes. I'm leaving. So what?"

For a long moment, everything is quiet. No footsteps echoing, no hum of traffic from outside. Just our tense, shallow breathing. Then he takes a deeper breath and says, "I want to leave with you."

It starts in my fingertips—the tingling itch of suspicion from before—and crawls over every inch of my skin.

"Why?" I demand.

"I told you. I have things to figure out."

"Well so do I—and I don't need you getting in my way."

"Getting in your way?" His laugh is sharp and irritated. "I'm the reason you got out of headquarters in the first place. Do you have any idea how much trouble I'm going to be in if my mom finds out I gave you that computer? Even though I *knew* you were going to use it to escape somehow. How exactly did you manage to trick her, anyway?"

"So you're running away because you're afraid of your mother?" I ask, ignoring his question about my methods. *The first secret to success: Never reveal everything you know.* Advice from my father that feels especially relevant at the moment.

"No," Jaxon says. "No, I'm running away because I want to see if I was right to help you. And because I want to find out firsthand what really happened to Samantha—which means finding your sister before anybody else, right? Because Huxley will twist any confession they get out of her."

"And so would your mother."

"Yeah. Maybe." His expression is pained. "Anyway,

Samantha was my friend—so, believe whatever you want about me, but I'm going to find out what really happened, for her sake. I just thought it made sense for the two of us to work together on this."

He sounds sincere. As always. But for all I know, delivering that line was just him following another order.

When I push by him this time, he doesn't try to stop me. But he does follow me.

"You don't have to go alone," he says to my retreating back. "I could help you. I have a car, and I can get Seth to come—he's annoying, but he can be useful too. He'll know how to disable the tracer on the Camaro, for starters, so we won't have to worry about that."

"Maybe I want to go alone." The words are automatic. They're not entirely untrue, either—even though he did just remind me of an important point: He has a car.

Finding Violet would be a lot easier if I had him to drive me around. Of course, that means trusting him more than I'd planned on ever doing again. But the alternative is walking. Or hitchhiking with complete strangers, since the ETS doesn't have any routes that go very far outside of Haven.

"So we form a truce," he's saying, drowning out my racing thoughts. "We forget what I did for now. Forget I'm CCA. Forget you're an origin."

Like I could honestly forget all of those things.

He *did* help me escape, though. And I don't think what he said about Samantha was a lie; they were friends. When I think about it, I can picture them in my mind, in vague memories of the two of them moving through the halls together, sitting at the same table at lunch, that sort of thing. I guess it's possible that he really *is* looking for the same answers as me, even if it's for different reasons.

More importantly, I'm tired of standing here arguing with him. Plus, he's proven ridiculously stubborn already—two days ago when he talked me into riding home with him, and practically every day before that when he tried tricking me out of the shadows with kind words and smiles, even long after anyone else would have given up on me.

I have a bad feeling that he's not going to give up on me now, either.

So maybe I should at least work this to my advantage if I can? We take his car. I get to where I need to go, and then if I have to, I'll find some way to ditch him. It's not the worst plan I've ever had.

I'm still searching for the precise, careful words to agree with this temporary truce, though, when I hear voices. They're only quiet, distant mumblings at first; but unless it's my imagination running wild and scared, they sound like they're getting closer. Jaxon moves closer too, and I can almost feel the unease rippling through him when his hand brushes my arm. And like I'm absorbing it from his touch, anxiety twists through me and dives straight into my gut.

I'm running out of time. The people following me are close enough now that I can make out what they're saying.

I know I saw her come in here.

We should have shot her the second she ran.

Would've meant one less Huxley freak for us to deal with later.

We should have shot her . . . should have shot her . . . They-shouldhaveshotme, freak, freak . . . Iamafreak—

"Fine." My own voice surprises me, because I don't remember the exact moment I made up my mind. All I know is that I'm past the point of changing it now.

Jaxon looks equally shocked. "Really?"

"Yeah. Come on." I give him a little shove. "But I swear, if you try anything funny—"

"I won't. Trust me."

Don't count on it, I think as I step past him, cautiously making my way back toward the lights of the city.

CHAPTER EIGHT

Persistence

"This is creepy." The sun's coming up now, and Seth is squinting at Jaxon from underneath a hand that isn't blocking out much of its light.

Looking around, I have to admit that I agree with him; this place isn't exactly well kept up. Grass and weeds grow wild and free in every direction, and most of the headstones are cracked and crumbling, their inscriptions unreadable. Only a handful of the stones have flowers or any other sort of memorial decorations to brighten them up. Not surprising, when you consider the distance we are from town and the poor condition of the road we had to take to get here.

That, and the fact that this is a quarantine graveyard.

We could never forget that, either, thanks to all of the biohazard symbols imprinted on every surface, from the headstones to the random, vine-covered signs spaced evenly throughout the rows of graves. This is one of the areas designated by the government as an acceptable, safe burial spot for the infected like my mother, and any others—such as her children—who might have been exposed to her enough to contract her "disease." It was a response to public outcry and the fear, mainly, that decaying bodies of the infected might somehow contaminate cities like Haven. If people bothered to learn the facts, they would know that none of the mutagen's effects ever proved to be contagious; but they're too busy being afraid to see that, I guess. And fear can make a truth out of a lie faster than anything I know of.

"Why are we here again?" Seth asks.

"There's something I want to see," I say. My tone might be a little shorter than necessary. But an hour-long car ride with Seth Lancaster—and his horribly off-key singing—will do that to you. It doesn't help also that the only words he's said to me the entire trip have been thinly veiled insults at best. The only reason I don't protest his coming too much is because Jaxon insisted he'd be useful in case we ran into any trouble; apparently, Seth has a way with weapons and a collection of them that would rival the arsenal of the entire Haven city police force.

I don't know why Jaxon thinks we need all the fire-power. Mostly I'm trying not to think about it—which means not arguing about it either.

"You could wait in the car," Jaxon says, glancing back over his shoulder at Seth.

"Good idea. And when I see the police and the CCA guys pull up looking for us, I could just leave you two here and haul my own ass to safety," Seth says. "Every man for himself and all that."

They keep bickering as we make our way through the graves. It's easy to believe they're brothers now; blood related or not, they definitely tease each other and fight like siblings. I let my focus drift away from them, paying only enough attention to make sure I get out of their way when they start shoving and punching each other. Playfully. I think. But then, sometimes I'm not sure I really understand guys.

I know where my sister's grave is, not because I've been to it frequently but because I remember the hill that it sits on. It's off by itself, and there's a lone, skinny tree at its crest, bending in the breeze like a flag someone just happened to plant there. I remember thinking on the day of my sister's funeral that the tree looked dead, like one decent storm might uproot it and finish it off completely. It's not much healthier looking now; the limbs are bare, the gray bark weathered and all but completely stripped off. It's still standing, though.

That tree is all I focused on during the funeral. Counting the scars and knots on its trunk is what kept me from crying, and I automatically start doing the same thing now, trying to keep myself from being overwhelmed by the sudden surge of emotion that hits me.

I should have braced myself better, I guess; after all this time, I just didn't expect coming here to still be this hard.

The grave is in much better shape than most of the others, and it's obvious that someone's visited it recently. The site is free of weeds and dead leaves. There's a bunch of fresh purple wildflowers piled at the base of the headstone, all the way up past the biohazard symbol etched in the center of it. I'm still staring at them when Jaxon walks up behind me.

"Your sister's clone?" he asks.

I nod.

"Why does she come here?"

I shrug, partly because I'm still not ready to open up to him again—about anything—and also because I'm not really sure. I've always just assumed it was that persistence of life that drives her to this place; the persistence of the old Violet's memories that are never far from her mind. Because it's not like she doesn't know she's a replacement. Our parents may blindly insist that she's the same as the one who came before, but they can't change the hateful things that other people say to her. Or to me. However angry I might be with her for disappearing and causing me all these problems, when I think about that, I still feel a quiet sort of sympathy for my sister's clone.

It isn't the first time I've felt it either. It's just that I always try not to dwell on these kinds of thoughts, because they inevitably lead to bigger questions that I can't answer. Questions about what's really going on in this Violet's head, about why she really does any of the things she does. And all the questions I'm not supposed to ask, of course, like how different things would be if this grave wasn't here, and the first Violet wasn't six feet underneath me.

Not as different as the CCA and all of those news reports are claiming; I feel like I should be sure of that much at least. Because no part of my sister is a murderer. She wasn't before and she isn't now. She *can't* be.

I keep running these thoughts over and over in my mind, and soon they start to feel like lines I'm rehearsing, like I'm trying desperately to force myself into character. I'm just not sure who that character is anymore. Who am I playing now? The loyal sister? The persecuted voice of truth? The delusional hero?

And if I can't get a read on this part, then how am I supposed to know how to play it?

The wind picks up a bit, and I absently reach for my arm, trying to smooth away the bumps that rise on my skin. The action makes me think of my mother. Of her constantly tugging on her sleeves, constantly trying to cover up her scars. It's no different, maybe, from the way they bury the quarantined so far away from the city—almost as if keeping things out of sight will make them less real. Or less scary, at least.

And now I find myself wondering, What if people are right to be afraid? What if I'm the one who's got it all wrong about everything?

What if I should be afraid too? Because if what President Cross said was true and I've inherited my mother's sickness, what happens then? My parents can keep trying to hide these things from me, but they can't stop them from happening.

The wind's grown calm again, but my skin still feels cold.

"Company," Seth says suddenly. I hear him, but I'm still so focused on my sister's grave that my reaction time isn't what it should be. Jaxon takes care of that for me, though—by throwing his arm around my waist and pulling me to the ground with him. I break the fall with my elbows, the right one falling on top of a sharp rock. I ignore the pain and lift my gaze toward the cemetery gates. A group of armed men are filing through them, the one in front giving orders in a loud, booming voice.

Seth drops down beside us a second later.

"See?" he says. "This is why I didn't leave all the guns in the car." He leans over on his side, reaches into the cargo pocket of his pants, and pulls out something that looks like a small silver pen.

"I thought Mom took that away from you," Jaxon says.

Seth shrugs. "I got it back."

"Why would she take it away?" I ask. It doesn't look especially dangerous.

"Because it's an illegal weapon," Jaxon says, reaching over me and forcing Seth's hand—which is already aiming the pen-weapon—to the ground, "and the laser in it is powerful enough to cleanly slice a person's arm from their body at a close-enough range."

"Oh."

"Key words there are 'at a close-enough range,'" Seth says. "It would only leave a little burn on those guys from here. Stop trying to make me look crazy."

"Pretty sure it's not me that's making you look crazy," Jaxon says.

The man shouts another order, and my gaze snaps back to him. And as if he can feel my eyes on him, he suddenly stops. Then he glances in our direction, and even from here, I can see the way his eyes narrow suspiciously. He lifts his gun and then uses his free hand to gesture for the others to follow him.

They're moving straight toward us. Fast.

"We can't fight all of them," I say, terror filling my lungs and making it hard to even whisper the words. "I feel like we need to move."

"And I feel like I agree with Clonie for once," Seth says. I jerk my head around to tell him—for the millionth time—to quit calling me that, but he's already army-crawling his way toward the back side of the hill. The crawl quickly turns into a dramatic roll down the steep slope. We catch up with him at the bottom, regroup, and head for the nearby trees. Once we've weaved our way deep enough into the forest that we can't hear the men behind us anymore, I turn back to Jaxon.

"Who were those people?" I ask, my heart still pounding and the words coming in between sharp gasps for air. The question—and the sick feeling that Jaxon knows the answer—has been eating away at me since the second we left my sister's grave.

But I'm not surprised when he claims he has no idea.

"So they're not CCA?" I press. I can tell the question frustrates him, but I don't really care; I don't see any benefit in pretending to trust him at the moment.

Seth is watching Jaxon out of the corner of his eye, and when his brother doesn't answer me this time, he jumps to his defense. "If they were CCA, do you honestly think I would have been pointing a weapon at them? Ten to one says those were Huxley creeps—and who knows how many more we've already got chasing us."

"They weren't exactly chasing *us*," I point out. "We

don't even know that they were looking for us."

"Right," Seth says, his tone bitingly sarcastic. "My bad. They were probably just out searching for new friends. Should we go back and introduce ourselves?"

"She has a point," Jaxon interrupts. "They could have been looking for her sister's clone, or for anybody, really."

"Or hell, maybe they were just out for a leisurely stroll."

"I'm serious, Seth."

"Of course you are," he says, glaring at me now. "You agree with her. Big surprise." His chest rises and falls with an irritated sigh, and the tension that filled the car on the way here is suddenly back, suffocating us even in the wide-open space. I'm relieved when he turns and starts to walk away from us.

"Come on, Seth," Jaxon calls after him. "Where are you going?"

"To get a better angle on the situation. I'll let you know when the coast is clear and we can get away from this place. Assuming those guys don't blow up the car on their way out."

"Don't joke about things like that," Jaxon says, sounding a little faint.

"Casualties of war, man," Seth calls back, waving a dismissive hand behind him.

I wait until he's out of earshot before commenting. "He's pissed."

Jaxon shrugs. "Give him thirty minutes and he'll be making inappropriate jokes again," he says. He's trying to sound casual, but there's a note of brotherly concern in his voice that I can't help but notice. And then it hits me the same as it did when he talked about Seth in the CCA headquarters yesterday: that feeling of something familiar settling between us. He knows what it's like to have to worry about someone else constantly, the way I do with Violet. Is that part of the reason he left the city with me, I wonder? Because he understands what that's like?

"You're worried about him," I say. It's not a question, but he nods anyway.

"He doesn't think it's a good idea, being out here," he answers. "Being with you."

"He might be right."

"He probably is."

"And yet here you are."

His lips slide into a half grin. "Here I am."

"For reasons neither of us can guess."

He picks a stick up off the ground and starts absently stripping the bark from it. "Would you believe me," he says after a minute, "if I told you I just prefer the view out here to the dirty, crowded city?"

"No."

"Yeah. Somehow I didn't think you would." He tosses the stick aside and glances up at me from underneath raised eyebrows. "So. Where to now?"

I don't answer him right away; mostly because I'm still trying to figure out the answer myself. If she was the one who put those flowers on the grave, then it means Violet did leave the city, just like I thought. And with everyone searching for her, and all of the police and everything swarming around our house, something tells me she won't be in a hurry to go back anytime soon. I'm not really in a hurry to go back either—maybe because now I have even more questions than I had when I left. I want to know who those people in the cemetery were. Were they from Huxley? And are they hunting for my sister? What do they plan on doing with her when they find her?

I'm afraid to think about it. So I know there's no way I can stop searching for her now. I can't just go back to my house and wait, and listen to my parents' lies about how everything is going to be fine. Because I know they're lies now. Nothing about any of this is fine.

But thinking about my parents just confuses me more, because if those people are hunting for Violet, then who's to say they won't take their guns to my house next? I'm not sure what I would do if I was there, but part of me wants to go back anyway.

Jaxon is still looking at me expectantly.

"I don't know," I say. "Maybe we should go back."

His expression doesn't change.

"What?"

"You don't want to go back to the city," he says. His matter-of-fact tone annoys me. Because he's right. I don't *want* to go back—it's more of a need. I just need to know my parents are okay.

"Seth doesn't think this is a good idea, right?" I say, diverting the conversation so I don't have to admit how easily he's managed to figure me out. "So maybe we should at least take him back." And while we're there, I could always check in at my house. It doesn't mean my parents have to see me, or even know I've been there; it wouldn't be the first time I'd gone unnoticed by them.

"He won't stay there if I'm still out here with you, so there's no point." He casts an anxious glance back toward the graveyard. "Because I'm not leaving you out here—especially not with those guys running around, whoever they are."

It would be stupid to argue with him now. He's proved useful so far, and as long as he's still willing to help me find Violet, I know I should take advantage of that. So I just nod and suggest we try to catch up with Seth.

But I trail a little behind him as we walk, my phone in my hand and my house number pulled up on the screen.

It isn't the same as seeing them. And I don't know what I'll say when they pick up the phone; I can ask them if things are okay back at the house, but I can't trust anything they tell me. They'll want to know where I am, but I'll have to lie to them. They can't know what I'm doing. Who I'm with. I can't tell them about any of this.

I might not even speak, I decide; just hearing their voices would be enough for now.

So I hit call. And I listen to it ring over and over, piercing the thick morning silence around us. I keep waiting. Keep listening. But no one answers. I try my father's cell next. Same result.

Mother's number takes me straight to her voice mail; no ringing, just her perfectly rehearsed words telling me to please leave a message after the beep. I remember her standing in the kitchen in her shirtwaist dress and heels, re-recording that message nearly ten times and trying to get it right.

Maybe if I could run through all the things I want to say ten times, I'd be able to decide on the right words to use.

But instead, I just end the call with numb fingertips and slip my phone back into my pocket.

CHAPTER NINE

Infatuations

"Where are we?" I ask.

We've been driving for what feels like hours before we finally slow to a stop. My legs are cramped, my shoulders stiff. I'm not complaining, though. At least we still had a car to ride away in when those people at the cemetery finally left.

"On what used to be Main Street, Lenoir," Jaxon answers. "Hopefully there'll be someplace safe to spend the night here."

Lenoir. The name doesn't ring any bells, and the place looks completely abandoned—just one of the hundreds of other ghost towns the war left behind. The scarcity of supplies and the difficulty of shipping over the decaying road system meant that smaller towns like this often got overlooked, and after years of struggling to get by, most people just gave up and migrated to larger cities. There are a few that manage to self-sustain, but not many.

The sacrifice of towns like this has actually been part of the government's ongoing rebuilding efforts; with limited manpower and resources, the idea was to purposely focus growth and financial support in a few designated Restoration Cities, and to then allow the eventual outward spread of population and commerce to occur naturally. It's a slow process, though. So while places like Haven—which is one of those designated cities—are currently bustling, most of the areas around it are far from lively.

And this town looks a lot like some of the pictures I've seen in Social Studies class: buildings with crumbling faces and weathered, barely readable signs; broken, dirty windows; gravel side roads that have been all but overtaken by weeds. It's a depressing scene. Because despite its rundown state, it's still obvious that there was once life here. If I squint, I can almost see people rushing in and out of its many shops, and in the low whistle of wind I swear I hear laughter and the chatter of gossip, the sound of someone crying, and maybe even someone singing nearby.

"This is your first time in one of these actual ghost towns, I'm guessing?" Jaxon offers me a hand and pulls me out of the car. "It's eerie, isn't it?"

I take another look around, watch an empty tin can roll back and forth in the wind. It clinks and clatters over the broken pavement, and the sound echoes between the buildings. It drowns out any laughter, any singing I might have been hearing. To think this is all that's left of the entire lives built here, that those people had no choice but to leave everything behind. . . . "Eerie" isn't the right word, I decide.

"It's . . . sad."

"That, too, I guess," Jaxon agrees.

"Is anybody going to help me with these bags?" Seth calls. "Or did you two just bring me along so I could be your personal slave?"

"We're coming," Jaxon shouts back. He's frowning. Probably because those are the first words Seth has said to either of us since we left the graveyard. The thirty minutes Jaxon insisted we give him have passed, and Seth isn't exactly back to his joking self. Far from it, actually. And I know it's my fault—that I'm the wedge driving its way between them. But I'm not sure what I'm supposed to do about it. It's not like I'm doing it on purpose.

We go around to the trunk of the car, where Seth is standing over a pile of backpacks and a suitcase that's almost as big as me. He's got a gun in one hand, and in the bag slung over his shoulder I can see the barrels of three more sticking out.

"You weren't kidding about all the guns you packed, were you?" I ask. I'm just trying to make conversation. As long as we're together, I figure I should probably try to smooth out some of this tension.

But he doesn't answer me.

"Just out of curiosity," I say, still keeping my voice as friendly as possible, "did you pack anything *besides* guns?"

He finally stops messing with the bags and looks up at me. "If you're asking if I packed all your girly necessities, then no," he says. "Jaxon told me I had twenty minutes, and to worry about essentials only. So we're roughing it. No nail polish or hairspray or frilly little hair bows or anything like that. Sorry." The smile he gives me is razored with annoyance.

"For the record," I shoot back, "I haven't painted my nails in almost eight years." The first Violet and I used to do that sort of girly stuff together before she got sick—I guess I kind of grew out of it after she died. I'm not sure why I feel like Seth needs to know that, or why I have this weird, sudden urge to convince him that I'm not as bad as he seems to think I am. To do more than simply get rid of the tension.

Since when do I care what anybody thinks about me? Especially Seth Lancaster?

I'm glad when Jaxon steps between us and rescues me. "Probably not a good idea to hang out in the middle of the street like this," he says. "How about those bags?"

Seth shrugs the bag of guns from his shoulder and tosses it to him. "Here," he says. "You can carry those; they'll make you look tough. Less like a girly man."

"Thanks," Jaxon says, picking up the bag and rolling his eyes.

"Just looking out for you," Seth says, cracking a grin that's a little closer to genuine.

Jaxon grabs the huge suitcase and heads toward the nearest building. I grab two of the backpacks and sling them over either shoulder, then follow him into what we quickly decide used to be a mini department store. The space is huge and open, with broken mirrors lining the walls and graffiti-covered elevators in every corner. Tons of racks and shelves have been left behind, and a few of them still have faded, dust-covered clothes left on them.

We move through the ghostly silence. Jaxon is tense, and without meaning to, I find myself mimicking his stiff, cautious movements. Seth, on the other hand, seems to be slowly returning to his loud, careless self; we've barely made it out of sight of the road before he's grabbing a sequined cocktail dress off one of the racks and holding it up to Jaxon.

"This one is definitely your color," he says.

"Are you kidding me?" Jaxon says. "That cut is all wrong for me. It would make me look dumpy."

"You say that about everything I pick out. Sometimes I think you just have self-esteem issues."

I can't help but join in. "You could pair it with this hat," I suggest, swiping the most ridiculous-looking fedora I've ever seen from a nearby shelf. It's bright red—even through the layers of dust—and has a huge white feather tucked into its band. Even Seth laughs at the sight of it. "It would draw people's attention away from how dumpy you look."

"There's an idea," Jaxon says, holstering his gun and taking the hat from me. He wipes away the dust, turns it over in his hands a couple times, then plops it down on top of my head. It's too big on me, and the front of it slips down over my eyes until all I can see is a blob of red with Jaxon's shadow behind it. "It's better on you, though," he says. "Somehow you manage to make it look good."

"I don't know," I say, "I don't think red's really my color."

He tips the hat back so he can meet my eyes. "I'm going to have to disagree with you there," he says.

And I almost slip.

I almost let myself get caught up in the warmth of his voice and in that spicy scent that clings to him. I almost, *almost* let my thoughts drift with the hazy summer air and into a daydream of us—one that doesn't take place here.

One that's somewhere less complicated. Someplace where he never lied to me. Where I'm not an origin, Samantha isn't dead, and his mother isn't trying to hunt down me and my sister. We go to school. Wave to all our friends. He takes my hand, and nobody thinks twice about it. There are no cameras, nobody's shouting or whispering things like "freak" as I walk by.

But deep down, I know that place doesn't exist. I know that he's spent his whole life surrounded by CCA members. How many awful things has he been told about clones, about origins like me, I wonder? And some part of him must believe those things. That's why he took me to his mother in the first place, isn't it? Because he thinks families like mine are a danger to society. Because we've been born and bred to be enemies.

When I think about that, the possibility of us lasting past anything more than this strange infatuation seems so far-fetched that it's almost laughable. Like a cruel joke the universe is playing on me. And standing so close to him is doing nothing but dragging out the terrible punch line.

So for once I'm thankful when Seth's big mouth interrupts, calling to us from the back door. "When you two are done making out," he says, "there's something back here that I think you might be interested in."

But Jaxon doesn't move; not until I clear my throat and slide past him. I can feel his eyes watching me go, and I force myself not to look back at him.

You can't trust him, I remind myself fiercely. *Don't be stupid. You have more important things to worry about, anyway.*

I take the hat from my head and let it fall behind me as I walk to Seth's side.

"Check it out," he says, pointing down the narrow street that runs along this side of the department store. It's lined with more run-down buildings, mostly; but at the end of the street is a sign that's actually still readable, even though the *H* is almost completely gone: HOTEL.

Inside, the hotel isn't much better looking than it is on the outside. Most of the furnishings are missing; though after a few minutes of searching, we do manage to find a room with two lumpy beds and pillows—which seem like extravagant extras when you consider the moldy ceiling and the piles of tiny bones and dry feces left by who knows what kind of animals. The walls are cracked, their paint, peeling. But at least there's no writing on them, no graffiti or anything that would suggest this place might be frequented by other people.

"Home sweet home," Seth says, fluffing one of the pillows and sending a cloud of dust into the air.

"I'm going to go see if I can find some better blankets and stuff," Jaxon says. He hasn't really said much—or even looked at me—since I hurried away from him in the department store, and I can't help but feel like he's making up this excuse to get away from me; the blankets in here aren't *that* dirty or holey. And I don't think he's going to find better-looking ones anywhere else.

"Good luck," Seth says.

"Try not to kill each other while I'm gone," Jaxon says.

He sounds relatively cheerful, but I don't miss the way his eyes jump right over me when he takes one last look around the room. He disappears into the hallway before I have a chance to say anything else.

With a sigh, I get up and move to the table on the far side of the room, where Seth neatly stashed most of the weapons he brought. I pick up gun after gun, studying them, asking him every question I can think of about them. It gets Jaxon out of my mind at least, and, besides, it seems like a good idea to know all I can about these weapons.

You know. Just in case.

For everything I ask, though, Seth only has a curt, one-word answer.

When I run out of questions, I give up and start sifting through the other supplies he brought. The suitcase that Jaxon carried in is crammed full with clothes on one side and vacuum-packed nutrition pills and other equally non-exciting foods on the other. As unappetizing as the food looks, though, my stomach still spasms with hunger at the sight of it; I can't even remember the last time I ate.

I take one of the pills, unwrap it, and bite it in half. It has a chalky texture and bland vanilla flavor, but I force myself to swallow the other half too. These pills aren't manufactured for their flavor, I know; I wasn't expecting them to be any better. They're lingering products of a struggling postwar economy: cheaply made, mass-produced, and genetically enhanced so they pack in almost an entire day's worth of nutrition.

I'm lucky because I haven't had to eat much of this

sort of food, but some of Haven's poorer families exist almost entirely on it. I know that because I've read plenty of the e-mails and petitions lobbying my father to do something about nutrition standards, poverty levels, and everything else that's wrong with the city. I used to help him sort through almost all of his mail, actually; we spent a lot of late nights at the computer together, and there was a time when I saw myself growing up to be just like him—working in politics, trying to make some sort of difference in the world like I always believed he was doing.

Then Violet died.

Her replacement came, and suddenly that's all people seemed to write about anymore: cloning and Huxley and *what-sort-of-moral-standards-are-you-setting-Mayor-Benson?* That, and insults. Threats. And then one night my father told me he would take care of the e-mails himself. He locked the door to the home office, and it was still locked when he left for town hall the next morning. I spent at least an hour trying to break the door's security codes while Violet kept watch for Mother, but it was useless. I never managed to get back in.

A few minutes after eating the nutrition pill, my stomach is still growling, still unsatisfied, but my head has already started to clear. I'm about to close the suitcase when something sticking out of one of the interior pockets catches my eye. It's the hilt of a pocketknife, but it's much more ornate than any of the other weapons here. I pick it up and turn it over in my hands, studying the intricate carvings along the handle.

"Do you make a habit of going through other people's things?" Seth asks, suddenly right behind me. For someone with such a big mouth, he moves incredibly quietly.

"I was hungry," I say, holding up the empty wrapper. "Thought everything in here was public domain."

"That isn't." He holds out his hand so I can deposit the knife in it. "I don't know how it got in there."

"It's yours?"

He looks reluctant to talk about it at first. But just as I start to turn away and go find something else to distract myself with, he quietly says, "It was a birthday gift. From my—from President Cross." As he talks, he flips the knife open and closed with precise flicks of his wrist, his eyes focused intently on the blade. "First time anybody bothered to celebrate the day I was born. We had a party and everything—just me, her, and Jaxon, but it was nice, you know? So I keep this close. Reminds me that there are at least two people who know I'm alive."

"What are you talking about? Half the school worships you. Everyone knows you."

He laughs humorlessly. "The same way everyone knew Samantha Voss. And I'm guessing that, as of today, her death is already old news." I make a disgusted face, but he just shakes his head. "Come on, Cate," he says. "You're in Theater too; you know how it goes: 'Out, out, brief candle! Life's but a walking shadow, a poor player that struts and frets his hour upon the stage' and all that crap."

"I never liked that play."

"Whatever. Point is, if I was gone this time tomorrow, there are two people who would miss me. And one of them, for reasons I'm still not sure I understand, has become rather infatuated with you."

I have a sudden, sick feeling that I know exactly where he's going with this. Why he's telling me all these things.

"But you already knew that, didn't you?" he says. "Because it's come in handy."

"You're kidding me, right?"

"I'm not, actually," he says. "I actually don't think there's anything funny about you taking advantage of my best friend. It's probably the only thing in the world that I see zero humor in." He takes a step closer to me. "So. I don't know how you did it, what sort of crap you pulled or what lies you told to get him here, but—"

"I didn't tell him *anything*," I say, my temper flaring. "He offered to go with me."

"And you've tried really hard to convince him to leave you alone, have you?"

At first all I can do is shake my head in disbelief. And then the only words I can manage, over and over again, are "You've got it all wrong."

"I don't think so, Benson. You aren't fooling me."

My cheeks are flushed red hot at this point, the heat so intense that it burns away any hope of this turning into a rational conversation. But I don't want to fight him either. I've spent my whole life avoiding him and the rest of his crowd, ignoring all the stupid things they said about me and my family; why should things be any different now? He's just as obnoxious out here as he was back at school.

This isn't school, though.

And things *are* different now. Because as much as I want to turn away from Seth—to put on that stone-faced mask one more time and march myself to someplace with better scenery—I can't. Not as theatrically as I want to at least, since all my dramatic plans of storming off and slamming doors in his face are tempered by one thought: *Jaxon.* Wherever we stand now, it wouldn't feel right to just walk away and leave him behind. Not after everything he's risked to leave the city and stay with me.

I'm beginning to wish that he and Seth weren't a package deal, though.

I take a deep breath through my nose. The pill wrapper makes a crinkling noise as I squeeze my hand into a fist, and then I walk over and throw it away in the tiny metal wastebasket in the corner. As wrecked as the rest of the room is, there's really no point in properly getting rid of the trash, but the movement gives me a chance to finish clearing my head.

"If you're so convinced that I'm the bad guy," I say, turning back to him, "then why did you agree to help me?"

"I didn't. I agreed to help Jaxon. Whole hell of a lot of difference." He saunters over and flops down on one of the beds, lies back, and flips the knife open again. I search for something else to distract myself with and end up back at the same suitcase, taking things out of it only to cram them all back in again. Seth doesn't stop talking. "And I only did that because I made a promise to his mom a long time ago— and over and over since—that I would watch out for him the same way she did for me. He's too soft to be out here on his own. Sees too much good in people." The sound of the blade puncturing and sawing through the mattress makes me glance over at him. "Lucky for you, right?" he says.

"He isn't just out here for me," I fire back. "Don't *you* even care about what really happened to Samantha?"

"Knowing isn't going to bring her back. Dead people don't come back." He stops carving up the mattress, props himself up on his elbows, and gives me a thin smile. "Or, at least, they don't always." The words are bitter, and suddenly I remember what Jaxon told me about Seth, back at the CCA headquarters.

Both his parents are dead, we think.

And what about the rest of his family?

One of my mother's favorite ways to try to explain away people's hatred of us was to accuse them of jealousy, of wishing that they'd taken the time or resources to prepare themselves for the unexpected the way she and my father had. I've never given that reason much weight before, but now I can't help but wonder: What if Seth hadn't lost anyone? For good, I mean?

Would he still be glaring at me the way he is now?

I shove my hands into my pockets to force them to stop messing with the suitcase's contents, and I wander toward the hall. The sound of his sigh reaches me all the way out here, and the relieved creaks of rusty bedsprings accompany it a second later.

"Come on, Benson," he shouts after me. "If you run off, I'm going to get blamed for it."

He appears in the doorway at almost the exact moment that glass shatters somewhere in the distance. Pounding footsteps follow. Then a loud crash, and an involuntary terror slams my heart against my chest. I look back at Seth, and he's already walking toward me.

"What was that?" I ask. He passes by me without answering, breaks into a jog, and disappears around the corner up ahead.

I hear Seth calling Jaxon's name. I don't hear Jaxon answering him.

I take a deep breath, and before I know what I'm doing, my feet are carrying me after Seth's voice. And then I'm running, up one hallway and down the next, until I come to a window that looks newly broken, judging by the dust still swirling and settling around it. There are plops of bright wet blood scattered amid the dust and shattered glass. A fresh wave of fear courses through me, raising the flesh along my arms and neck.

I hear Seth's voice again, and I break into a sprint.

I hurtle around a corner, into a damp, musty-smelling room with a tarp-covered pool in the center.

And the good news is that I no longer have to worry about where Violet is. Because she's standing right there, at the edge of the pool. Less than ten feet away.

The bad news is that she has a shard of glass pressed like a dagger against Jaxon's neck.

CHAPTER TEN

Wrong

My sister doesn't answer when I call her name.

She doesn't even look at me.

Over and over I'm shouting at her to stop, but it's like there's some sort of invisible wall between us and my words are just slamming into it and falling uselessly away.

This can't be happening.

Only it is. And I have to do something about it. Now. I know how strong Violet is; I know how fast she is. And I don't know what the hell she thinks she's doing right now, but I *do* know how easily she could shove that glass into Jaxon's neck, make it come right out the other side and cut every vein along the way. But maybe if she sees me, maybe if she realizes I'm here, maybe—

I go for the arm holding the glass. I wrap myself around it, throw all my weight into trying to drag her to the ground, or at least away from Jaxon. I've caught her by surprise, but she's stronger than I am—*so* much stronger—and she just braces her arm and swings me around until there's suddenly nothing underneath my feet except flimsy black tarp. I manage to get my left foot balanced precariously on the crumbling edge of the pool, but the right one sinks down, flooding the tarp with water.

Would it have been too much to ask for the hotel owners to have drained the pool before they left?

Because—more bad news—I can't swim. My mother never saw fit to teach me, since she didn't approve of the way "girls these days parade around half-naked when they go swimming." I think the thought of the press taking a picture of me in a bathing suit horrified her.

I look frantically at Violet and find her staring down at me through dead, emotionless eyes.

"What are you doing?" I demand through clenched teeth.

This time, the sound of my voice makes her flinch. She blinks. Crouches down along the pool edge so we're face to face.

"What are *you* doing?" she asks. "Do you know who this boy is? Do you know who his mother is?"

"Of course I do!"

"Then why are you with him?" Her voice is chillingly calm. Out of the corner of my eye, I see Jaxon start to take a step. Violet's gaze snaps toward him.

"I thought I told you not to move," she says.

I throw more of my weight against her arm, trying to bring her attention back to me.

"Leave him alone," I say as evenly as I can manage. "He's not . . . he's not what you think. I can explain, okay? Just pull me back up and I'll explain everything." Her eyes are hollow again as she turns back to me. I take a deep breath. She knows I can't swim. She's not going to let me drown. She's going to pull me back up now—

And she does pull me. She jerks me so hard that the one foot I had up slips, and both my knees slam into the side of the pool with a sickening *crack*. Then she gives the arm I'm still clinging to a vicious shake, trying to knock me off.

That's when I lose my temper.

I dig my nails into the skin of her arm, gripping tighter than ever. I press both my feet against the side of the pool for leverage, grit my teeth, try to ignore the ungodly pain in my knees, and then push off. Hard. Violet goes flying over my head and lands with the sound of crumpling plastic and a muffled *splash* behind me. I feel her sinking, the water pulling away from me as her body drags it down, and a new panic floods through me; because I know she can't swim either. Or at least, the first Violet never could. She was terrified of water.

Did I just kill her?

I scramble desperately for the edge of the pool, kicking and flailing until a hand grabs mine, and I hear Jaxon's voice telling me, *be still,* and, *I've got you, don't worry.* But I'm not worried about me anymore. It makes absolutely no sense now, not even to me; but all I can think about is *her.*

"She can't swim," I sputter out, along with a mouthful of dirty water. "Violet can't—"

"Cate!"

Jaxon's eyes go wide, and he tries to pull me the rest of the way up with one strong heave—but he's not fast enough. I look back just as Violet explodes out of the water behind me. The glass shard comes down across my face, and her arm slams into my stomach, hooking around me and dragging me down, down, *down*. My fingers slip out of Jaxon's, and a second later I'm under water.

We tumble deeper and deeper, the tarp twisting around us. She's going to drown us both. She has to realize that. Maybe she just doesn't care. She's not even trying to swim back to the surface, even though it's obvious now that she can; instead she stays twisted and tangled with me, hacking wildly with the glass that's somehow still in her hand. The water slows down her swing, but not enough to prevent her cutting several nasty gashes along both my arms, and across my hip when we reach the bottom of the pool and I try to push my way back up. Soon, the murky water is blossoming with clouds of my blood, and my vision starts to blur. The deep, cold water steals the feeling from my hands and feet. Then it takes the pain, too. And then I am weightless, floating without feeling, aware only of the shadow of a figure descending over me.

My sister, coming to kill me.

I shut my eyes. Tightly.

Pain. Behind my eyes. In my knees, my arms, my shoulders—everywhere, from my skin down to the very core of my bones. So much pain that for a long time I don't realize the miracle of my own breath rising through my trembling lips.

Things come back to me little by little after that. The feel of rough concrete beneath my fingertips. The choking scent of chlorine. The sound of water drip, drip, dripping somewhere close by.

And then a voice.

"Cate? Please say something. . . . say something—anything. Do something so I know you can hear me . . . please?"

He sounds scared. And I'm hit with an uncomfortable feeling in my stomach as I realize, *So am I.* For him and for me, because I was almost too late, because my sister . . . my *sister* . . .

Why is this happening?

I open my eyes.

"Finally," Jaxon says, cupping a hand on either side of my face and pressing his forehead to mine. He stays like that for what feels like a long time, his hair dripping beads of the dirty pool water down onto the side of my face. The harsh scent of chlorine that's masking his normal scent makes it hard to breathe, but I'm too numb to push him away.

He pulls himself back after a moment, and we just stare at each other the way people stare at a burning building or a car wreck or some other kind of catastrophe—our eyes discreetly downcast but desperate for details. For answers about what really happened, however twisted and gruesome the facts may be.

Jaxon opens his mouth several times to speak, but he stops every time.

Because what do you say about something like this? I don't even know what to think.

The only thing my mind is processing now, over and over with the cruelest kind of clarity, is a memory. The memory of that call, of my father's voice, the buzz of hospital noise in the background, and the only three words I heard out of everything he said: *She's gone, sweetie.*

The memory of dropping the phone and then going into Violet's room and just sitting there, cross-legged in the middle of that ugly green throw rug, staring up at the poster of the solar system that I got her as a birthday gift after she told me she wanted to be an astronaut. I felt exactly the same then as I do now: *lost.* Empty. Like someone split me open, took out all the important parts, and then didn't even bother to close me up again.

But Violet's replacement came quick enough back then, and she filled up some of those empty spaces, stitched me together with threads of safe, familiar things before I had time to completely fall apart.

It's different this time, though. It feels like she's died all over again, only this time I can't see how she's going to come back.

And I don't know what I'm supposed to do about that.

"Why did you jump between us like that?" Jaxon finally manages to ask. His voice is so quiet that, even as close as he is, it's almost lost in the wind breezing through the windows, scattering leaves and trash around us. "Are you insane?"

"I didn't think she would . . ." The rest of me is soaked, but my mouth is so dry that talking actually hurts, each word a knife in my throat. "I don't know what happened," I choke. "I don't . . . I don't know why she did that."

He sits the rest of the way back, moving into a bright patch of moonlight that's streaming in through the dirty glass roof, and I get a good look at a face that doesn't seem like it could be his. There's no trace of his usual smile. All of his features are strangely gaunt, his skin pale and ghostlike. Like his hair, his clothes are still dripping wet and clinging to his body. There's faint red, splashed like watercolor paint, all down the right side of his shirt. Blood.

Mine? Or his?

I'm not sure which would be worse. I don't like the thought of my sister hurting *anybody*. Not Samantha, not me—and definitely not the boy I've been daydreaming about since sixth grade, even if he is the son of the CCA's president. Because regardless of what's happened between us these past few days, all I know is that he's still here now. He still hasn't given up on me.

What sort of mess have I pulled him into, exactly?

I slowly lift my hand to the place that hurts the worst—my head. My fingers trail down across my cheek, and I feel it all over: the sticky, still slightly warm blood. It's dried in some places too, and with even the smallest movement it pulls at the little hairs along the side of my face.

"Don't touch it," Jaxon says, his fingers closing around my wrist and gently pulling my hand back down.

"Is it bad?"

"It's . . . It's going to be okay. Don't worry." I can tell he's trying to keep the anxiety out of his voice. "Seth is going to be back in a minute, after he takes care of your sister's clone, and then we'll—"

"Where is she?" The thought of Violet sets off a throb of pain, right between my eyes.

"In the room. Unconscious." His voice is colder than I've ever heard it. "Seth hit her with several shots from the tranquilizer gun. She'll be out for a while, at least."

But not out long enough, his tone suggests, and my chest tightens, squeezing the air from my lungs and sending the room into a tailspin. Because I know everything else he's thinking, all the other unspoken words that come loaded in that tone. As much as I hate to admit it, I'm thinking the same things.

I'm thinking I might have been wrong.

Because now I know.

If Violet could have killed me, then she could have killed Samantha Voss.

CHAPTER ELEVEN

The Shadow

There's nothing but soft moonlight illuminating our sad little hotel room when I open my eyes who knows how many hours later.

Everything that's happened comes flooding back all at once. My sister, my family—my entire world feels as broken and bruised as my body. All I want is to be back in my room. In my safe place in the closet, hidden away where no one can find me ever again.

I would cry, but I can't find the strength for it; I'm so, so tired. My body. My mind. Everything. And for being made of nothing but lumps and springs, this bed is surprisingly comfortable. I don't want to leave it behind. I don't even want to move, but I force myself to stretch out, to unbury my face from the pillow that—courtesy of me—now smells like chlorine and blood. The first place I look to is the bed across from me, where my unconscious, possibly murderous sister was resting when I collapsed here earlier.

She's not there.

I feel much stronger all of a sudden.

"Where . . ." I bolt upright in a panic, and a rush of dizziness hits me. I spin away from my sister's bed, reaching for the wall on the other side of me—for something to brace myself against. But my hand doesn't reach the wall. It hits a person instead. I blink several times in the darkness, hoping I'm not seeing what I think I'm seeing. But then Violet speaks.

"Hello, Birdy," she says, using the nickname that the first Violet gave me, and that she's always insisted on calling me by even though she *knows* I despise it. And I didn't think it was possible, but I hate it even more now. Because we're so bitterly far from the moment Violet first came up with that name that it just sounds wrong. I don't want this Violet using it. Especially not while she's sitting there, giving me this huge grin while her voice is light and cheerful.

It's like she's completely oblivious to the fact that she nearly killed me just a few hours ago.

"Are you feeling better?" she asks.

I don't think. I just throw my covers off and dive at her.

She jumps back in surprise and lands in the small crack between the bed and the wall, but leaps back to me just as easily, moving with that speed and refinement that's borderline inhuman. The bed sinks below her, old springs squeaking and groaning as she crouches in front of me.

"What the hell, Birdy?"

"Okay, one: Stop calling me by that stupid nickname. And two: What the hell, *Birdy*? Are you *serious?* How about what the hell, *Violet?* You almost killed me! And Jaxon! What were you doing? And what are you doing now? Why are you here, and what about . . . what . . ."

I twist around, fear suddenly seizing me. Because I just

realized: She's awake, and there is no one in this room except us.

Jaxon. Seth. Where are they? What happened? *What did she do now?*

"Jaxon was gone when I woke up," Violet says. I jerk my gaze back to her. She's studying her nails intently, like the possibility that she chipped one is much more concerning than the terror in my voice. "I think I scared him off," she adds with a smile that's almost mischievous. "And as for Seth . . . I simply got even with him."

My breath catches in my throat.

She motions toward the second bed. I jump up and rush to the other side of it, only vaguely aware now of the pain in my every step. And there Seth is, sprawled out on the floor behind the bed. I drop to my knees beside him and feel for a pulse.

Slow and faint, but still there.

I barely have time to sigh with relief before I sense my sister behind me. I straighten up, take several deep breaths, and try to get my own raging pulse under control. But I can't. My hand raises and flies straight for Violet as I turn to meet her. She's too fast, though, and she stops the slap just centimeters from her face. Her fingers clench my wrist and she holds it there, studying it like she's not sure why I feel like slapping her.

"I didn't think you liked Seth," she says, still not lowering my arm.

"That doesn't mean I wanted you to *shoot* him!"

"He shot me first, you know."

"Because you were trying to kill me!"

Something flickers in her eyes. I want to call it regret, but I'm afraid that might be wishful thinking at this point. She does finally let go of my wrist, though. For a long time she's silent, looking from me to Seth's unconscious body, then back to the cuts on my arms and face.

"I wasn't trying to *kill* you," she says, quieter now. "I just—"

"Oh, and I suppose you weren't trying to kill Jaxon, either, holding that glass to his neck like that?"

Anger flashes in her eyes. "All I did was ask him where you were. He wouldn't tell me. He just kept following me, demanding answers about Samantha, calling me a murderer—and so yes, I eventually lost my temper, and he got what he deserved." She looks close to losing it again and has to take several deep breaths before she continues. "What does it matter, anyway? You said you knew who he was. That he was CCA." She spits out the letters like she's trying to rid her mouth of a nasty taste. "So it's me that should be asking the questions, isn't it? Because I would so love to know, my *dear* little sister, exactly what he's done to you to convince you to join his side."

I almost laugh, because of how incredibly wrong she is. Except then I decide it's not very funny at all. Because they haven't convinced me of anything, of course—I've been running all over to find proof that she's innocent, and that I was right not to help the CCA find her. But all I've found out is how very wrong *I* am, and the thought of that doesn't make me want to laugh.

It makes me want to vomit.

Suddenly I feel incredibly stupid, and incredibly embarrassed to be standing here in the wake of all her violence. With Seth unconscious beside me, and with fresh blood still trickling free from the cuts on my arms every time I move them. Stupid, stupid, stupid. And naive.

How could I have been so naive?

"So you aren't going to deny it, then?" she asks. Her mouth twists into a knowing smirk, and any trace of what might have been regret—of what suggested the old Violet I knew and loved—disappears. I don't want to see her like this. But no matter how many times I try to look away, I can't.

I can't overlook that maybe President Cross was right. That maybe this isn't my sister at all, but only a shadow of her—something much darker, something much emptier than the actual thing. An impersonation. And that remorse I saw in her eyes was nothing but a piece of my real sister that she's only copied, along with all the thoughts and memories of us.

"So much for sibling loyalty, I suppose?" she says.

"Did you kill Samantha Voss?" I ask, because I can't take another second of not knowing.

Violet's eyes narrow. "Would you even believe me if I told you I didn't?"

"Just answer my question."

But she doesn't. Not right away. And that smirk doesn't fade, either. It doesn't even twitch; the only movement she makes is with her eyes, her gaze sliding toward Seth, and then back to me without losing any of its venom.

"Maybe I don't remember what happened that night."

"This isn't a joke, Violet."

"I'm not laughing, am I?"

"Answer my question," I repeat. "Tell me the truth. Tell me the truth or I swear to God—"

"Why don't you tell *me* the truth first? Why are you helping CCA members track me down?"

"It isn't like that. And this isn't about me, anyway."

"Isn't it, though?" she says, smoothing a hand through my hair. I shiver at her touch, even though it's so hot in here I can barely breathe. "About me and you and all of Huxley's wonderful plans for our kind—"

"Have you lost your mind?" I say, jerking away from her touch. "There's nothing *wonderful* about any of this, and I'm not going to be a part of any of Huxley's plans— and neither are you, so just . . . just stop it, all right? Stop talking crazy."

She makes no attempt to close the distance between us. The confusion from before flashes in her eyes, but she blinks it away just as quickly. Then she simply smiles and says, "Soon. You'll be gone soon, and the new Catelyn— the real Catelyn—will understand."

The words slide like ice against my skin, lifting the little hairs along my arms. I fumble for the edge of the bed, searching for something, anything, to brace myself against. What I really want to do is collapse down beside it, to crawl up underneath and somehow get away from all of the awful things she's saying. But I can't. So instead I make myself look her in the eyes, and I very quietly say, "I understand right now. I understand that Huxley has brainwashed you, that they're filling your mind with lies and trying to turn you into something . . . something that's all wrong." I have to fight to keep my voice from breaking. Realizing that President Cross might have been right and forcing myself to accept it are two totally different things.

They aren't the same person. I can believe that—I *have* to believe that. But I still can't let go of the pieces of my sister that I see in this Violet. I don't want to let go of them, because I'm afraid that letting go will lead to forgetting.

And I'm not ready to forget.

"You're so desperate for someone besides Jaxon to be the bad guy," she's saying. "If anyone's been brainwashed, it's *you*."

I don't answer immediately, because I'm not sure what to say. It's not like I can say he's never tricked me before, or that I completely trust him after everything he kept from me. Still, though, there are bad guys and then there are *bad* guys. And I don't want to think that Jaxon is either one, really. I just want to tell Violet, again, that she's talking crazy. I want to tell her to shut up. But all I end up doing is turning away, hoping that she might drop it if I refuse to argue back.

That tactic has never really worked with her, though, so I'm not surprised when it doesn't work now.

"Would it make any difference," she asks, her voice low and cold, "if I told you that *he's* the reason Samantha died that night?"

I keep my back to her. I don't want her to see the pained confusion that crosses my face, or the frustrated tears threatening to spill from the corners of my eyes. "What are you talking about?"

I hear her take a step closer to me, but she doesn't answer. Not until I wipe my eyes dry and spin around to find her watching me with a smug look. "You trust him so much," she says then, "so why don't you ask him for yourself?"

"He's here to find out what happened to Samantha. That's the whole reason he decided to help me find you." The argument that sounded so convincing coming from him seems weak and flimsy in my voice. I'm just tired, maybe. Tired of fighting, and of trying to make sense of all this.

"You just believe everything he says, then, do you?"

"I have to believe something, don't I?" I practically shout. "And it's hard to believe *you* about anything when you're holding weapons to people's throats, or else drowning or *shooting* them!"

She glances over at Seth's still body, and her mouth twitches into a perplexed little smile, as if she'd forgotten about him. "So that's it, then?" she says, her gaze flickering back to me. "Now we know whose side you're on, plain and simple. I wonder how long it will be before Huxley decides to come for you now. Sooner than they'd planned on, I bet."

So is that true too, then? What Cross said about Huxley going after origins? What else was President Cross right about? Everything? Was I wrong not to cooperate with her?

"I do so hate the thought of them sending someone else to initiate your replacement, though," Violet says, taking another step toward me. I stumble back and trip over Seth's outstretched arm. I catch myself on the bed and crawl over it, putting as much space as I can between us without taking my eyes away from her. Something is off about the way she's looking at me; it's the same as it was in the pool room—a sharp, terrifying sort of focus. Only now it's narrowed on me instead of Jaxon, and there's no one else here to stop her.

"Stay away from me," I warn.

Her eyes light up with a terrible sort of excitement. "All these years we've pretended," she says, voice smooth as silk, "pretended that things were the same, that you and I were so *dear* to each other. So close. Just like sisters should be." She moves around the bed toward me, her steps quick and quiet. Like a tiger stalking its prey. "Sister, sister, sister," she sings. "Does it bother you, when they call me that?"

No. Tell her no.

Why can't I tell her no?

I feel around behind me, searching the nightstand she's backed me up against for some kind of weapon. There's nothing but the dusty lamp. On the table on the far side of the room, I can see the glint of guns in the moonlight, but there's no way I'll be able to get around her and get to them before she stops me.

"Because you know I'm not your sister," she says. "I've seen the way you avert your eyes when people talk about me. I've seen the way your lip curls in disgust when they tell you we look so much alike."

"That's not true."

God, I wish it wasn't true.

"You're not the actress you think you are," she says. "But it's okay. Because I'm a little disgusted with the masquerade myself—which is why I think maybe I should end it."

My hand finds the narrow part of the lamp base, and I grip it as tightly as I can.

"Because maybe you're not my sister either," she continues. "Maybe my sister is sleeping, safe and sound at Huxley. And all I have to do—"

I swing. The lamp hits her in the side of her head and shatters, pieces of ceramic showering the floor. I drop what's left of it and jump to the bed, bounce off it, and land hard on the other side, sending a jarring pain shooting up into my knees. Violet lets out an enraged scream that I'm surprised doesn't wake Seth—even as drugged up as he is—and dives after me.

I try to twist out of the way, but I'm not fast enough; she slams into me and sends me spinning into the wall. My head hits hard enough to leave a dent, and sends little flecks of plaster raining around me. Blood trickles down from the reopened cut beneath my eye; I lift a shaky hand to try to wipe it away and turn around to find myself face to face with Violet.

She doesn't touch me. Doesn't speak. She's just *there*, with barely a breath of space between us, and she's just watching me with that familiar frenzy of a smile on her face.

But then her eyes drift to the cut. To the blood drying against my cheek. To my shaking fingers. That smile twitches a little, and she slowly lifts a hand and presses it to the back of her head. Something like pain spasms across her face.

"You were six," she says suddenly. "You were six, and Mother told you not to climb on the slide like that, but you did it anyway."

At first I think I must have hit my head harder than I realized, because I can't pull any sort of significance from her words. But then I see the way she's still watching the blood winding its way down my face; our eyes meet, and I slowly start to understand, to relive the same memory that this moment must be reminding her of.

"You fell off," she says.

"And hit my head on a rock." There was blood everywhere then, just like now. I ended up needing ten stitches.

"And you blamed me for pushing you." She takes a step back, talking more to herself now. "But I never touched you."

"I didn't blame *you*." My voice is sharper than I intended; the exhaustion, the confusion, the pain—I'm tired of all of it. I just want this conversation to be over. I want to go back to sleep, and to wake up and find that everything that's happened today was only a nightmare.

"It wasn't you," I say, quieter. "That memory doesn't belong to you."

"But I have it all the same." Her eyes are vacant, staring at me and straight through me at the same time. "No matter how many times they try taking it away, it keeps coming back." She's whispering now, and her lips are trembling in a way that almost makes me think she might cry. Except I don't think I've ever seen this Violet cry before—I'm not sure she even knows how. The thought of it happening stuns me into a silence that stretches at least a full minute before she interrupts it.

"Samantha wasn't supposed to die," she mumbles. "Not that night."

Her voice was so quiet that I'm almost sure I've misheard her. And she refuses to repeat it. To explain herself any better, no matter how many times I ask or beg or plead. Soon I can sense tension coiling up around her again, frustrated aggression that I'm afraid may snap into action if I keep pushing her. I press slowly back against the wall, as far away from her as I can get without making any sudden motions. Maybe if I just wait. Maybe if I just let her calm down again . . .

Except then I hear him.

Jaxon. Calling my name.

The corner of Violet's mouth quirks. "Take care, then, little sister," she says. Without looking back, she turns and bolts into the hallway.

I grab the nearest gun and take off after her.

I'm never going to catch her, I know. I won't beat her

to Jaxon. I can only hope I get there in time again. That I can somehow stop her again. But all too soon my body is screaming at me, reminding me of how much blood I've lost today, and how deep the cuts in my arms and face are. Wind rushes into those cuts as I run, and the burning it sends through my skin is almost as unbearable as the fire in my lungs; all the adrenaline in the world couldn't make me oblivious to that. I don't know how I keep my legs moving. I just do. I pump them harder and harder, until I lose the feeling in my feet, until I've run up and down so many hallways that they all start to look the same, and I'm sure that this place is a maze built to torture and confuse me.

I take a sharp left, and I see Jaxon walking toward me, see the way his eyes widen at the sight of me. I'm going too fast to keep from slamming into him. We fall back, and both our guns and the bags of whatever he'd been carrying go tumbling over the floor.

"Catelyn? What are you—"

I throw myself over my gun, draw it, and climb to my knees. I don't trust myself to stand all the way up. Now that I've stopped moving, the pain threatens to overwhelm. Everything has started to spin and stir viciously around me. But I have to focus. She's here somewhere, she's close, I can feel it—

"Why were you yelling like that?" I pant, swiveling in every direction, the gun leveled and ready. *"What is wrong with you?"*

"I don't know," Jaxon says. "I got turned around. All

these rooms look the same. Plus I didn't want to sneak up on you guys and freak anyone out, and I—"

"Where is she? Did she come by here? Is she—"

"Where is who? Your sister? What's going on?" He appears beside me, his own weapon back at his side, and I turn so he can't see the bloody side of my face. When he speaks again, it's in that same cold voice he used by the pool—the one that makes me afraid for Violet even now. Even after what she did. "Catelyn? I swear, if she tried to hurt you again—"

"She didn't," I say quickly. Why am I still protecting her? Am I really that stupid? "No, I mean, we fought, but then she ran off, and I thought . . . I just thought . . ."

I thought she was coming after him. I thought I was going to be too late. That's exactly what she wanted me to think. She could have found Jaxon before I did, I know. She probably could have killed him just as easily, too. As easily as she could have killed Samantha. As easily as she could have killed me in the room. But she didn't.

Why?

I want to think it's because she still feels something for me. That she hasn't forgotten all of the times I've stood up for her. Or how I've tried so hard to look at her and see only my sister, and not my sister's replacement.

More likely, though, it's because there's no fun in killing us now. Why not drag it out and make me squirm with fear and confusion? This Violet has always loved a show, after all. And right now? She's messing with me. She has to be. For all I know, she's watching from someplace nearby, someplace safe, and waiting with that mischievous smile on her face.

She probably thinks this is hilarious.

"You fought in the room, you mean?" Jaxon's words are heavy with dread, and I can guess his next question before he even asks it: "What about Seth? Where is he?"

"He's fine." Okay, maybe "fine" isn't the best choice of words here—but he could be worse. And I'm afraid that if I tell Jaxon what Violet did, there's a good chance he'll take that gun in his hand and go after her, no questions asked. I don't want it to come to that. Not as long as I can help it.

I expect him to press me for more details, but his phone rings before he can, the shrill noise making me jump.

I don't ask him who's calling. But when I glance back at him and watch him silence it without answering, I can't help but wonder: Is any of what Violet said true? Am I a fool for still being with him? For wanting to trust him? He said he wanted to find out the truth about what happened to Samantha that night—but what if he already knows the truth and he's only trying to keep me and everyone else from figuring it out? Is that his mother calling again, giving him more orders?

"We should go back." I want to ask him all of those things, but I can't. Not right here, not right now. If Violet's watching me, I don't want to give her the satisfaction of seeing the fear and confusion she's caused.

Because I do know one thing for sure now: I'm not playing her games anymore.

CHAPTER TWELVE

Reasons

"I was gone for like thirty minutes," Jaxon says, voice still full of disbelief as he picks up Seth and lays him on the bed. I don't say anything; I just watch silently as he pulls the sheet up around Seth's shoulders, and a strange longing fills my gut.

Before the old Violet decided she wanted to be an astronaut, she used to tell everyone who would listen that she was going to be a doctor. She would make me pretend to be her patient, tuck me into bed the way Jaxon is doing now and take my temperature, treat my invisible wounds with bandages and hand sanitizer that she swiped from Mother's purse. I never really liked that game; the bandages hurt to pull off, the sanitizer stung my eyes, and I didn't like all of the gruesome diseases she would diagnose me with.

But it was still a lot better than the game we're playing now.

Jaxon goes on, "She was out cold. As many tranq darts as Seth pumped into her . . . she should have been dead to the world for twenty-four hours at least."

"She's not like us," I remind him. Saying it out loud twists my longing into something even more painfully fierce.

She's not the old Violet. She never will be. Why can't I just accept that?

I force myself back to what I was doing, and cringe as I press the alcohol-soaked gauze to the cut on my cheek. Medical supplies—that's what Jaxon had been carrying, and the only place he claims to have gone was an abandoned clinic a few miles into town; he went to raid it for whatever remained in its storage closets. Bandages, gauze, alcohol—all of it's spread out on the dresser in front of me now; there are even a couple bottles of painkillers. They're way past the expiration date stamped on the lid, and they probably won't work, but I swallow a couple anyway as Jaxon walks back to me. He picks up a wad of gauze and douses it in the alcohol.

"May I?" he asks, his fingertips resting light against my arm. "That cut along your cheek . . . it doesn't look so good."

"Knock yourself out," I say.

He works quickly and carefully, dabbing at the cut and apologizing every time I suck in a deep breath in response to the stinging pain. It's not until he starts to push strands of hair aside, trying to get to a cut along the side of my neck, that it occurs to me how uncomfortably close his fingertips are to the scar Huxley left back there. My body tenses automatically.

"Does that hurt?" he asks, hesitating.

I don't say anything. I just reach up, take his hand, and pull it down. I have every intention of letting go of it then, but somehow our fingers end up loosely intertwined.

I didn't realize my hands were shaking so bad until I felt them against the stillness of his.

"There's a number over an older scar back there," he says suddenly. "That's the one from Huxley, isn't it? From where they linked you to your clone?"

I freeze.

"I saw it when you were unconscious by the pool," he adds quickly, sounding almost embarrassed. "I mean, I wasn't looking for it or anything, but there was all that blood, and I was trying to clean it up and make sure there weren't any more cuts . . . and I couldn't help but notice it. Sorry. I was curious."

I flatten my hair over the back of my neck, trying to hide it even now. Even though he knows it's there, I still don't want him to look at it. I don't want him to look at me and see a number. I don't want him to think about my clone. I just want to be Cate right now. Not origin Cate. And I just want Violet to be Violet, not clone-Violet, and I want to forget about the CCA and Huxley and all this mess between them that we've gotten caught up in.

But Jaxon's still watching me, still waiting for me to answer him.

I guess we're way past the point of pretending that none of this is happening.

"Sometimes I wonder," he says, "about half of the stuff my mom's told me about Huxley—about whether all if it's true or not. The whole mind-uploading thing, especially. It sounds too crazy. And it doesn't seem right, does it? For them to have such free access to your thoughts and stuff like that. I mean, your . . . your clone, her brain is essentially just a computer that all that stuff goes to, right? Doesn't that weird you out at all?"

Free access to your thoughts.

I let out a curse.

"What?"

"Huxley knows where we are." I reach up and dig my fingertips into the scar on my neck. A crawling spreads from underneath my touch, all the way up over my scalp. It takes Jaxon a few seconds, but then his face lights with the same understanding.

"They're using your memory transfers to follow you?"

"And they're going to realize I'm with you, and then . . ." I trail off, thinking of what Violet said earlier. How long *will* it be before they come for me, once they realize I'm out here road-tripping with their enemy? I know they can see the things I'm seeing, that they can use them to track me down—because they've done it before. A few years ago, a young origin boy went missing from the ETS station in Westside, and his parents went to Huxley for help. It was all over the news, the way they downloaded his most recent memory transfers to help find him, and pro-cloning advocates had a field day celebrating what they saw as an obvious benefit of Huxley's work. But the skeptics all wondered the same thing that I'm wondering now: How easy was it to access such transfers? And just how much detail could they see from them? Just the simple visual things—or all the thoughts that went with them? Does Huxley see my doubts about them now? Is someone sitting at the lab right this moment and taking every single feeling I've ever had about Jaxon apart, picking through it like lines of code and searching for errors?

Suddenly, I want to rake my nails across the scar, to open it up and rip out that stupid chip so I can crush it in my hand. I don't want to give anything to Huxley right now. Or maybe ever again. Because even after everything Violet gave her clone, she's still turned all wrong, and *this* is all wrong, and all I want to do is just end the cycle somehow—I don't care if it means I'll only have one life to live. Maybe that's how it should be anyway.

I think about the knife Seth had earlier, and I wonder if I'd have the stomach to cut out Huxley's access to my mind. Probably not. I dart around the room all the same, searching through all of the bags and in the pockets of the jacket Seth was wearing, trying to find it.

"What are you looking for?" Jaxon asks.

"Nothing," I lie. But only because I realize that it probably wouldn't work; I've seen the diagrams on their stupid videos. The chip is so deeply embedded that I'd probably cause irreversible brain damage before I even managed to cut my way anywhere close to it.

I fling the jacket onto the bed with a frustrated sigh and watch as Jaxon walks over and picks it up, then folds it and lays it back by the nightstand. He seems entirely too calm about everything. "What exactly are we going to do about this?" I ask.

He's thoughtful for a moment, and then he says, "Given Seth's affinity for illegal things, I have a feeling there might be something we can use in the stuff he brought." He goes to the bags I've already made a mess of and starts rifling further through them, using his phone as a flashlight to check all of the zippered pouches.

"Aha," he says after a bit of searching, drawing out a small black object with two pronglike antennae. He holds it up to me.

"Is that what I think it is?"

"It's exactly what you think it is."

A signal jammer. The fine for getting caught with one of these kinds of devices is more than even my father makes in a year.

"I have no idea how it works," he says, "but you're good with this sort of thing, right?"

I frown. "Not with doing illegal things, no."

"You hacked the CCA's computer system, didn't you?"

"That was different. And they started it, anyway."

He gives me an incredulous look. "And Huxley *didn't* start something, using your mind uploads without permission like this?"

"Assuming they are—we don't really have any proof of that." He doesn't argue back, but I can tell he wants to. Not that I really blame him. I know I'm only making excuses now. Because that desire to disconnect from my clone is new, and it's strange, and in a way it's like admitting that I didn't know the truth about even one of the most routine and basic parts of my life. This chip in the back of my head was always a bit unsettling, but it was ultimately supposed to be a *good* thing. It was supposed to make it all worth it—all of those judgmental stares, all of that hate mail my father got; none of that mattered when I thought about what had happened to Violet. About how it could happen to me, too, and how that chip was the only thing that could undo it.

But now, even though I'm scared to think about it, I can't stop wondering what the *actual* cost of cloning is.

And more importantly, how is Huxley planning to collect their dues?

"Give it here," I say, crossing to Jaxon and holding out my hand. I don't want to admit it to myself, but I know he's right: We need to block any information the chip is transmitting, and then hurry up and get away from here. The brain uploads aren't continuous; they're scheduled and usually only occur once a day. So with any luck, Huxley won't learn—at least not from me—exactly what's happened, or where we're going from here. They'll realize something is up when my clone's memories for the past hours turn up as nothing except static, of course, but this might buy us some time at least.

While I work on trying to figure out how the tiny jamming device works, Jaxon finds Seth's knife. He cuts strips from one of the ragged pillowcases and twists them together into a sort of bracelet, fitting it around my wrist and leaving enough length to tie around the jammer's prongs.

"So," he says as he works, "you have that chip, and Violet has something like that too, right?"

"Hers is a lot more complex," I say offhandedly. "Her entire brain is a supercomputer, basically."

The rest of a clone's body grows completely from cells taken from their origins. However those cells are manipulated and redesigned, they're still essentially human—superpowered or not. But the brain proved too complex an organ for Huxley to grow properly, especially given the advanced-human-clone body that it needed to exert control over. Building a computer with the necessary functionality had simply been easier.

And Huxley freely explains this in all of those videos and brochures and information files that they give prospective origin families, all of which my father keeps in a messy folder on his personal computer. *Transparency and trust*, that's what the scientist in Mother's favorite video insists they are all about. *Because nothing about this science— these advancements with such possibility to change the world— should remain a secret.*

"A computer that Huxley has access to?" Jaxon presses. "That they could control remotely, even?"

I don't know the answer to that, and even if I did, I'm not sure I would tell him. Because I remember what Violet said. And it's crazy, maybe, but when he mentions *control*, the first thing I wonder is if what she said was true—am I the one being brainwashed? Is it really safe to be talking with him about all of this? I've been telling myself that I'm the one using him, but is it really the other way around? Maybe my sister was right to be angry with me for taking his side.

I turn the jammer over and over in my hands and pretend to study it. "I have no idea about any of that," I say. "But can I ask you something?"

"Can I really stop you?"

"No."

"Then go for it, I guess."

"Why are you still here?"

He sighs. "I already told you—I want to know what really happened that night Samantha died."

It sounds just as convincing as it did the first time he said it. Violet was wrong. She has to be wrong. He doesn't know anything about Samantha's death. He would have told me if he did.

You trust him so much, so why don't you ask him?

The memory of her voice makes my head spin. I stop messing with the jammer and close my eyes, trying to make it stop. "Where were you the night she died?" I ask quietly.

"Why does this suddenly sound like an interrogation?"

"It's just a question. You don't have to answer it if you don't want to."

A tense, hesitant silence stretches between us. One minute. Two minutes. Three minutes. And then of all the things he could do to break it, he laughs. "What did that clone say to you earlier? What did she tell you about me?"

"She doesn't matter right now," I say, my eyes flashing open again. "I'm the one who's asking the question—I can think for myself, you know."

"I *do* know that. Which is why I'm wondering what I have to do to make you stop thinking I'm the worst person you've ever met."

"Just tell me the truth. That's all I need."

His sigh is softer this time. "Look, I didn't even see Samantha the night she died. We were supposed to get together, to grab coffee before we went to this CCA meeting thing, but she never showed up. I didn't think anything of it, because it wasn't the first time it had happened. Her father doesn't particularly care for me, as you might have noticed the other day, so she's had to bail on me a few times in the past, whenever he managed to find out the two of us had plans. Then later, at the meeting, someone said she was sick and had stayed home. No big deal."

"You didn't think it was weird that she didn't call or text you or anything?"

He raises an eyebrow. "How well did you actually know Samantha?" he asks. "She wasn't exactly the dependable type."

Unpredictable. I think that was the word Violet used to describe her—it was what my sister had liked best about her only friend. I guess the two of them were a lot alike that way.

"I never held it against her, though," Jaxon says. "She could have turned out a lot worse, with parents like hers. And for all the crap people gave her about being rich and stuck-up, she wasn't really that bad." He shrugs. "At least not to me. And she definitely didn't deserve . . . you know, what happened to her."

There's another long, awkward pause, and again he's the one who breaks it. "I messed up, not telling you the truth about me from the beginning," he says. "I know I did. And I'm sorry. But I'm not lying now—I wouldn't keep something like this from you. I never wanted to keep *anything* from you."

His voice has changed. There's something vulnerable in it now, and that scares me more than the possibility of any of Violet's warnings about him being true. I absently untuck my hair from behind my ears and let it fall into my face, like that could hide me. He's not looking at me anymore, though. Instead, he takes the jammer from my hands and ties it into the makeshift bracelet, and then he fastens the whole thing around my wrist, somehow managing to barely touch me and avoid my gaze all at the same time.

"Probably not the best fashion statement you've ever made." It's a blatant change of subject, I know. But his tone still has that soft vulnerability to it, and it makes it difficult to keep fighting or to honestly doubt anything he's just said. "Hopefully it'll work, though," he adds. "Now we just need to get out of here as soon as possible."

The main problem, we agree, is Seth; until he comes around and we can tell exactly how hurt he is, we're afraid to move him any more than we have to. Not to mention we're both exhausted, and the thought of hauling all of our stuff to the car in the near pitch-black darkness isn't exactly appealing.

"Less than three hours until morning," Jaxon says, glancing at his phone.

"Might be enough time for Seth to start waking up," I think aloud.

"And for you to get some more rest."

I go and sit down on the bed, not because I'm planning

on actually going to sleep, but because all of the thoughts whirling around in my head are starting to make me feel dizzy again. "What about you?" I ask.

"It'll probably be a while before Huxley figures anything out, but we still don't know where your sister's run off to. One of us needs to stay up and keep an eye out for her." He grabs a spare pillow, props it in the corner between my bed and the nightstand, and then leans back and tilts his head against the mattress. "I think I'm past the point of sleep anyway."

I try arguing that it should be me who stays up—since I already had a few hours of sleep earlier—but he doesn't budge from his spot on the floor.

"You could at least sit on the bed," I say. "It would be more comfortable."

"Not a good idea," he says. "Something tells me I would get distracted from keeping watch." Out of the corner of my eye, I see the wry smile spreading across his face. I force myself to stare only at the wad of covers balled up in my fist.

But warmth is already rushing into my cheeks. Even now, with everything else I could be focusing on, and with all the doubt these past few days have left between us . . . why do I still not have any control over the butterflies he sets free in my stomach when he smiles like that?

What is wrong with me?

I draw my knees up to my chest and rest my chin on them, take a deep breath, and try to force my thoughts away from Jaxon. Away from all the possible ways I could distract him.

I shouldn't be thinking about things like that.

I can't stop thinking about him completely, though. Not when he's this close. Not when I'm having to make a conscious effort to keep from reaching a hand out and running my fingers through his messy hair. I should say something. Anything to divert my thoughts away from the roads they're trying to go down.

"Do you remember the first time we met?" I ask quietly. Not the best diversion, maybe, but it was the first question that came to mind.

"Vividly."

"The music room," I think aloud, and I'm instantly back there; back to the scent of instrument polish and the lingering cloud of floral perfume that our teacher always left in her wake.

"You thought you were alone that day, didn't you?" he asks.

"Of course. That was the only reason I was singing." The rest of the class was at lunch, but I wasn't hungry; so I'd wandered into the room the older students sometimes used for recording. There was all that fancy equipment, and the walls were covered in soundproofing foam. It felt so . . . *professional*. And for a moment, I forgot the disapproving looks my mother always gave me when I would sing, and I just closed my eyes and belted out the first song that came into my head.

When I opened my eyes, Jaxon was standing in the doorway of the room.

"That day . . . I'd never been so mortified in my life."

"I tried to apologize," he says, "but you ran away. You didn't even look back."

"And you spent the rest of that semester trying to get me to sing again." The whole thing seems kind of silly now that I say it out loud.

"Because you were better than anyone else I'd ever heard. You still are. Whenever I hear that song now—which I swear is all the time, because my mom plays it constantly—I hear you singing it. I don't even remember the lyrics, just your voice."

I'm staring at him again. I can't help it. His gaze, meanwhile, is distant and lost in thought.

"There was something in your voice that day that's never let me go," he says after a minute. "Something that's there when you perform in all those plays, too. And that's why I . . ." He twists around and rests his elbows on the edge of the bed. "I mean, there were other places I could have gone when I was blowing off my duties as an office assistant. But I knew you'd be there in the auditorium. And I'd watch you performing, and I'd get the same feeling I had the first time I heard you sing. That feeling I'm still trying to figure out." His eyes meet mine again. They're less anxious now. "So if you don't want to believe me about my first reason," he says, "there's another for you. That's the other part of why I'm here."

"I was only pretending when I was on that stage," I say, and suddenly all the nervousness is gone, replaced by a swift and strange sort of sadness. Because I hate to break this to him, but he's followed a fraud. His infatuation isn't with me; it's with the person I become when I put on whatever costume the play calls for.

"No one can pretend that good," he says.

"I can."

I can tell he still doesn't believe me. And it's frustrating—because I don't know how to make him understand how incredibly wrong he is.

Because he *is* wrong.

Isn't he?

It's then that I realize I can't even answer myself. I was wrong about who Violet was; who says I haven't been wrong about myself all this time too? How did this conversation even become about me, anyway? This wasn't supposed to be about me. I don't like talking about myself, and I don't like the thought of someone else knowing me better than I know myself. Especially when that someone else is Jaxon, considering I still don't know what to think about him.

I know what I *want* to think, though, don't I? I have to admit that. I want to think he's on my side. Though I'm not sure if that's because he truly is, or if it's because he's so dangerously persuasive and I'm so incredibly tired. Or maybe it's simply that, after what's happened with Violet, I'm just about desperate enough to hope anybody is still on my side. I don't know. Sometimes it would be nice to have even a tenth of that relentless confidence he seems to have about us.

I grab the pillow at my feet and toss it behind my head, intent on going to sleep and putting an end to this conversation before it becomes any more confusing. When I start to turn away, though, he grabs my wrist. I keep my focus on the pillow. I can feel his eyes on me, waiting for me to turn and look at him. But I don't know which face he'd see, or if it's even the right one anymore, so I don't move.

"Let go," I say.

"No."

"Excuse me?"

"I answered your question from earlier," he says. "Now I have one for you."

"What?"

"You found Violet. So where are you planning to go now? What are you going to do?"

I almost breathe a sigh of relief. Somehow, I find it easier to talk about my crazy sister than about whatever is going on between Jaxon and me. Though my answers are just as inconclusive about her as they are about him.

"I don't know." I try to pull out of his grasp; I think he sees the pain it causes me—the way my entire sore, broken body cringes with the movement—because he's quick to let go then. But he still stays close, his body leaning into the mattress and sinking me toward him. "But if you don't want to follow me around anymore, I understand," I say. "Especially after . . . after what my sister did to you."

"After what she did to *me?* Are you serious? What about what she did to *you*, Cate?" He takes my arm again, much more gently this time, and tries to meet my eyes. I do my best to avoid his. "Please don't tell me you're thinking about going after her."

I'd be lying if I told him the thought hadn't crossed my mind. It's not like we can just carry on as if none of the past few days happened; my sister and I are going to have to meet again. That seems inevitable. And I'd rather be the one tracking her down. I'm not going to spend the rest of my life looking over my shoulder, waiting for her to sneak up on me. If she's going to try to turn this into a game for her own personal amusement, then fine—but I at least want to be the one making the rules.

"I think it's time for a plan B," Jaxon is saying. "Even if she knows what happened to Samantha, do you really think she's going to tell you? You tried to talk to her, and she tried to *kill* you in response. Remember that? She doesn't really seem like the divulging type."

"Except she did tell me." I regret the words the second they leave my mouth, because I can't elaborate on them. I can't bring up that she *did* mention Jaxon's name, even though he's already guessed as much; it will only lead us back to our argument from earlier. I don't want to go there again. I want to believe what he's told me and leave it at that. And the only other thing Violet said was that Samantha wasn't supposed to die that night, but I don't know what she meant by it, either, so I'd rather keep that to myself too. Maybe I'm just afraid of what Jaxon would make of these things—that he might see something incriminating in her words, some sort of proof that I'm trying desperately to overlook.

All I really know is that he's watching me expectantly now, so I have no choice but to follow up with something.

I manage a stuttered, "I mean she *started* to tell me," which only earns me an exasperated look from him, since I guess we both know that all I'm doing is grasping for answers I don't really have.

Because whether it was supposed to happen or not, Samantha is still dead, and everything still points to it being Violet's fault.

"She tried to kill you," Jaxon repeats in a perfectly monotone voice.

"If she'd wanted to kill me, she would have." I realize how insane it sounds—to still be making excuses for her right now—but for some reason I can't make myself take it back.

Maybe because she *didn't* kill either of us, even though I know she could have. Easily. I keep thinking about that, and how that's the other part of the equation I can't make sense of. However violent and out of control she seemed tonight, my sister was still in there. She still had her memories of us, and the second she saw the blood on my cheek, she stopped.

It makes it seem like she's the one in control. Like maybe she hasn't been brainwashed by them at all. Not completely.

But that would mean it was actually Violet who let Samantha Voss bleed to death on those railroad tracks. The girl who is supposed to be my sister. Not some zombie being controlled by Huxley. If she can walk away and leave me and Jaxon alive, then she could have done the same thing with Samantha, right? If she was really there that night, she could have saved her, even.

Except she didn't.

I don't understand any of it. All I know is that the more I think about it, the more I want to scream. The more I want to track her down right this second and do whatever it takes to stop her from hurting anyone else—even though I'm afraid to think about what, exactly, that's going to mean.

"How do you know she won't kill us both next time, though?" Jaxon asks.

"I don't." The words are numb, lifeless. It's not on purpose; I think I'm just feeling so many different things at once that they've all mixed into one bland blob of emotion—like when you mix all the different paints together and get that awful brown color.

"I think you should stay away from her." There's something in his voice that breaks through the blandness of my thoughts; something violent, almost. And when I turn my head and meet his eyes, I see aggression shimmering there, just beneath the surface. "And if she knows what's good for her," he says, "she'll stay away from me—and from you and Seth—too."

Out of all the emotions inside me, anger is the one that fights its way to the surface. It's not really anger at Jaxon, I know; but my voice is still seething when I say, "You do realize that's my sister you're threatening, right?"

"No she's not, Cate. She's not the Violet you want her to be, and you can't keep protecting her like this."

Not the Violet you want her to be.

That's exactly what I thought earlier, wasn't it? That

this Violet was some sort of impersonator, a memory thief masquerading around in a part that she was playing all wrong. So why can't I stand to hear Jaxon say the same thing? It's like a kind of unwritten law, I think—that you can be as pissed off at your family as you want, but the second someone else has anything bad to say about them, you're suddenly ready to forgive even the most heinous crimes they might have committed.

Because other people don't get it. They don't know all of the good parts of Violet. They don't realize that she's as much a victim in all of this as anyone else; it's not like she *asked* to be Huxley's creation.

"I'm not protecting her," I say, "I'm only trying to—"

He's just watching me now and shaking his head in disbelief. It's irritating.

"You have no idea what it's like," I snap. "You have no idea what we've been through, so just . . . just stop acting like you do, all right?"

"Fine." For a moment I think that's going to be the end of it. But then he fixes me with a very serious look and says, "But I do know what she did to you, don't I?" That violence from before hovers at the edge of his voice, and suddenly his face looks like it did when I opened my eyes beside the pool; pale and sick, like we're reliving that moment here and now. "And I just . . . I just don't think any answers we want to find are worth you getting killed over. That's all I'm trying to say."

He stands up and wanders away from me then, his hands clasped behind his head and his chest rising and falling in attempts at deep calming breaths. Back and forth, back and forth he paces, and with every step he takes, arguing with him seems less important. At least for now. Because now there's no denying how genuinely worried he looks. The violence in his eyes grows a little fainter every second, uncertainty and fear taking its place. And at least in this moment, it's hard to believe that we're not on the same side. It's hard not to think that he's right about at least some of the things he said. I did find out the truth about my sister, didn't I? She's dangerous. After what she's done to all of us, I can't deny that. It would be stupid to deny that.

But there are still questions that need answering. Questions like who's in control of all this, and how do I make it stop? There has to be a way to make this stop.

Jaxon glances at Seth's unconscious body; his eyes don't linger, but I see it. And I see that uncertainty flicker across his face again. I know what he must be thinking. Seth is only here because he asked him to come. If anything happened to Seth, something tells me Jaxon would never forgive himself.

And I don't want anything to happen to either of them. So maybe we should just go our separate ways now? They should go back. It would be safer for them to go back to the CCA headquarters, and my next meeting with Violet would probably go a lot smoother if I didn't have to worry about keeping her from attacking them, too. It makes sense.

So I don't know why I find myself hesitating to speak, silently watching Jaxon lean against the dresser and turn his gun over and over in his hands, pretending to study it.

When I decided to leave the city, I had every intention of going alone. I never wanted them to come—and even now, I don't completely trust them. So why is it so hard to even think about telling them to leave? It would mean finding my own way back, and fending for myself from here on out. But I could handle that. Maybe what I can't handle is the feeling from earlier: knowing Violet and I aren't on the same side anymore, and that losing Jaxon and Seth would mean the only one left is me.

Thinking about that sends a wrenching loneliness twisting through my insides; I'm suddenly desperate for something familiar to hold on to, and I think of my parents—because I can still go home, right? Eventually. If no one else is on my side, I at least need to believe that much.

I arch up so I can reach into my back pocket and grab my phone. I know it's a waste of time, though—since it was in this same pocket when I went for my unplanned swim earlier, and Seth ended up retrieving it from the bottom of the shallow end of the pool. It didn't turn on earlier, and it doesn't now. I'm not sure why I was expecting anything different.

I drop it into my lap, mumbling about how the stupid thing was *supposed* to be waterproof. A second later, Jaxon's phone lands with a soft *thump* in the covers beside me. He doesn't say anything. Doesn't ask who I want to call, or why; he's not even looking at me anymore. And I'm kind of ashamed to admit it, but my first thought isn't to thank him or to dial my house's number.

It's to find his recent calls.

To figure out exactly who was trying to reach him in the hallway earlier, and who he might have been trying to reach while I was asleep. I can't bring myself to follow through with it, though. Maybe because I'm afraid of my suspicions being right, or because I want to see this phone as some sort of peace offering—an attempt to put our shattered trust back together again—and I'm not going to be the one who ruins it.

So I focus on trying to reach my parents. Once again, though, I'm not surprised when they don't pick up. I convince myself that, if my phone were working, I would have at least ten messages from them by now. That it's still perfectly normal for them to not be answering this call. After all, in the past, when we've found ourselves in the middle of a media storm, my parents would always see to it that we dropped off the radar until things calmed down. Which meant not going anywhere. Not socializing. Not answering the phone, even—especially not from a number like this one, which they wouldn't recognize.

Never mind that it might be their daughter calling.

They're too busy trying to keep the stone wall around our family from crumbling, so of course they don't have time to answer.

"Calling home?" Jaxon asks softly.

I nod without looking up.

"No one's there?"

"Maybe not. I probably just missed them." I shrug. "Communication's never been our strong point," I add with a quiet laugh. I sound perfectly composed. Perfectly fake. My mother would have been proud to hear it.

Keep it together, Catelyn.

She may as well be right beside me, speaking those words into my ear. I clench the phone in a trembling fist until my knuckles turn white, and it's all I can do to keep myself from throwing it at the wall.

Jaxon appears at my side a second later, gently pries the phone from my grip, and tosses it back onto the bed. He takes my shaking hand in his, and the concerned look on his face tells me that I must look at least as bad as I feel. I think about pushing him away, about telling him I'm fine even though we'd both know I was lying.

But, at least for the moment, I'm tired of keeping it together. I'm tired of walls. I don't want to be like my parents, always building up and never breaking down, no matter the cost.

So instead I meet Jaxon's calm blue eyes and very carefully tell him the truth: "I know it's dangerous to go after Violet. But I have to. I can't go home without her."

There is no home without her.

I expect him to keep arguing. But he doesn't. He just pulls me close, rests his chin on top of my head, and breathes deeply in and slowly out, warm air breezing through my hair and sending shivers down my neck. I stop thinking about pushing him away. My hands stop shaking. My body is still against his and for the moment, at least, everything feels strangely peaceful.

If my sister is a hurricane, I think, then maybe Jaxon

could be the eye to her storm. A patch of blue sky, calm and centered even as the winds whip around and around us—that's what he was before all of this. It's what I want him to be now. I want to trust him again so much that it's painful. However stupid, however desperate, and however loud my mother's warnings are echoing in my head—

Don't give anyone the illusion that anything they do can affect you. You can't give them that control, because there's no telling what they'd do with it.

She's right, too. I don't know. I could wake up in a few hours, and he could be gone. He could promise to stay, promise to help me, and all that could turn out to be more lies. Or not. There's really no way of knowing, and maybe at some point you have to decide who's worth the risk, even if there's a chance they'll wind up hurting you in the end.

And right now, this feels worth it. So I don't pull away from him. My cheek is still resting against his shoulder when I ask, "Does this mean you're staying out here with me?"

He keeps his arms tightly wrapped around my waist but leans back enough so that our eyes can meet.

"I'm not going anywhere, Cate."

CHAPTER THIRTEEN

The Rules to the Game

"Wake up."

Jaxon's voice is quiet, muffled by the pillow I've got wrapped around my head. I don't open my eyes right away. I want it to be a dream, like it always was before, like all the times I drifted off in class and daydreamed about him softly calling my name.

Because he's calling it now. But it's not the same. His tone is all wrong. Fear edges his voice, and I feel that same fear in his touch a second later when he grabs my shoulder and gently shakes me until I sit up to face him.

It takes only a quick glance at him to tell me that I was right. Something's wrong.

"There's someone in the hotel," he says.

"Who?"

"Someone from Huxley—a half dozen of them, actually. I saw their trucks, and more were pulling up as I came back inside. Apparently, we didn't have as much time as we thought."

"How many trucks, exactly?"

He doesn't answer, but that look in his eyes tells me that we're in trouble.

I jump up from the bed, grab the nearest bag, and start

throwing things inside it. My body is still weak, still sore, and some of the bumps from earlier have turned into ugly, discolored bruises; but I don't have time to baby my injuries right now. After this first bag is filled, though, the next one I grab is the one with medical supplies. I take the pain pills out of it, swallow a couple, then throw both bags over my shoulder. Jaxon glances over his shoulder at me and almost smiles.

"I wish Seth was as enthusiastic as you in the morning," he says. He's got his brother propped up with one of his arms around his shoulder, but the second Jaxon tries to pull him to his feet, Seth collapses to the ground with a *thud*.

"You're going to have to carry him," I say. "He's still too out of it."

He nods, and while he lifts Seth onto his back, I scurry around the room, collecting everything else in sight.

A minute later, we're in the doorway, breath held, bodies tense, eyes scanning the hallway on either side of us.

"Why are you carrying me?" Seth groans, "I can walk. I can walk . . . so good . . . I can . . . *so good*—you don't even know, man. . . ."

I bring my face very close to where his rests limply against Jaxon's shoulder. "Shut. Up," I whisper. I hate to be mean to him right now, because he looks awful—his normally tan skin is pale and glistening with sweat, his chocolate eyes dull and lifeless—but he's being entirely too loud. And I swear I just heard footsteps.

I lean farther out into the hallway, listening.

My sister's words from last night crash into my head:

everything she said about Huxley, about how they would probably be coming for me even sooner than they'd planned on.

As soon as now?

"Your girlfriend's rude," Seth mumbles behind me. "And I think you should dump her."

"So which way do we go?" I ask, ignoring Seth.

"Good question," Jaxon says. "We should have mapped this place out better last night, had a better escape route planned. We should have—"

"We were busy fighting off my psychotic sister last night, remember?"

"Still."

I try to focus on the parts of the hotel I've been to, try to remember the layout of the halls I ran up and down while I was searching for Violet. It's mostly a blur, though.

"We need to go out the way we came in," Jaxon says. "So we can head straight to the car—the less time we're running around outside, the better."

"But if anyone sees us, we're screwed," I say, frowning. "We're not going to be able to outrun them while you're carrying him."

"You have to leave me," Seth groans, stretching a hand dramatically into the air. "Save yourselves—"

"Tempting, but no."

Jaxon gives me an anxious look. "So what are you suggesting we do, then?"

I don't think I even realized what I was thinking until he asked. But now I do.

"One of us is going to have to create a distraction—"

"No."

"—so we can get Seth safely to the car—"

"*No.*"

"—and it's going to have to be me. I can't carry Seth. We'll make our way toward that exit, and then you guys hide in one of the rooms while I draw everyone away from it."

"And then what?" I can tell he's fighting to keep his voice at a whisper.

"I'll catch up," I say, starting into the hallway. He reaches for my arm, but I twist out of the way and keep walking. Someone has to move. Otherwise, at the rate we're going, we'll still be standing here arguing about what to do while the Huxley creeps drag all three of us away. I can't let that happen.

"How, exactly, do you plan on getting out?" Jaxon demands.

The pool room flashes back into my mind. I remember it more vividly than anywhere else, and I remember a door tucked into the corner of the room and so covered in dust and grime that it almost blended into the cracked concrete walls. It wasn't that noticeable. They might not be guarding it. And I *think* I remember how to get back to it.

"When you get to your car," I tell Jaxon. "Drive it around until you can see the pool room. I'll get out through there and meet you at the road."

I press against the wall and peer around a corner into the next hall. It's clear. But the hairs on my arms and all along the back of my neck are already sticking straight up now, every nerve ending in my body anticipating the worst.

Am I crazy for thinking we can actually make it out of here alive? All three of us?

"You can see one of the main exits from the pool," Jaxon says, grabbing me and pulling me into an empty room. "There will be people guarding it. You'll be shot the second you step outside."

"I'll run really fast."

"I'm not joking, Cate."

"Me either."

I slide one of the bags from my shoulder and start to dig through it while Jaxon backs slowly toward the corner of the room, crouches down and lets Seth slide from his back and to the floor with a quiet *thump*. I ignore him as he returns to my side, still trying to argue with me the whole time; I'm more focused on the small, diamond-shaped weapon that I've finally managed to find. It's one of the weapons I'm glad I asked Seth about last night—capable of filling an entire room with smoke in an instant—and it was the first one that came to mind when I thought about distractions.

I give the diamond another glance, reminding myself how it works. Jaxon tries to snatch it out of my hand, but just then we hear voices in the hallway, followed by footsteps, and he freezes with his fingers still outstretched toward me.

The voices get louder, and my heart pounds faster; I

clutch the diamond to my chest and stumble away from Jaxon. I don't have time to argue with him anymore. Seth mumbles something from the corner, and my thoughts jump back to the pain, the uncertainty, that I know Jaxon was feeling last night; I know he's feeling it now, even though he'd never admit it.

"You have to make sure Seth gets out," I say, because I know that will make him stay. I know he can't argue with that.

Jaxon only calls my name once as I sprint out of the room. He's stubborn, but not stupid; if he can't stop me from doing this, then I think—I hope—he knows better than to screw it up by drawing any attention to himself and Seth. Something tells me he's going to be pissed when he sees me again, though.

Assuming we actually see each other again.

I follow the sound of the voices to the end of the hallway and peer around the corner into a mini lobby area that I vaguely recognize. My guess is that it was grandly decorated at one time, judging by the intricately carved arched doorway I'm leaning against. There are still a few paintings on the wall as well, though they're faded beyond recognition and covered in cobwebs and dust. There's even a crumbling fountain in the center of the room.

And that's where they are. Two men in Huxley uniforms, gathered around that fountain. There's a third one leaning against the left wall, right next to the little corridor that leads to the entrance we originally came in through. They're talking casually. Laughing, even.

Like this is no big deal, them being here to kill me.

I pull the diamond from my pocket and move swiftly and silently to the hallway farthest from the entrance-corridor. I size up the main room, trying to decide the best place to lob the weapon so that it makes it hard for them to see and follow me but not so thick that Jaxon and Seth don't have a clear path to escape.

Laughter echoes through the room again, sinking into my skin and further fueling the rage growing inside me.

I swipe the activation dial on the weapon and step into plain sight of all three of them. And then I start shouting. They turn in unison and lift their guns at the exact moment the curtain of thick, black smoke billows up between us. But they've already seen me. The bait's been laid, and as I turn and sprint for the nearest hallway, I keep yelling, keep giving them the sound of my voice to follow until I'm sure they're on this side of the smoke wall, and Jaxon and Seth are safely moving behind it on the other.

A blaze of white-hot energy hits the wall to my left. I turn, trying to see how close the shooter is, and look back to the path ahead just as another man in a Huxley uniform rounds the corner. He sidesteps to avoid our collision, grabs my shoulder, and slams me against the wall so hard that it knocks my breath away. While I'm still disoriented, he roughly grabs my chin and jerks my face up to meet his.

"Are you the one causing all the commotion?" he hisses.

I answer by slamming my head into his as hard as I possibly can. He stumbles back, but not far enough to make any difference—I still don't have enough room to slide out from underneath him. And now all I've done is make him angrier. His skin is a terrible, blotchy red, his beady brown eyes almost bulging from his skull as he looks back at me.

I feel like I don't have long before he loses his temper completely. So I don't waste any more time; I throw my hands at his face, fingers clawing for eyes. I catch a nail in his right one and he roars in pain; his hand flies toward my throat, wraps around it tightly enough to make me choke. He throws me to the ground and I hit chin first, biting my tongue and flooding my mouth with the tart taste of blood. I scramble up to my hands and knees, turn, and find him drawing some sort of gun from his side. It looks a lot like the tranquilizer Seth was carrying around earlier. And I hope that's all it is, because within seconds he has it aimed at my chest.

"We could have avoided this part if you were a bit more cooperative," he says. I search my pockets frantically for something I can use—a distress disc, another smoke diamond, a gun I know isn't there—but I have nothing. I wasn't thinking that far ahead when I left Jaxon and Seth behind.

And now it's too late. The gun makes a strange clicking noise, and the man's finger itches toward the trigger. I take a deep breath. Brace myself for his shot.

But someone else fires first, from somewhere behind me. The shot eats a clean little hole right in the man's temple, filling the air with the scent of his sizzling flesh. A single trail of smoke spirals up from it, while a thin coil of blood oozes down between his eyes. He slumps forward, and he's dead by the time he falls at my feet.

I look back, and Violet is behind me, lowering a gun to her side.

"Hello, Birdy," she says, that familiar cat grin spreading across her face.

"What are you doing?" I scramble away from her and get unsteadily to my feet, not taking my eyes off that gun.

"Saving your life."

"Why?"

"Because you are my darling little sister, and I love you so."

"You are a psychopath," I say, inching away from her, "and I don't have time for your games right now." Not to mention I really don't like the idea of playing without any sort of weapon.

"This is pretty serious for a *game*, wouldn't you say?" She gives the Huxley man a little shove with her foot. He rolls over, and his dead, unseeing eyes are still wide open. I can't stop looking into them. The sight makes me sick to my stomach.

Almost as if his lifeless body rolling over was their cue, suddenly I hear the shouts of more men in the distance. They sound like they're moving closer. Violet throws an irritated glance toward the noise, while I force my eyes away from the dead man and swallow the bile rising in my throat.

"And here I was hoping we'd have a little more time before they caught up," she says, looking back to me. "Because there's something I wanted to talk to you about. Questions I wanted to ask you."

"Questions about what?" I ask, backing farther away from her.

"About something you said last night." I don't like the strange gleam that lights up her eyes as she says the words; maybe it's just a trick of the low lighting in here, but there's still something unsettling about it. "You said I was something all wrong," she continues, her voice missing some of its usual indifference. "What did you mean by that?"

"That's a bit of a loaded question." I mutter the words under my breath, but the frown that crosses her face tells me she heard them. And something about that frown makes me stop midstep. It's too real, almost.

Too real for a psychopath, at least.

I know better than to trust it now, though. I'm not sure what she's trying to do, saving me like that, and looking at me the way she is—but I don't have time to deal with this right now. I need to get out of here. Jaxon is probably outside waiting for me by this point, and if I don't show up soon, something tells me he's going to come charging back in here after me. And I can't think of any possible way that could end well.

So when Violet steps toward me, I quickly take another step back. And another. One step back for every one she takes forward. I try to turn away, but she catches me by the elbow with a grip like steel.

"I have to go," I say. I try to pull free, but it's useless; she's too strong.

"I know," she says, her gaze drifting back toward the sounds of the approaching men. "So we'll meet again soon, then. Tonight. In the woods, north of the graveyard."

"What are you—"

"You know where I'm talking about."

"You're crazy."

"The three of you should head back toward Haven, anyway," she goes on, as if she's having the conversation with herself and I'm just an unfortunate audience member.

"Why?"

Her gaze goes distant for a moment. She looks like she's having a hard time focusing on the words she wants to say. Then she closes her eyes, gives her head a little shake, and says, "Because. Things are happening."

"Don't be vague or anything."

She still looks confused, unfocused for a few more seconds. But then her familiar smirk returns. "Outside the city walls is no place for you anyway," she says, her fingers tracing the cut along the back of my arm. "You might get hurt."

"You're the only reason I got hurt," I snap. "And I left the city to find you."

"Well, here I am," she says. "Well done. You found me. And tonight you'll find me again, in the woods north of the graveyard. Only you, though. The other two stay behind."

"You honestly think I'm going to meet you *alone* in a dark forest? After what you've done?"

"Either you come to me or I find you. And then I get rid of Jaxon and Seth so that you and I can have some privacy for our little chat."

My mouth is unbearably dry all of a sudden. So much

for making the rules to the game. "You leave them out of this," I say.

"So long as you cooperate, I have every intention of doing exactly that." Her eyes harden. "Even if I am something *all wrong.*" I ignore the stab of guilt that her tone causes. Because I'm not taking those words back; I'm tired of apologizing for my own thoughts.

Was I right to think that about her, though? She just killed one of Huxley's own personnel. That doesn't seem like something their scientists would have brainwashed her into doing.

All of my questions about that are going to have to wait, though, because Violet's already turned away now, and I don't have another second to waste in this hallway. But still, I can't help myself: I call after her one last time.

"Where are you going?" I ask. Because it looks like she's heading directly toward the men, and even after everything she's put me through, I still can't help but worry about what might happen.

She doesn't seem concerned, though. If anything, she looks bored. "To take care of them," she answers, "so hopefully you can manage to get out of here without getting yourself killed. Now hurry up and go. You're going to be late for our meeting if you stay here much longer." She picks up her pace and disappears around the corner. I watch the spot where she disappeared until I can't hear her footsteps anymore.

And then I turn and face the long hallway stretching out in front of me, and I force myself to start walking.

CHAPTER FOURTEEN

Monsters

"So why, exactly, are we stopping again?" Seth asks, propping himself up on the armrest between me and Jaxon.

A muscle works in Jaxon's jaw. He hasn't been in a good mood since we left the hotel, and I don't think Seth's helping. A fact which, unsurprisingly, Seth seems oblivious to. I'd blame it on the tranquilizer still fogging up his brain, but I don't know if he deserves that much credit.

"I'm just curious," he goes on. "Because it seems like the definition of a bad idea to me—you know, given how many people have tried to kill us in the past twenty-four hours? I mean, if it's all the same to you guys, I'd like to keep a little distance between us and—"

"We're going to have to stop and charge the engine at some point," Jaxon interrupts. "We have no gas, and we won't make it back to Haven on the power we've got now." He glances over at me, his expression unreadable. "And Cate wanted to stop here. So this is where we're stopping. Any more questions?"

"Actually—"

But Jaxon already has his door open, and he slams it behind him before Seth can finish his sentence.

For a minute the two of us just stare after him. Then Seth clears his throat, and I feel his gaze shift to me. *"Cate wanted us to stop here,"* he says in a terrible impersonation of Jaxon's voice.

"Shut up."

"You've been using your voodoo devil-woman magic on him again, haven't you?"

"Seth, if I knew devil-woman magic, I'd use it to take away your voice. Forever."

He hoists himself up and swings into the vacant driver seat. "You know, I don't doubt that. So I guess that only leaves one explanation." He leans back against the seat with a sigh.

"What are you talking about?"

"My boy is completely and totally whipped."

I roll my eyes. "He didn't stop just for me," I say. "You heard him—we need to take care of the car."

"I should have seen this coming," Seth says, shaking his head and groaning as if he's in actual pain.

"I think you should go get the charging pad ready," I say pointedly. "Preferably before all those people who want to kill us show up."

"I could have saved him—"

"I'm serious, Seth."

"He was so young—"

"Okay, I'm leaving now."

"You stay away from him, devil-woman!" he shouts at me as I shut the door. Even though part of me would rather stay behind. At least Seth is in a joking mood, since he's thrilled that we're going back to the city after all. But Jaxon was more than a little suspicious about my sudden change of heart. And that, on top of the fact that he's still incredibly ticked off about the way I ran off in the hotel, is at least part of the reason I'd rather just crawl into the corner of the backseat and somehow make myself invisible to everyone and everything around me.

But I can't do that. Not now.

It's gotten much cooler out since we left the hotel, which makes it even more impossible not to think about how late it is. The sun is hanging dangerously low in the sky. I wander toward the graveyard gate and lean against it, lift my gaze toward the woods in the distance.

Tonight . . . Only you . . . The other two stay behind.

I made it this far, at least. I managed to get Jaxon to stop here by telling him I wanted to visit my sister's grave one last time before we headed back into Haven. Now I just have to figure out how to get away from the two of them, and how to keep them from following me.

Because I can't let them anywhere near Violet. I want to think she was bluffing when she said she would get rid of those two if she had to, but I'm not stupid. I still can't trust her. And I can't—I won't—run from her anymore either. So this is what it comes down to, I guess.

"If you're going to go visit your sister's grave, you need to hurry up." Jaxon's voice makes me jump. "We're leaving as soon as the engine's done charging."

I force myself to turn my back on the woods and face

him. I can't run from him, either, no matter how much I might want to right now.

"You're still mad at me, aren't you?" I ask. I don't know why, out of everything else I should be worried about, those are the first words that come to my mind. I guess I just don't like the thought of leaving him when he's still upset with me. Just in case I don't come back.

"I'm not mad," he says. But his shoulders are stiff as he leans on the fence next to me, and his tone is obviously irritated; he's never talked to me like this before. His phone is in his hands, and instead of looking at me, he focuses on tossing it back and forth between them.

"You're lying," I say quietly. Maybe I shouldn't push him, but I don't have time to wait for him to decide to admit his feelings to me.

He stops tossing the phone and gives me a sidelong glance. "I'm not mad. I mean, besides the way you left me standing in that room, after using Seth as a bargaining point so I had no choice other than to just watch you run off to your possible death, why on earth would I be mad at you?"

"What else was I supposed to do?" I ask. "We're out here because of me. Seth was barely conscious because of me. It was the least I could—"

He turns angrily toward me, closing the space between us and crowding me back against the rusty iron gate. The bars dig into my back, and the whole thing creaks under my weight. "Stop. Doing. That," Jaxon says, his voice low and hardly containing his anger. "You didn't come out here for yourself. You aren't the one who knocked Seth unconscious. Stop blaming yourself for the things that clone has done."

"Stop calling her that," I warn. I don't bother trying to keep my voice as quiet as his.

"You mean stop calling it what it is?"

"She's not just an *it*."

"What would you like me to call her, then?"

I try to push him away, but he just grabs the bar behind me and braces his arm against it. His body is so close to me now that I can hardly move, much less get any kind of leverage to shove him away with. "I'd like for you to call her by her name," I say through clenched teeth. "And I'd also like for you to get out of my way. Now."

"I'm not calling her anything but a monster. Because that's exactly what she is. Just like Huxley and all their creations—and I knew it from the beginning. But I followed you out here to find her anyway. I was going to *keep* following you, for some stupid reason, I wanted to think you were right, that you—"

"Well I didn't ask you for any of that, now, did I?"

I also didn't ask for this argument. I don't have time for this either.

"It doesn't matter," he says. "All that matters is that we're going back to the city now, and we need to talk about something before we get there."

"Talk about *what*?"

"About how we can't keep pretending like this."

"I never—"

"Violet's clone needs to be stopped. I realize that now. *You* have to realize that now, and you have to know we can't do it alone. Things are just . . . they're getting out of control. This is bigger than you and me. Way bigger."

"You're just scared."

"Of course I am," he says, shaking his head. "I've almost lost you twice now. Do you have any clue what that's doing to me? The thought of anything happening to you—the thought that no matter what I do, I can't keep you safe. I can't stand it."

His voice is softer now, so I try hard—really hard—to take some of the edge off mine when I say, "I'm sorry, okay? I just don't know what I'm supposed to do anymore."

"It's obvious, isn't it? You cooperate. With me, with the CCA, with—"

The back of my neck burns. "With the people who have terrorized my family since practically the day I was born."

"With the people who will help protect you, if you'd just work with me here."

"Right," I say, eyes narrowing in disbelief. "I guess I should have just cooperated from the beginning, huh? Just helped you all destroy my sister's clone before you even had any evidence that she'd done anything wrong."

"She's a clone," he says, his tone hardening again. "What more evidence did we really need?"

I slap him. As hard as I possibly can.

"Jesus, Cate—"

"Get away from me. Now."

"Calm down."

"Let me go, Jaxon, or I swear, I'll—"

"*Please* calm down. I'm sorry, okay?"

I raise my hand, threatening him with another slap. But he grabs both my wrists and gently but firmly pushes them back against the bars behind me. The phone slips from his hand and falls at our feet.

"Was this your plan all along?" I ask, my gaze falling with it. "To wait for the perfect moment to drag me back to the CCA? Is that who you were calling? That was who called you in the hotel, wasn't it?"

I was stupid to let him get so close to me last night. I was stupid to think—even for a second—that he was actually different from the rest of those monsters at the CCA. That he was on my side and that he'd actually be able to understand why I can't help anyone hurt Violet.

"Do you really think this is what I wanted? Have you listened to *anything* I've told you? I didn't want Violet to be a murderer. I didn't want my mother to be right—about Violet or Huxley or anything. And I just want all of this to be over with now." His voice is calm, but there's still fire smoldering in his eyes.

"What if it was me?"

"What?"

I didn't really mean to ask the question out loud. But now I can't take it back; the way he's looking at me gives me no choice but to keep going. "What about when my replacement comes?" My voice is shaking so badly that he probably can't even understand what I'm saying. "Are

you going to be the one to track her down and kill her?"
I demand. "Because she'll remember you, you know. My
clone . . . I bet she'll think about you all the time. At
least at first. Maybe she'll be exactly like me at first too,
and so she'll want to trust you in spite of everything, and
she'll be easy to trick. So you'll be the perfect person for
the job! And I bet you think it will be *easy*, don't you?
That you're going to be able to look at her and then just
destroy her, simple as that, because she's just a clone in
the end, isn't she?"

"Stop it. Don't say things like that."

"Like what? Like the truth?"

"That isn't the truth. You're not going to be replaced."
He takes his hands from my wrists and brings them up on
either side of my face instead. "I won't let that happen, all
right? I'm not going to let anything happen to you."

Wouldn't it be nice to believe him, I think. Wouldn't it
be nice if I could just keep staring into his eyes like this,
and if just focusing on his touch was enough to make me
forget what we'll have to face once we get back to the city?
Assuming we both make it back, of course. Assuming that
losing myself in the blue sea of his eyes somehow makes
the darkening sky—and the looming meeting with my sister—irrelevant.

If only.

"You shouldn't make promises you can't keep," I say,
and this time when I put my hands on his chest and shove
him away, he doesn't fight back. He just stares at me, his
shoulders slumped and a torn expression on his face.

I realize then that this is how it's going to happen. This is how I'm going to get away from him.

And it's going to suck.

"I don't need you to make all those stupid promises anyway," I say, my voice quiet and as angry as I can force it to be. "I don't want anything to do with them. I don't want anything to do with you—I never should have had anything to do with you in the first place."

"You don't mean that."

"Yes. I do. I just haven't been able to say it until now. But I'm done, okay? We're done. This—whatever this is between us—it's done. Now get away from me."

"I'm not just going to leave you out here." He reaches for my arm, and I'm so into this act now that I respond without even thinking about it; I grab the gun from his belt, lift it between us so quick that it takes him a moment to realize what I've done. He stops reaching for me and lets his hand fall slowly back to his side.

"Why are you doing this?"

"You're CCA. I'm an origin. We're enemies, Jaxon. We always have been, and we were stupid to think we could be anything else."

Enemies. Even now, the word makes me feel like someone is taking my heart in their fist and clenching it as tightly as they can. I take a deep breath and try to imagine myself on stage, try to convince myself that these are just lines I'm reciting. It's all made up. Fake. Everything is fake.

Everything except the hurt in his eyes.

"Put the gun down, Cate. Come on."

"You wanted to stop pretending. So here you go. I'm not pretending anymore."

"Cate, please . . ."

"No!" I have no choice but to shout it; no choice but to take my performance to the next level if I'm going to convince him to let me go. "Go back to Seth. Go back to the city, and stop thinking about me, stop worrying about me, stop following me everywhere. It's pathetic, all right? Surely you have better things to do."

The words have exactly the effect I wanted. He doesn't just look hurt anymore; he looks angry, too. More angry than I've ever seen him, and who could blame him?

Have I mentioned how much this sucks?

It only gets worse. Because as angry as he looks, he still doesn't speak. Or move. He only glares at me until all I want to do is dig the deepest hole I can and just crumple down into it and never climb out again. But I can't crumple now. All I can do is take a deep, shaky breath and tell him good-bye in the steadiest voice I can manage.

And then I turn and walk away, praying he doesn't follow.

CHAPTER FIFTEEN

Expectations

He doesn't follow me.

I didn't expect him to. I didn't want him to. So why does it still hurt so much when he doesn't call my name, or even once tell me to stop? I don't know if he even watched me walk away before going back to the car, because I don't trust myself to turn around to check. I can't see him again. I can't look at the hurt on his face again, because I know it would be my undoing, and I can't afford to come undone now.

I try to calm myself down. I try reciting lines from every play I've performed in; try softly singing lyrics from every song that I can think of. But with every word, my voice only gets shakier.

The sky is a dusky shade of purple by the time I make it to the edge of the woods.

My palm is covered in sweat. I set the gun down while I dry my hands on my shirt, and I stare at it for a long moment before I convince myself to pick it back up again. It would be foolish to meet Violet unarmed. Even if I probably won't be able to shoot her, if it comes to that. Not to mention I'm not sure what type of gun this is, or if it could actually stop a clone. Though judging by the way

Jaxon looked at it when I pointed it at him, I'm guessing it would at least slow them down.

But hopefully I won't have to find out.

I linger around the outskirts of the woods. Watching. Waiting. My whole body tingles with nervous anticipation, and several times I start into the dark web of trees, only to double back out into the open. She could be anywhere in there. If she really wants to see me, she can come out here and meet me. I'm not playing psychopath hide and seek with her.

At least thirty minutes pass. The sky fades from purple to a deep, starless black, and I feel like shouting at the trees, demanding that they stop hiding her. After what I had to do to Jaxon to make it here alone, I'm going to be seriously pissed if she doesn't show up.

Maybe I should stop waiting. Maybe I should track her down myself and refuse to let her make me look any more stupid; but how do I know she's even anywhere close? How do I know she didn't just suggest a meeting at the first random place that came to mind? My cheeks burn, and my grip tightens on my gun as it occurs to me that that's probably *exactly* what she did.

I should never have come here.

I spin around and am about to head anywhere but this place when I hear it: a scream, cut short by a terrible choking sound.

And it sounds a lot like Violet.

I should keep walking.

After everything she's done . . . god, how I wish I could

keep walking away and let whatever is in those woods take care of my problem for me. But then I hear another scream—quieter, weaker this time. My stomach sinks, and the sick feeling in it makes my decision for me.

I turn and race back toward her voice, tripping over roots and brush, stumbling through the darkness. Limbs and briars grab at my arms and face, scratching bloody trails across my skin. A patch of briars catches me by the hair and jerks me to a stop, and while I try to unsnarl the strands I'm holding my breath, listening, trying to hear what I can't see in the shadows around me.

A twig snaps somewhere close by. I twist toward the sound, yanking out a fistful of my hair in the process.

No one's there.

"Violet?" I call softly, uncertainly.

No answer.

I draw my gun and maneuver carefully around the thorn bush, moving on silent feet toward the sound of the breaking twig. After about ten steps, though, I hear something else. Laughter. Then a man's voice, directly ahead of me.

And then another man's voice.

How many of them are there? What are they doing in here?

I really, really don't want to know. But I'm going to have to find out—because the next voice I hear is definitely Violet's, and though most of what she's saying is lost under the frantic pounding of my heart, one word is still terribly clear: *Stop.*

Either this is her most horrible trick yet, or she's in trouble.

I'm not sure what I'm going to do about it—especially if I'm outnumbered—but I have to do something. The thought of going back to Jaxon and Seth for help briefly flashes through my mind, but I dismiss it just as quickly; there's no time. Jaxon probably wouldn't help anyway. Not after what I said.

I slip from tree to tree, picking up my feet so they don't drag noisily through the brush. Soon I can hear the voices more clearly, and I pick out at least three distinct people— the two men, and what sounds like an older woman. I press close to a wide-trunked tree that's missing most of its bark. I draw the gun back to my chest, just as the light at the base of the barrel glows the green of a full charge, and then I dart to the next closest tree that's big enough to conceal me completely. Keeping as close as I can to the trunk, I curve around and scan the woods for someone, anyone—

There.

To the left, less than twenty feet away, I see a light— the pale blue fluorescent of an electric lantern. The bodies are hazy in the harsh light, but there are clearly three of them, surrounding a fourth person who's on the ground, her body doubled over at an odd angle. A mass of wild, tangled black hair hides her face. But I don't need to see it. I already know it's her.

Violet.

I draw in a sharp breath just as the man closest to her

kicks her hard in the side. She rolls over with a muffled groan. The man draws his foot back for another kick but stops as Violet's groan transitions into laughter—soft at first, but then louder and louder still until it echoes through the muggy night air.

"You've got a strange sense of humor, clone," the man says. He grabs her arm and jerks her to her feet, while the one beside him holds a gun to her forehead. My stomach lurches. I shrink back against the tree, close my eyes, and try to take a deep breath.

"You won't be laughing much longer." It's the woman talking now. Her voice is like ice water drenching me, leaving me cold and shaking. "Not after we take you back to the lab and have you properly dealt with." I don't have to be able to see her to know those last words were accompanied by a nasty snarl. And whatever feelings exist between me and my sister's clone, that still sends a tremor of fear skipping through me.

Back to the lab? So these are people from Huxley, treating a clone like this? And *dealt with?* What does she mean by that? What are they planning to do to her?

"But don't worry," the woman continues, "we're going to find your sister, too, and bring her along so you won't be lonely. President Huxley is very, *very* interested in the relationship between the two of you."

"There is nothing interesting about us," Violet says, her voice sharp and afraid. I assume it's from the fear of herself being dragged back to Huxley, or at least of the gun that's pressed to her forehead now. Until, in a calmer voice, she says, "And you won't find my sister, anyways. She was supposed to meet me here several hours ago, but she never showed up. My guess is that she's on her way back to Haven—probably already there. You'll have to face the CCA if you want her now."

She's lying.

For me.

The fear in me tangles with confusion, into a ball that sinks deep into the pit of my stomach. I don't know what I'm supposed to feel; for the second time today, she's defying Huxley to protect me. It would make sense, maybe, if the cuts she gave me herself weren't still burning in the tiny bit of breeze slipping through the trees.

"Lying to your superiors," says the man's voice from before. "Do you honestly think that's going to help your case, clone?"

"You are not my superior." Violet laughs.

I hear a vicious slap, the sound like a whip cracking. I swear I feel it across my own skin. The pain is white hot, stinging through the half-healed cut on my cheek. And for the millionth time since this Violet came to live with me, I find myself silently willing her to just shut up. To just *stop* provoking everyone within a ten-foot radius of her.

At least long enough for me to take aim.

I crouch down until I'm level with a low-lying branch, then press my gun into the crook between it and the trunk to steady it. The first shot will have to be perfect, and the next two will have to be perfect *and* impossibly quick. I'm hoping this gun recharges fast and that by some other combination of miracles I'll be able to stop all three of them before they even know where I'm coming from.

Stop them.

I have to stop them.

The words are nearly a battle cry in my thoughts, but I still find myself hesitating. How is this gun going to stop them? Is it going to be permanent? When I stop firing, will I have to avoid the dead stares of these three, the same way I tried to avoid the eyes of the man Violet killed earlier?

I'm not like her.

Am I?

I don't want to think about it. Not right now. I'm running out of time to think, anyway; because just then the communicator clipped to the woman's belt lights up, and after only a few seconds of conversation I can't hear, she angrily tosses it aside and draws some sort of skinny, cylindrical weapon in its place. It looks terrifyingly similar to that illegal gun Seth had in the graveyard the other day. The one that Jaxon said could cut a person's limb cleanly from their body.

She aims it at Violet's chest.

"This is your last chance," she says. "All you have to do to make this stop is tell us where, exactly, your sister is— and why we haven't been able to get a clear mind upload from her for hours now."

The terror in Violet's eyes fades, and that crazy, defiant gleam comes back to them. "If I knew where my sister was, you would be the last person I would tell," she says.

Then she spits at the woman's feet.

All at once there's a flash of light, the smell of burning flesh, and the terrible screech of my sister's pain.

Something inside me snaps.

I fire. The gun kicks back more than I was expecting, but the recharge is even faster than I'd hoped. I take aim again. The woman is on the ground now, and my only thought is to make the other two follow her. The silent, stoic man with the gun seems like the next most important target; my first shot grazes his side. Not enough to stop him, but enough to make him trip and drop the gun. Violet grabs it. She doesn't move as quickly as she normally does, but she still manages to get the gun turned around and aimed at the last man still standing, and when he makes the mistake of turning to shout at me, she fires. His shout dies in his throat. He staggers a few more steps toward me and then falls face-first to the ground, stirring up the leaves and twigs and dust around him.

The man that my second shot hit lets out a groan. Violet lifts her gun to his head.

"Don't!" I shout, lowering my own weapon.

Her arm drops slowly, reluctantly. Even just that little bit of movement makes her eyes tighten with pain. Once she recovers from that, she lifts her uncertain gaze to me.

"He's unarmed now," I explain. "And I want to talk to him." I want to know exactly what's going on here, and you can't get answers from a dead man.

"He deserves to be shot," Violet says smugly. But the strength seems to be fading from her body even as I watch;

the hand holding the gun starts to shake, and then she drops it and collapses back to the earth.

"Violet?"

She doesn't answer me.

That fear from before emerges with a whole new strength, and I rush to her side, crouch down, and lift her into my arms. It's then that I finally get a good look at her.

It's awful.

There's a bruise already forming all along the right side of her face. Blood trickles from the corner of her mouth and from the blistered, burned skin along her chest and up across her neck.

I try to remind myself that it's not as bad as it looks. That she's not human like me. Her body is different. Even as I watch, the edges of one of the deepest burns starts to glow with that strange scanning red light that eventually spreads over the entire wound. I've seen it before, and I know it's the electronic sensors in her body communicating with her supercomputer brain, surveying the damage and initiating the necessary biological reactions. Within seconds, scar tissue begins to build—the artificially engineered cells regenerating themselves at insane speeds.

But her breathing still comes in weak trembles, each one making her eyes roll a little farther back into her head.

"Violet?" I gently pull the strands of her hair away from where they've stuck to her bloody lips. My hand lingers against her cheek, and she tries, halfheartedly, to pull away from my touch.

"You shouldn't be here," she says quietly.

"You told me to meet you here."

"After everything I've done, you're still listening to me?" She laughs weakly. "Stupid."

I shake my head. "Are you honestly calling me names right now?"

"I'm your sister. That's what I'm supposed to do, right?" Her eyes close again, and she's quiet for a long moment before she asks, "But I was never the same, was I?"

"Don't talk like that." I don't like the note of finality in her voice. Or the way her skin feels cold and clammy against my hand. She's too pale. Too corpselike.

Too much like the first Violet the last time I saw her alive.

"Why do you always have to be so dramatic?" I ask, and I try to laugh too. Like this is all one big joke. It must be a joke, because the universe can't be cruel enough to make me watch my sister die twice. It can't be.

So why is her breathing getting slower and slower? Why is she so still, so silent, even as her body continues to put itself back together right before my eyes? Is there damage inside that I can't see? Damage that even the most advanced technology can't heal fast enough to save her?

"Why did they do this to you?" I whisper. Just for myself to hear, because I'm not really expecting an answer this time.

But her eyes flash open. When she tries to focus them, though, her gaze still ends up distant and hollow. "I guess I just didn't live up to their expectations either, did I?" she says.

"Forget about Huxley and their expectations." A terrible, numbing rage courses through me. "They're going to pay for this. Me and you are both going to make them pay. So you better keep your eyes open. We have people to get even with."

Her head shifts just slightly in my hand. She's trying to shake her head no. Eventually, she gives up, and with a feeble cough, she rolls her head away from me and spits a dark red glob of blood onto the ground.

"You should go." She coughs. "Before . . . before . . ."

"Before what?" I ask, shaking my head. Violet doesn't answer me.

Someone else does.

"Before it's too late for you to get away," says a voice from somewhere behind me. A voice that's so impossibly familiar, I have to turn around. There's a gun pointed at me, but my eyes linger on it only for a fraction of a second. I'm much more interested in the person who's actually holding the gun.

Because there's no mistaking it. That fierce smile. Her father's blue eyes. That white blond hair that she claims is natural but that I know for a fact she's been bleaching since she was five years old.

That's Samantha Voss staring back at me.

And she's supposed to be dead.

CHAPTER SIXTEEN

Control

A million different questions and fears and possibilities race through my head. Luckily, one single thought manages to make itself heard over all the others: *Move.*

I grab the gun from Violet's limp hand and roll out of the way just as Samantha fires a shot that burns a clean, smoky line along the forest floor. It radiates so much heat that I can feel it even as I dive aside. I'd be surprised if it didn't singe the hairs off my arms; I don't stop to check them. I sprint for the closest tree and scramble behind it. I'm not going to run from her and just leave Violet there—but I need a second outside the line of fire so I can get my body and my thoughts to stop shaking. Otherwise there's no way I'm going to win this fight.

"Come on, origin," Samantha calls. "I'm not going to kill you. They want you brought back alive. And if you cooperate, maybe I won't even hurt you." I hear the low hum of a weapon charging. "Maybe."

They want me brought back alive? Does she mean Huxley? Is she working for them, too? But that doesn't make sense. Because her father . . . her father—

The side of the tree explodes in a blast of dust and splintered bark. My heart feels like it might explode through my chest, and my face and the back of my neck break out in a cold sweat. I take a deep breath and creep as quickly and quietly as I can to another tree, and then another, keeping to the darkest shadows in hopes that she won't be able to follow my movement. Before long, she's firing at every tree around me, clearly unsure of exactly where I'm hiding.

"You're going to make me work for this, aren't you?" She laughs. I close my eyes and focus on that mad laughter, on the trees that it's bouncing off and the direction the wind carries it from. She's to my left, I decide. And she's searching in a sweeping circle, judging by the way the laughter gets louder, then quieter, then louder again. I lift both of the guns in my hand.

I managed to hit those people earlier, but they were standing still, and I had plenty of time to aim. This is going to be a much harder shot. Not to mention that I actually *know* Samantha—obviously not as well as I thought I did, but still; the thought of shooting her makes my heart pound even faster, until every beat actually starts to hurt.

But then one of her shots hits the tree in front of me, and the reality of the situation becomes even more painfully clear: It's her or me.

It's not going to be me.

I listen for her next shout, and without hesitating I roll around the tree and toward the sound. And there she is, no more than fifteen feet away, her back to me and her body half-blocked by a thick tangle of tree limbs. My first shot misses her but hits one of the largest of those limbs, cleanly separating it from its trunk with a quick *snap*. Samantha ducks out of the way as it falls, and as she straightens up and turns around, the shot from my second gun hits her square in the chest. She stumbles backward, trips, and falls spread-eagled to the ground.

Once on the ground, she doesn't move.

I can taste the vomit rising in the back of my throat, and I know I have to keep moving. Away from her, away from the other still bodies, away from these woods—away from all these things that will have me curled up on the ground and sobbing if I stop long enough to think about them.

I rush back to the clearing where I left Violet, and a small wave of relief washes over me when I see that she's still conscious. She's trying to climb to her feet, even. I go straight to her side and offer her my shoulder to lean on.

"Where is Samantha?" she asks, eyes wide with a terrifying, feral sort of fear that almost makes me draw away from her.

"I . . . I shot her. She's back there—" I point vaguely toward the trees. "She wasn't moving, and I just wanted to get away from—"

"Are you sure you hit her? Are you sure she wasn't moving? At all? Was she conscious?"

"I—"

"*Are you sure?*"

"I mean I didn't check, I—"

"Go." She shoves me away with a ridiculous amount of force, considering her condition. "*Go!*"

I start to argue but trail off at the sound of footsteps dragging through the brush. Fear grips me, stopping my heart and freezing the breath in my lungs for a long, terrifying moment.

I hit her dead on, I try to reason with that fear. *There's no way. . . .*

"New plan," Violet says under her breath. "Don't go. Don't try to run. She'll catch you before you make it a hundred feet."

"She . . . how can she . . ."

"And we should aim for the back of her head," Violet says. "Because that's where her brain's CPU is."

"CPU . . ." My eyes widen in realization. "She's a clone?"

"Ding ding ding," Violet mutters, "let's tell her what she's won."

And then Samantha bursts out of the shadows, a terrible blur of rage and fury with shaking hands and bloodshot eyes. She doesn't even bother with a gun anymore; she just runs straight toward me, grabs my arm, and jerks me away from Violet. She swings me against the nearest tree and presses in close, blocking off any chance of escape. Over her shoulder, I watch Violet stumble a few steps, lift her gun and aim it straight at the base of Samantha's skull.

She fires.

The gun lets out a high-pitched whine. But other than that, nothing happens.

"You've got to be kidd—"

Samantha grabs my throat and slams me harder against

the tree, pinning me more securely before glancing back at Violet. "That's what you get for trying to switch sides," she says. "Serves you right, traitor."

She turns her attention back to me. Her fingers push deeper into my neck, making breathing almost impossible; my vision starts to blur, and a strange prickling sensation starts at the tips of my fingers and travels up my arms. I have to glance down to make sure I still have a gun in my hand, because I can't feel it anymore. Samantha follows my gaze with her own. Her free hand shoots out and wraps around my wrist, and she gives it a vicious twist, trying to force me to loosen my grip on the gun; I'm so woozy from barely being able to breathe that I don't feel much pain. But I do hear a sickening popping noise—and I doubt that means anything good.

I grit my teeth and struggle, trying to squirm my way out from underneath her. When that doesn't work, I knock her hand away from my throat and try to hold it off long enough to get a decent breath of air. Then I focus every bit of strength I have left into driving my knee into Samantha's stomach. I hit her hard enough that she doubles over and falls back, leaving just enough room for me to slip away from her and the tree.

I switch the gun to my other hand, since I'm now painfully aware of my throbbing wrist. I make it about five steps before Samantha dives after me, tackling me at the knees. Without thinking, I throw out my empty hand to catch myself; my wrist gives out instantly on impact, snapping back so hard that if it wasn't broken before, it has to be now. I fall the rest of the way forward, my momentum still going, and slam my head into a rock. It leaves me dazed, but not as dizzy as before; at least I can still breathe this time. Now if I can just keep it that way.

I kick as hard as I can, over and over until I've freed my legs from her grip enough that I can roll over onto my back. I slap her across the face with the barrel of my gun, then drop it and thrust my hand up, grab her by the hair on the left side of her head, and push her away. When she starts to fall back on top of me, I get a foot between us, pressed squarely against her stomach. With my adrenaline pumping uncontrollably, and the ground to brace myself against now, my next kick sends her flying.

I snatch the gun and stagger to my feet. So does Samantha. She's moving much more slowly now, though. Pain slices through my broken wrist. Blood drips down into my left eye, clings to my lashes so that the part of the world I see through them takes on a strange pinkish tint.

Samantha walks straight toward me, seemingly unfazed by the weapon I have lifted between us.

Violet is behind her, still messing with the faulty gun. If she gets it to work, Samantha's clone is as good as gone— but would Samantha even care? Can she even think of anything other than Huxley's orders? I don't think so. She seems different from Violet, somehow. There is no hesitation with her, no question in her eyes about what she's supposed to do, or who she's supposed to be. There's only a mad, wild determination. She's going to kill me, or I'm going to kill her. It doesn't seem as if something like this should be so simple, but—at least in this moment—it is. And that scares me worse than anything.

Aim for the back of her head. I remember Violet's words, but there's no way I'm fast enough to get behind Samantha. So when I manage to catch Violet's eye a second later, I make a decision that I really hope I don't end up regretting. I throw her my gun. She catches it one-handed, and in a single fluid motion she lifts it and fires before Samantha even has a chance to turn around.

I take the first decent breath I've had in what seems like forever.

Once Samantha hits the ground, Violet isn't far behind her; she drops to one knee and braces both hands against the ground, breathing heavily.

"You okay?" I call, moving cautiously forward, my gaze jumping between her and Samantha's still body. My mind is still working double time, trying to process everything that just happened. Trying to make sense of not just my sister now, but also of the fact that Samantha Voss had a clone running around. What does that mean? What about her father?

"I'll be fine," Violet says as I reach her side. Then she looks up at me and asks, "What about you?" And maybe I'm delusional after having my head bashed against a rock, but I'd swear she looks genuinely concerned. More concerned than I've seen her in a long time. Nothing like stopping a homicidal clone together to strengthen that sisterly bond, I guess.

"I've been worse," I say. I think about reminding her

of that one time she almost drowned me, but I decide not to bother. It feels like there are bigger things—more important things—to worry about now. "Although I don't remember the last time I was this confused," I say, offering Violet a hand and pulling her to her feet. "Samantha's father is vice president of the CCA. Why would he have a cloned daughter?"

"He used to work for Huxley."

"I know, but so did President Cross—they left together to form the CCA."

"Except he never really left," she says, wiping at some of the dried blood around her lips. "He's been working as a double agent for years now, and as close as he was to President Cross, he was the natural choice when Huxley decided to put their master plan into motion—starting by tearing the CCA apart from the inside. And their first target was the president herself. Or her son, more specifically, since he would have been easier to take out first."

My stomach flip-flops. *Jaxon.*

Maybe it wasn't just me they were after at the hotel.

Where is he now?

"How do you know that?" I ask, starting to walk. I'd run if the world didn't insist on reeling from the pain in my head and my wrist.

"I know because Samantha's origin knew, and she told me. She found out about her father's plans for Jaxon."

"But why him? Surely there were more important targets they could have focused on. Just because he's the CCA president's son doesn't mean—"

"I don't know why, all right? From what Samantha told me, all this drama between these two groups sounds a lot more personal than I would have guessed, so maybe someone was just out looking for revenge? I know Cross made a lot of people mad when she left Huxley. The important thing, though, is that Samantha knew about her father's plans not just for Jaxon, but for *her*—the eventual plan for all origins."

I almost tell her to stop, because I'm starting to piece things together myself now. And I don't want to look at the ugly, nightmarish picture they're forming. I'm too focused on trying to block out the pain and keep my feet moving at the same time, though, so I don't manage to find my voice before Violet continues.

"Samantha was afraid of being replaced. So she got the foolish idea that she would prove herself more useful than any clone that could replace her."

"By doing her father's job for him?" I guess.

"She wasn't supposed to die that night," Violet says, quieter now. "Jaxon was."

"And why didn't he, exactly?"

My gaze meets hers, and she traps me with that same stare as before, that wild fear and uncertainty dancing in her eyes. And I'm still so unused to seeing this Violet afraid—of anything—that I can't help but freeze midstep. I don't know what to say, though. Because there's no more denying it now. We both know the truth.

For whatever reason, she *is* the one who killed Samantha. My sister is a murderer. And I guess I am too now—

because I helped her kill all that was left of Samantha Voss, the clone I left lying back there in the woods, the same way Violet left Samantha's origin lying alone on those railroad tracks.

"Things got out of control," Violet is saying as I stumble on, too dizzy to walk straight but determined to get away from this all the same. "I was only trying to stop her—I couldn't just stand back and let her become a murderer. She would have been caught, locked away for life. I went to reason with her but I . . . I was just a lot stronger than she was."

"You killed her." The words hum through my brain, numbing as they go. "You actually *killed* her."

She grabs the sleeve of my shirt and jerks me back to a stop. "I didn't mean to do it." I turn and find her watching me, eyes wide and desperate as the next words fall frantically from her mouth. She takes a deep breath. "Look. I know I'm all wrong. I know I started messing things up for you the second I got here, and I never really figured out how to stop doing that—never really figured out how to be what you wanted me to be. Because you didn't want anything to take your sister's place. I know you didn't. So I couldn't be her, but then what else was I supposed to be?"

"How about anything except for a murderer?" I deadpan, pulling away from her.

"It was an *accident*, Cate." She folds her arms and hugs them to her chest, looking cold and alone and so much like the old, sick Violet that it makes my breath hitch into a quiet cough. "That night, I just . . . I thought I was doing the right thing. For once." Her eyes slide out of focus as she trails off and wraps her arms even more tightly around herself. And even with her so close, even with her telling me these deep, dark things, it still feels like it so often has with this Violet: like we're in two different places and I'm never going to find my way to where she is.

Though not for lack of trying. Because I'm searching desperately for the right words to say, for a way to understand all of this—a way to understand her—but I don't know how to get there from here.

All I keep thinking is that Samantha isn't coming back, and now I know why. I came out here looking for the truth, but in my heart I think I already knew what I wanted it to be—that Violet was framed, that those witnesses were lying, that she had *nothing* to do with Samantha's death. That she wasn't even there that night. But this? This is all wrong. This is not how the story was supposed to go.

I take a deep breath.

It was an accident, Cate.

I can forgive an accident, can't I? I've forgiven her for everything else; why should this be any different? I've spent the past four years picking up the pieces of nearly every mess she's made; I should be a pro at it by now. I should be able to fix this—to fix us—just like I always have. And besides, I've told myself from the beginning that my sister would never *purposely* hurt Samantha. They were friends. I know that. I believe that.

So why does it still feel like so much of this doesn't make sense?

I'm still quietly trying to force some sort of meaning onto it all when we reach the edge of the forest. It's started to rain by this point; heavy, quick drops that don't help my pounding head as they smack against it. I rake the hand not attached to my aching wrist through my damp hair and leave my palm pressed against my temple. Blood pounds against the skin there, a dull, relentless thumping in my ears that makes it hard to concentrate. The signal jammer doesn't help either; now that we've stopped talking, I can hear it emitting a garbled, high-pitched static. Broken, it sounds like. I don't remember hitting it against anything, but I was a little distracted earlier—so who knows.

Even with all the pain and the noise, though, I eventually manage to single out a question, plucking it from the crowd of them swarming through my thoughts.

"If you went after Samantha to protect Jaxon," I ask, my voice rising to compete with the trees creaking and groaning in the wind, "then why did you attack him at the hotel?"

"Because." Violet shuffles uncomfortably, starts to move out of the woods only to double back around to face me. "What you said last night was partially right. Sometimes I'm not as alone in my head as I'd like to be—one of the many things Huxley leaves out of their lovely informational videos."

"So they sent you?"

She moves away from the trees again, glancing up into their dark branches as if she's afraid of them overhearing, and this time she doesn't look back. I have to jog to catch up with her.

"They wanted me to go after you," she says. "To see if I would actually do it, I think. Because I worried them, thanks to everything that happened with Samantha. When I stopped her from killing Jaxon, they decided they needed to figure out exactly *why*—they probably saw it as me protecting him at first, which, since he's CCA, went against the most basic programming of any clone. A quick glimpse into my memory uploads would have shown them that I only did it because I cared about Samantha— enough to override any brainwashing or command or they might have given me. Which is apparently *all wrong* for a clone like me, and which led to this experiment to see if I would be able to override it again, and exactly *how* and *why* I was doing it. With Samantha gone, though, they needed another dependent variable to factor in." Her eyes lock with mine. "And, of course, there was really only one other person that I cared about nearly as much."

The lump that rises in my throat is so huge that I manage to choke out only a single word: "Me."

She nods, her gaze falling back to the path ahead. "The day after I killed Samantha, I started getting flashes of terrible things. Not straightforward *commands*, but more like pictures, scenes I felt compelled to make happen—I don't know how else to explain it. But they . . . they were all of you. Awful things they were trying to make me do to you. And the longer I resisted, the worse they got. That's why I left town, because I thought if I could put some distance between us . . ."

The lump in my throat swells even larger. I'd been so

angry with her for running off, when all along she'd only been trying to protect me.

"You weren't supposed to follow me," my sister says.

"You should have known I would," I answer quietly. The wind is blowing the rain almost sideways into my face now, hard enough that it stings the back of my hand when I try to block it out. "I always have."

She smiles, but it's a sad kind of smile that quickly wilts in the corners. "Right. Because you're an idiot," she says, shaking her head. "You could have been killed last night, you know. If I hadn't found Jaxon first, if he hadn't started shouting at me about Samantha . . ." She takes a deep breath. "He confused me. By the time you showed up, my mind was a wreck, but at least everything Huxley had tried dumping in there was scrambled and confused too—especially after the tranquilizer darts. I keep thinking about what I could have done, about what I—"

"But you didn't do it. You wouldn't have done it." Even if I couldn't understand anything else she's telling me, suddenly I know that I'd still understand that much. "You would never have done it," I repeat. "Not to your sister."

Her step slows. I keep walking, but I can feel her watching me in that intense way of hers, waiting for me to say more.

"You aren't some robotic creation of theirs," I say. "You've proven that, haven't you? You're not like Samantha's clone. She was different—she wasn't thinking about anything except what Huxley wanted. I could tell."

I'm sorting everything out even as I say it now, and

those last few words send a chilling realization through me—one that quickly makes everything else seem a lot less important. "And what about the rest of the clones?" I ask. "If Huxley sees you as a flaw in their plans, then most of the other clones must be like Samantha, right? And that would mean . . ."

I let the thought die on my tongue, as if not saying it out loud will somehow prevent anything like it from ever coming true. But Violet finishes my sentence for me.

"It would mean they potentially have a terrifyingly strong army to control. And there's really no telling what they could do with that sort of power, but I'm starting to doubt that anything about their plans was ever really as just-in-case as they claimed."

I'm thankful for the rain, suddenly; for the cold drops hitting my skin, washing over me and keeping me awake and alert. Because as much as I'd like to drift away from all of this, to let all of me succumb to the same shock that's threatening my mind, I can't. I know exactly what they could do with that sort of power. Every word of the conversation I had with President Cross is ringing clearly through my memory now, all her warnings of Huxley's plans to replace the population with their perfected, manufactured clones. She was more right than she could have guessed—and now we have proof.

And we have to do something.

"We have to tell someone," I say. "About what Huxley was doing to you, about the clones, about what really happened to Samantha, about—"

"About what really happened?" She laughs bitterly. "Yes—let's tell them that a clone killed a defenseless young girl. That's an *excellent* idea. I'm sure it won't cause any rioting mobs to form or anything like that."

"We'll make them understand!"

"You can't force people to understand what they don't want to, Cate."

"You've managed to fight off whatever it was that Huxley is trying to do. You're proof of what's really happening at their labs—we can't just keep that to ourselves. There are people who will believe us. The CCA, even."

"You really do trust them, then?"

"No, not all of them, but we could start there, at least. And with our parents, and whoever else we—"

She cuts in front of me so quickly that I slam into her.

"I'm not going back to the city," she says, her gaze not breaking mine even as I shove her away.

"Violet—"

"I left because I was afraid of what I might end up doing. And yes, I'm fighting Huxley *now*, but these past twenty-four hours have been hell. What happens if I slip again? What happens if they catch me and figure out a way to 'fix' me, and I become just another brainless member of their army?"

"That isn't going to happen. You're stronger than that—and since when have you *ever* listened to anything anyone's told you to do?"

"I'm not going back," she repeats, shaking her head. "It's too late, anyway. It's already begun. If Samantha's clone was activated, then it means her father has most likely dropped the double-agent act and that President Cross knows the truth about him. Huxley might not have been ready to start their war with the CCA yet, but thanks to Samantha, they have one on their hands now—and I don't want to get caught up in it anymore."

"There has to be something we can do to stop all of this." I wish I could keep the telltale fear from my voice. That I could somehow sound at least a little more confident than I feel. But I can't. And soon that fear starts to feel more like frustration, because there is no quick fix that I can see for any of this. Everything just keeps getting more complicated. Our lives were never what most people would call "normal," I know; but we had *our* normal.

I just want our normal back.

But it won't be the same without her.

"You can't just run away."

"Yes, I can."

She's looking at me like I'm the crazy one now, as if running is the only thing left to do.

And I try, but it's hard to be completely annoyed with her, when I want so badly to hide myself. It's what I've always been best at, after all—and there isn't a lot I wouldn't give to be able to leave all of this fear and confusion and uncertainty behind.

I'm not entirely sure why I keep walking toward it, pushing past Violet and setting off at a run through the rain-slicked grass. But I do. For a long time she doesn't follow; I keep looking over my shoulder just to see her staring back at me, her body the only disruption in the sheets of water falling to the earth. I've nearly lost sight of her when she finally decides to move.

She closes the distance between us easily. "Running has been my plan since the beginning," she says. "I was going to get away from all of this. But then you insisted on following me and bringing Jaxon and basically setting the entire stage for Huxley and their sick little games—"

"So you're blaming me again," I snap, whirling around to face her. "How fantastically original of you." It's all I can do to keep my voice from shaking. Angry tears sting my eyes, but at least they won't be noticeable when they fall, thanks to the rain already streaking down my face.

Violet slows to a stop, staring uncertainly at me. Then she takes a single step back—a hesitation that seems weighted with decision, and somehow that small motion annoys me more than anything she could have said.

"And what am I supposed to tell our parents if you don't come back?" I ask. "Because I'm tired of making excuses for you. I'm tired of everyone coming to me for answers, of having to explain away all of the stupid things you do. I don't even know what to say anymore."

She shrugs. "Tell them I'm gone. For good this time." Her voice is much calmer than mine. Peaceful, almost, like someone with their eyes closed, ready to float off to sleep. "I was always just for show, anyway. It's not like anyone is honestly going to miss me."

I will.

In spite of everything, I know I will, because I still love her. And part of me hates her for that.

I can't find my voice, and I can't look at her anymore, so I turn and continue in silence back to the graveyard. I pick my way through the headstones, feet slipping and squelching through the muddy pathways until I'm past the iron gate and back to the place where I left Jaxon behind. Only then do I glance over my shoulder to see if Violet is still with me.

She's not.

And then I turn back to the empty darkness in front of me, and I realize, no one else is either.

CHAPTER SEVENTEEN

Chasm

My thoughts shift violently away from my sister and crash into worst-case scenarios about Jaxon and Seth.

They have no clue about Voss, about how complicated and cataclysmic everything surrounding Samantha's death really was. And now I'm too late to tell them. Too late to stop them from going back to the city and walking straight into the center of this mess. I knew I would be, but I was still hoping against hope that Jaxon would have stayed, that he would have waited for me even if I didn't deserve it.

But I guess my performance was even more persuasive than I thought.

Because he and Seth are nowhere in sight, and they aren't answering me, no matter how loudly I shout their names.

I wander toward the run-down groundskeeper's house and circle around and around it, stubbornly searching. He can't have just left. Not without me. How many times did he promise me he wouldn't go anywhere? I know I made him mad earlier, but mad enough for him to abandon me?

What am I supposed to do now?

I slump back against the house. The rough concrete

siding scratches through my soaked shirt, and my eyes drift to the dark highway, to the broken pavement funneling streams of water into potholes oozing with mud and debris.

Twenty miles to Haven. At least.

It's going to be a long walk.

And when I get there, what then? If Huxley really has decided it's time for an offensive, then what's happening between them and the CCA? Am I going to be running straight into a war zone? I think of what happened in the woods, of the weapons they used against Violet. Of Samantha, and her terrifying strength and speed. And she was just one clone. What would an entire army of that be like?

I think about my parents, about Jaxon and everyone else trapped in the city and caught up in that war zone, and I feel sick.

Maybe Violet was right. Maybe it's too late to stop any of this.

But there's only one way to find out.

I pull my swollen wrist against my chest, trying to brace it and keep it still. And then I push off the wall and start for the road.

Almost as soon as I reach the pavement, I hear the splash of quick footsteps coming from somewhere nearby. I keep walking. But I cast an anxious look around, expecting to see Violet and thinking—hoping—that she's done being dramatic and has decided to come with me after all.

Still no sign of anyone, though.

I've been on this eerie, empty highway for less than two minutes, and I'm already hallucinating. I give my head a little shake. "One foot in front of the other," I chant quietly to myself. "One foot . . ."

I start to turn my full attention back to the path ahead, and that's when I see it: Directly to my left, the misty rain is bending at strange, impossible angles. My mind immediately tries to dismiss it as another delusion. But hope flutters defiantly against my insides, and my feet move on their own, carrying me toward the space. I reach into it, and my fingers brush smooth, curved metal.

Jaxon's car.

He's used the opacity adjustor. And between the rain and the dark it's near impossible to see, but it's there. So where is he? I try shouting his name again, and listening closer for some response, any response—and I get one. Voices. But they're not his.

I hear Seth first, and then Violet.

I sprint toward the sound, and I'm almost back to the graveyard's gates before I can make out their bodies in the darkness. They're standing dangerously close to each other, muscles tense and weapons drawn.

I curse under my breath and run closer, feet sliding over the mud one second and getting stuck in it the next. By the time I reach them, I have flecks of it splattered all the way up to my arms.

"Wait a second, Seth," I pant. "It's okay, she isn't going to hurt anything—"

"Claims the girl who pulled a gun on Jaxon less than

two hours ago." His glare shifts from Violet to me instead. "You'll forgive me if I don't exactly trust your word on this."

I don't think Seth would actually hurt me, but I've never seen him look quite this pissed before—so I'm glad when Jaxon walks up beside him, grabs his gun arm, and forces it down.

He doesn't say anything, though. And his eyes are perfectly guarded as they meet mine. I can't help the disappointment that crashes through me; I mean, I didn't expect him to be happy to see me after what I did, but surely he has to realize that I had a reason for doing it. That I didn't mean what I said. I'm not *that* good of an actress, am I?

"I had my reasons for doing that, Seth," I say. "I swear I did, but I don't have time to explain it—not right now. Because right now we need to talk about what I saw in the woods."

"When you went to meet her," Jaxon says. "Alone." His tone is unbearably even as his gaze shifts to my sister's clone. I can almost see the wheels in his head turning, and I don't want to know what he's thinking—what explanations he's coming up with for why I went to see Violet. Because I know they're all centered around the same things: betrayal, and the lines I drew when I walked away from him earlier.

I'm an origin. He's CCA. We're not on the same side, and I couldn't have made that any clearer than I did when I showed back up with my sister's deadly clone.

I have to find some way to undo the damage I've done—quickly. So I blurt out the quickest explanation I possibly can about Huxley, about Violet and Samantha and what really happened. But when I finish, Jaxon's eyes only narrow, studying me in disbelief.

"Voss is the vice president of the CCA," he says. "He and my mother have worked together for almost two decades."

"All I know is what I saw."

"She—"

"This is a bunch of crap," Seth interrupts, jerking his arm out of Jaxon's grip and spinning away from him. He starts to lift the gun toward me, but Violet springs forward and grabs his wrist, twists it, and gives him a vicious shove. They both tumble back and slam into the saturated ground. They roll back and forth, Violet shouting and Seth stringing entire sentences together out of just curse words until he finally manages to kick her off. When Violet straightens up, Seth's gun is securely in her hand.

I step between them before she can even think about aiming it at him. Jaxon follows me, gets his arms locked around Seth's, and holds him back until he finally stops struggling and starts to calm down.

With Seth restrained, I look back at Violet. Anger flickers across her dark features. I brace myself but don't move; not until her shoulders rise and fall in a deep breath and she flings the gun into a puddle at my feet. Then I bend slowly to pick it up, not taking my gaze off her.

Her lips curl back into an almost-snarl. "Next time I won't be here, and he can just shoot you," she says.

Before I can answer her, I feel Jaxon's hand on my arm. "You're sure it was Samantha?" he asks quietly. He's watching Violet out of the corner of his eye, a worried frown on his face.

I nod. "You need to warn your mother."

Jaxon's face turns several different shades of white at the mention of his mother. He pulls his phone from his pocket but doesn't say anything. He just takes a deep breath—an attempt to calm himself, I think. But still the phone trembles just slightly in his hand, and I see the way his arm tightens, the muscles trying to keep it from shaking.

And all at once, I realize why.

"You did try to call home earlier, didn't you?" I ask.

He lifts his head, but his eyes never quite manage to meet mine. "No one answered."

I should be angry at him for trying to contact them behind my back, I guess; but he looks too miserable to be mad at. And when I think about how badly I've wanted to hear my parents' voices over the past couple days, all I want to do is put my arms around him instead.

"We should have enough of a charge to open the comcenter," Seth says, wiping a speckle of mud from his cheek. "Maybe I can reach her through messaging." All of his attention is focused on Jaxon now, his fight with Violet abruptly forgotten. He's watching him anxiously, waiting for some sort of reassurance, maybe. He doesn't get it. All Jaxon gives him is a silent nod. It's enough to make Seth move, though, to send him racing toward the car without another word.

"He's not going to reach her, is he?" The cynical question escapes me before I can stop it.

Jaxon's chest rises and falls with a deep breath. "Sometimes I feel like she's been waiting for something like this. For Huxley to make some sort of move. For a reason to fight, to prove that she's right."

I don't question him on that, because from just my brief encounter with his mother, I have no trouble seeing her as the kind of person who doesn't like being wrong about anything.

Does anybody, though? Not everyone is as confident about it as President Cross, but maybe deep down we're all convinced that we're the heroes of our own stories, and that we're the only ones with good enough vision to see the truth. Which would explain why there are so many different versions of it flying around lately.

I think I understand now—maybe better than the president herself did—what she said a few days ago: *Most of the things that are bad in this world started off as someone's idea of good.* And I'd be willing to bet that more evil has been done in the name of righteousness than for any other reason. That's what started all of this, isn't it? My sister set out to do what she thought was the right thing, and it just ended up all wrong. And Samantha had her own good reasons for what she did, and they made sense to her.

I just wish I could figure out what makes sense to me.

"So you think your mother will have already started to fight?" I ask Jaxon.

"I think . . . that I need to get back to the city," he says. "I think I need to know that she's okay."

Because right or wrong, good or bad, I guess she's still family.

"Are you coming with us?" he asks, his eyes finally meeting mine.

I can feel Violet watching me too. Still hoping I'll say no, I think. That maybe I'll decide to run away with her after all.

If only I had the time and the words to explain to her why I can't.

But when Jaxon turns and heads for the car, I hesitate only for a moment before following—just long enough to ask Violet one last time to come with us. She refuses. And with every shake of her head, with every second of her silent stare, I imagine the ground between us opening a little wider, until it's a chasm that I'm not sure either of us will ever be able to cross again.

I catch up with Jaxon, and in an attempt to take my mind off of where Violet is going to go from here, I say, "I thought you'd left. When I came back, when I didn't see you—"

"I tried to leave," he says, his gaze directed straight ahead. "I couldn't. Not without knowing what would happen to you." He glances over at me. "It's pathetic, I know."

I slow almost to a stop, the words bouncing around in my brain. I'm not sure what to say. How to fully accept that even now, he really did refuse to leave me behind. He must have been worried when he couldn't reach his mother. But despite that, despite every hateful word I said to him, he was still here when I got back. And that's . . .

Well, it's not pathetic.

We reach the car—which is now back to full opacity and to that pearly blue color I love—and he opens the door for me without a word. I wipe my shoes off in the wet grass as best I can and climb into the backseat, thankful to finally be out of the driving rain. Seth doesn't look up from the comcenter or acknowledge me in any way. I hold in a sigh and wipe off the foggy rear window so I can look back toward where Violet stood, watching me walk away. I can't see her now, of course. It's much too dark. If she's there at all, she's blending in with the hazy gray rain and the black backdrop of sky.

My fingers reach for the door handle. It's an automatic reaction, and I have to fight to keep myself from flinging that door open and rushing back to find my sister. I can't keep doing that. I've spent too much time stumbling around in the dark, trying to find her, and I've lost sight of so much else because of it.

"What's taking it so long?" Jaxon asks.

"It's searching for satellites," Seth replies. "And the rain's not helping. Just give it a second."

In the rearview mirror I can see Jaxon, and how his face has grown paler still; I wish there was something I could say to bring the life back to his eyes, and the color back to his cheeks. I wish I could make the message go through. I wish I could somehow guarantee that his mother would answer from the other side and tell us everything is fine. That she's fine, and this is all some misunderstanding, and nobody is fighting about anything and it's all going to be okay.

But all I can do is stare at the LCD screen blinking CON-NECTING over and over in a bright green font, and shiver in my soaking-wet clothes, and hope, and hope. . . .

"Here." Jaxon's voice makes me jump from my practically catatonic state. A canvas jacket lands in my lap a second later. "Your lips are turning blue," he says, looking at me in the mirror. His tone isn't quite as harsh as before. Progress, at least.

"What about me?" Seth asks.

"What about you?"

"She holds a gun to you, and she still gets the jacket?"

"Yeah."

"That's messed up." Seth twists around in his seat so he can see me, and mouths, *Whipped*. And I'm about to smile, just because I'm glad that Seth isn't ignoring me anymore, but then the comcenter beeps.

All three of our heads jerk toward the screen.

We have a connection. The contact list loads along the right side, and after a few frantic seconds of searching, I find their mother's name. Third from the top, grayed out with a little offline icon beside it.

"She's never offline," Seth says. "She's always working." His voice is barely audible over the rain that falls like pounding hammers against the roof of the car.

We're all silent for a minute, holding in a collective breath, suspended in a moment that feels poised on the edge of chaos.

And then Jaxon turns the key. The car roars to life, and the tires squeal as we turn back toward the city.

CHAPTER EIGHTEEN

Last Chance

The sun breaks the horizon in a hundred different places—reflected in a hundred different buildings—just as we reach the city limits. I've had so little sleep that I'm beyond the point of tired. My eyes are burning, bloodshot, and as we drive, the edges of Haven blur and run together into a spinning canvas of silvers and blues.

Even though I'm half-asleep, I still can't help but notice how strangely empty the city is. It's close to seven a.m. The streets should be packed with people going to work, but we have the road almost entirely to ourselves, and I count only a few dozen people on the sidewalks. They all seem blissfully unaware of the desolation around them— one of them even looks like he's whistling to himself, which for some reason sends a shiver up my spine. Most of the stores and restaurants still have their lights off, and several of them have the metal security walls pulled over the doors and windows. Everybody has those walls; after all, the people who built Haven are the ones who lived through the war. Even so, this is the higher-end district of the city—the safest district—and people in this part of town almost never use them.

Something is definitely wrong.

My house is only a few miles from here. Do my parents have our security system engaged too? Are they safe? I almost ask Jaxon to turn down the next road, which would take me to them, but I know that finding out what's going on at the CCA headquarters is more critical right now.

Still, when we pass the street, I find myself gripping the armrest for strength and breathing deeply through my nose, commanding myself not to panic. I sink back against the seat, and though I'm trying not to think about her, Violet's words are the first thing that drop into my head.

It's too late. . . . It's already begun.

We can't turn back now, though. Because suddenly we're in that same abandoned parking deck that Jaxon brought me to just days ago, and he opens the door for me just like he did then. Except this time he won't look at me.

Everything is so different now. We're so much more complicated. And out of everything else that's weighing on my nerves, out of all the anxiety and worry, the way he averts his eyes is somehow worse than anything else.

Because suddenly I realize: Standing here, I still feel the same as I did before. After everything we've been through, I want to trust him even more than I did the very first time we stood here together. I can't stand the thought of him still being angry with me. Especially not now—not when I don't know what we're about to face, or if I'll have another chance to apologize and set things right between us. Maybe there's no time for that sort of thing now. But when you're faced with the possibility of the end, it's hard not to think about all the things you should have started.

Seth is busy digging through the trunk, pulling out weapons left and right. Jaxon is taking more time than necessary to mess with the opacity adjuster—I'm guessing because it gives him something to look at instead of me.

This may be my last chance.

That's the last thing I think before I walk over, grab Jaxon's arm, and pull him to the corner of the garage.

"Cate, what are—"

"I'm sorry. I'm sorry about what happened earlier. About everything I said." The words tumble breathlessly from my mouth.

"Okay. It's fine. Let's just—" He tries to maneuver his way back around me, but I stop him.

"It's not okay."

He sighs. "We really don't have time for this."

"No—I mean, I *know* we don't have much time, but that's just it, isn't it? We don't have time, so I . . . I have to tell you that I'm sorry."

"You already did. I heard you the first time."

"Not just about earlier. About everything."

He stops trying to fight his way around me.

I take a deep breath. There are so many things I've thought about saying in this moment—lines that I've rehearsed, words that I thought would be so perfect if only I could find the courage to say them. But the words that come out of my mouth are not what I planned; for better or worse, they belong to this moment and this moment alone.

"I'm sorry for not trusting you," I say. "I'm sorry for

all of the times I looked away when you tried to catch my eye in the cafeteria, and for pretending not to notice you when you came into the auditorium. Because I knew you were there." I take another deep breath. "And I guess you've always been there, but I've always been too scared to admit that to myself, but now . . . I mean, after everything we've been through it just seems really, really stupid to be afraid of telling you all this, and so I think you should know that walking away from you earlier was one of the hardest things I've ever had to do. I couldn't do it again if I tried."

By the time I finish, his eyes are locked with mine, watching me like we're the only two people left in the world. I exhale. Slowly.

"So . . . yeah. There's that. And now I'm really wishing you would say something," I whisper. I need to hear him say he feels the same. I want him to tell me how hard it was to watch me walk away, or how he plans on always being there for me, just like he always has been. Something. Anything.

But he doesn't say a word.

"Okay," I breathe. "So you're not going to say any—"

He stops me with a kiss. At first it's slow—almost shy—but then he takes my face in his hands and crushes me to him, and for one beautiful moment I forget everything except for the taste of him, and the feel of his fingers pushing back into my hair, pulling me eagerly, almost greedily, into his kiss. I forget that there are people out to kill both of us. I forget about the dead city all around us. I forget about how caught up we are in the lies this world has told us, and in this war that's building and threatening to cave in on us. Right now, the only thing I'm caught up in is him. Again and again I'm caught up in him—in his amazing scent, in the warmth of his skin against mine, over and over until we're so close, so tangled up in each other, that it's hard to tell where he ends and I begin. And when he finally pulls his lips away from mine, we stay like that, his arms wrapped tightly around me, his heart pounding against mine.

We don't have time to catch our breath before the trunk of the car slams shut. I turn my head in time to see it fading out of sight, adjusting to the opacity level of the rest of the car. Seth is walking toward us.

"Good thing we don't have anything important to be doing right now," he says, raising an eyebrow.

I feel myself blushing. Jaxon kisses my forehead—lets his lips linger there for just a few seconds—before stepping away.

Seth clears his throat. "And I'm not only complaining because you two just took my role as third wheel to a whole new level of awkward," he adds. "We're just on a bit of a tight schedule here."

He hands me a weapon I've never seen before—a sleek black thing that resembles a tiny crossbow. I force my attention to it, away from the lingering taste of Jaxon's kiss. Overall, the gun's incredibly light, but in its center is a weight that helps steady it when I practice aiming it at a pillar on the far side of the garage.

"Cybow," he says. "It's a well-balanced gun, and you should be able to shoot it with just one hand." His eyes fall to the swollen wrist at my side; we ripped up a box that was in the car's trunk and used it and some of the medical tape and gauze Jaxon took from the clinic to make a sort of splint for it. "That's your dominant hand, isn't it?" he asks.

"Unfortunately."

"Yeah, so you're definitely sticking with the Cybow. It's easy as crap to aim, even with your lame hand. It is, however, one of my favorite guns, so don't you dare lose it."

"Hopefully you won't have to use it, anyway," Jaxon says, grabbing his own weapon and starting toward the elevator.

"Always the optimist," Seth says. But Jaxon's moving so quickly that he's already too far away to hear. We jog to catch up with him, and then the three of us keep up that pace, moving as fast as we can while still keeping an eye on our surroundings. Not that there's any need; the garage is just as empty as it was the first day I came here.

Even so, by the time we start our descent in the elevator, the back of my neck is damp with nervous sweat. Anxiety is like a fourth passenger in the cramped space, walking between us, wrapping her arms around us so tightly, it's difficult to breathe.

The elevator lurches to a stop, and Jaxon steps in front of me. "Stay close to me," he says, and we brace ourselves as the doors slide open.

CHAPTER NINETEEN

Aftermath

Inside, the room stretches emptily before us—quiet and strange with no chatter, no bustle of people or clicking and beeping of computers like last time. The only noise disrupting the deathlike stillness is the sound of our own uncertain footsteps, and the occasional flicker of the fluorescent lights above. And even though I know we're all thinking it, no one asks the obvious, terrifying question: *Where did everybody go?*

We draw our weapons and head for the president's office.

It's empty. Just like everywhere else. The chair at her desk is overturned, and on the floor there's a broken picture of her and Jaxon, alongside a man I can only assume is Jaxon's father; but other than that, the room looks undisturbed. I linger in the doorway while Jaxon picks up the picture, and Seth searches the room a little closer, checking recent messages on the president's computer and comcenter. A series of screens on the far wall catches my eye, and I move to Jaxon's side, motioning toward them.

"Part of a security system?" I ask.

He nods.

"Maybe we can find out what happened," I say, joining

Seth at the computer. My fingers have already started flying across the screen, trying to navigate around the security control program, before I notice that Jaxon is still watching me silently. And I think I know why.

Because if I manage to pull up the footage of the last twenty-four hours, who knows what it's going to show.

What will he have to watch happen to his mother?

I take a step away from the computer. "Or maybe we should just go. Obviously it's not—"

"No," Jaxon interrupts. His eyes are on the computer, not me, and they have a strange, glassy look about them. "No, it's a good idea. We should find out what we can."

He takes my place at the door, keeping an eye out, and I reluctantly go back to work.

The system is more than a little intricate. There are over twenty-five cameras being operated by this computer, and it takes a solid minute or two for me to just work out which files represent which rooms. And even after I manage that, trying to gain access to any of their past surveillance feeds just earns me an administrator password prompt that I can't get past.

I'm starting to get frustrated, when I find a group of camera folders labeled "low profile"; they don't require administrator access, only program passwords—which are easy enough to bypass. A few more clicks and setting adjustments later, three of the monitors on the wall blur to life.

"I couldn't gain access to this room's cameras," I explain. "I'm not sure where this one is, but it looks like this it's a live stream, so hang on, let me adjust the date and time and see if I can—"

"Wait a second," Seth says, "check out the bottom-left screen."

Jaxon leaves his place by the door, and together we tread softly to the tiny display and crouch down in front of it. The scene playing out on it isn't as clear as I'd expected—but it's clear enough to see what Seth's talking about.

There are no fewer than a half-dozen people on the screen in front of us. And I recognize every single one of them from school. Lacey Cartwright is front and center, her smile tight and menacing as she points to something offscreen. They're in what looks like some sort of storage room, surrounded by steel racks stacked high with computer equipment and crates of old discs. Most of them are sifting through the crates, but it's hard to tell if they're looking for something, or just trying to make as big of a mess as possible.

Suddenly, almost as if Lacey can feel us watching her, she turns and looks directly up at the camera. Her smile widens. I stumble away from the screen, trying to catch my breath; but it feels like the air's been punched straight from my lungs.

"They're CCA, right?" I ask, glancing back at Jaxon. "Please tell me all of them are CCA, and that's why they're here."

He shakes his head, and I look back at the screen just as a petite brown-haired girl—a sophomore whose name is Brittany, I think—grips the edge of one of the steel racks and lifts it, single-handedly, into the air. Her strength is obviously inhuman, but it's nothing compared with how quickly she moves, how her entire body blurs with speed and grace as she flings the rack aside. An instant later we hear the crash—not over the video feed, but reverberating down the hall outside.

My gaze snaps toward the door.

How close is that room, exactly?

There's another crash, followed by shouting and loud peals of laughter. When everything grows quiet again, it's Seth who finally moves; he goes straight to the door without a word, then shuts and secures it. It slides closed with a painfully loud metallic *thump* that echoes around the room. I want to think that it only seems so loud, that it only makes me jump because of the panic settling over us.

But when I finally feel brave enough to look back at the screen, most of the people—the clones—are gone.

Seth turns off the lights and slowly makes his way back to us, his face illuminated by the soft glow of the monitors. No one interrupts the silence; we're all too busy listening, and probably wondering the same things: Did they hear the door shut? Do they know we're in here? And where did they go now?

The seconds crawl by. I take Jaxon's hand, focus on the warmth and weight of it, and slowly, slowly force my breathing back to something like normal. Seth starts to speak several times—probably to try and break the tension with a joke—but stops. He settles instead for just passing the minutes by tap, tap, tapping them out with his fingers against the desk. The computer fans kick on, whirring faintly in the darkness.

Someone pounds on the door.

I bite back a scream. I don't know why I bother, though—because there are so many voices talking and laughing outside now that they probably wouldn't have heard me anyway.

It sounds like there are even more than I counted on the screen.

I rush to turn off those screens now, unplugging them along with the computer—trying to hide every sign that anyone is in here. Without them on, the room is almost pitch black. The three of us scramble blindly for some sort of cover; Jaxon and I end up underneath his mother's desk just as there's another pound against the door and the ear-splitting sound of steel peeling away from steel. A jagged ribbon of light appears on the back wall, and with a sick twist in my gut I realize: they're punching a hole through the solid metal door.

"Knock, knock . . . anybody home?" Lacey's voice is as sickeningly sweet as ever, and crystal clear now that there's less and less door separating us. Someone punches the door again, and the spot of light against the back wall grows wider.

Jaxon's arm brushes mine, and I glance over and see him swiping the safety off the gun in his hands. Wherever Seth ended up hiding, I imagine he's doing the same thing. So I do too, even though I can't help feeling that it's pointless now.

There's another slam against the door; it sounds like someone threw their whole body against it this time, judging by the way the steel screeches and groans under the weight. I shut my eyes and try to imagine I'm anywhere else, but open them a second later when I feel Jaxon move past me. He's inching his way out from underneath the desk, getting dangerously close to the light flooding in from the hole in the door. I grab his arm just as he lifts his gun.

"What are you doing?" I whisper, jerking him back.

"They just know that someone's in here," he says. "They don't know how many. So if they find me—"

"Don't be stupid."

He turns and presses me into the back corner of the desk. "They don't know you're here," he whispers, a forced calmness in his voice that terrifies me. "And you are going to stay right here, and you are not going to make a sound, or do *anything* that lets them know otherwise."

I want to argue. But I don't want to make any more noise—because he's right; it would be stupid to let them all know we're *both* in here. I can't seem to find my voice, anyway, so instead I just stare at him and silently shake my head. He gently pries my hand, finger by finger, from his arm and starts to pull away again.

He freezes at the edge of the desk, at the exact moment I think we both notice how quiet it's suddenly become. No one's pounding on the door. The voices outside have stopped. We hold our breath and listen for a minute, two minutes. . . .

The footsteps that break the silence are impossibly close. A shadow blots out the light on the wall a second later, and Jaxon dives around the corner of the desk, gun raised, in the same instant Seth says, "They're gone."

I let out the breath I've been holding and crawl out from underneath the desk to find Seth with his hands in the air and Jaxon slowly lowering the gun.

"I almost shot you, idiot."

"I know," Seth says, still eying the gun nervously, "I was there. Saw the whole thing, complete with my life flashing before my eyes."

"Why would they just leave?" I ask, my voice still not rising above a whisper.

"Because they want us to follow them for some reason?" Jaxon says. "I'm pretty sure this is a trap."

It's obvious now that he says it. And it's also obvious that we don't have any choice but to walk straight into that trap—because it's not like we can stay in this room forever.

The closest exit, Jaxon and Seth decide after a bit of arguing, is a set of elevators on the other side of the main meeting room. It's a straight-enough shot from here to there, but it's still not exactly close.

Every hallway we have to turn and walk down seems narrower than the last. Soon it starts to feel as if the building itself is closing in on us, but there's nothing to do but keep moving. I hold my breath around every corner, expecting each one to be the last we ever turn, and Lacey's terrible smile to be among the last things I ever see.

We make it to the main room without encountering anyone.

I'm about to sigh with relief when I notice the first body.

Seth almost trips over it. He mutters several curse words as he tries to regain his balance, and I cover my mouth and turn away, even though the corpse's charred, twisted face is already burned into my mind. I stumble a few feet before I dare to turn back, making sure I don't look down at the body. It's then that I take my first good look at the room—and the aftermath of what was obviously a horrible fight.

There are burn marks all over the walls and the steel rafters above us. Light fixtures are dangling, and almost all of the bulbs themselves are shattered, leaving the room bathed in a hazy half darkness. From what I can see, most of the computers and other equipment is lying in melted, twisted pieces on the floor. Half of the desks are over on their sides—used as makeshift bunkers, judging by the gunfire scars and warped metal across their tops. The pungent scent of burnt flesh and blood saturates the air, and scattered in between all the destruction is the occasional still body. I don't get too close to any of them, but Jaxon and Seth are already racing through the room, checking pulses and identifying the ones that haven't been burnt past recognition.

My knees feel weak. Seth pointed out the exit elevators the second we stepped into this room, and my gaze drifts back toward them now. The lighted panel above them is like a beacon cutting through the darkness, and suddenly

I'm walking across the room, thinking only about how badly I need to get far, far away from this place.

I'm in such a trance that I don't realize Jaxon and Seth aren't following me, not until I've made it almost all the way to the elevators. They're still behind me, still moving through the bodies. Still searching. Because they knew these people, of course. And because the president is still missing.

I don't want them to find her. Not here. Not like this.

"I should have come back sooner," Jaxon says, walking up beside me.

I look at him but don't say anything. I'm not sure there's anything I could say that would make any of this any better.

"If I'd been here, my mom—"

"Wherever she is now, I'm sure she's glad you *weren't* here when this happened."

He shakes his head, shoves past me, and rejoins Seth on the other side of the room.

"We can't keep searching forever," I call after him, my voice breaking. "You know we can't."

He doesn't look back.

I hug my arms against my chest and wander closer to the elevators. We've been here too long already. I don't know what we're going to do about his mother, but I do know we need to figure it out somewhere else. Somewhere safer. Somewhere less . . . creepy. The room seemed so deathly silent at first, but the longer I stand there, shifting my weight from foot to foot and begging the guys to hurry up, the louder everything around me becomes. Distant whispers of voices, the metal creaks and groans of the structure settling around us, the hiss of the ancient heating and air unit. And with the noise, I see faces blurring through my mind now—the familiar faces of Lacey. Of Brittany. Of so many other Haven High School students. I knew Brittany was an origin, and same goes for most of the others we saw on the monitors. Lacey was a surprise, though. I've never seen her name listed in any of the databases Huxley has available to the public—and those are supposed to be thorough. Complete. It's against the law for them *not* to be.

How many other clones don't we know about?

Movement. Somewhere to my right. I jerk around, and out of the corner of my eye I see the shadows shifting, the light changing. I take a deep breath, smooth a hand over the chilled skin on my arms. It's nothing but my mind playing tricks on me, I know. Jaxon and Seth are both to my left, and the only other people in here are all dead. And dead people don't move.

But something above us is moving. Something *smacks* against the exposed ceiling beams and sets off a metallic ringing that bounces around the room and sinks straight into my bones. And it isn't just in my mind this time, because Jaxon and Seth are both frozen in place too, their eyes wide and gazing toward the darkest corner of the ceiling. It's too dark to see anything, though.

They slowly inch their way back toward me and the elevators, and the three of us reach them just as the screen above lights up with the number of our floor. A high-pitched *ding* fills the air. The doors open and Dr. Atticus Voss steps out, flanked on either side by several armed men.

There are so many people, but Voss is the only one I can look at.

Samantha had her father's eyes.

Does he know what happened to her clone? Does he know she's gone forever now?

I spin around, thinking about running back the way we came. But Lacey and the rest of the clones from earlier are blocking the path. And still more of them are stealing silently into the room, out of every adjacent hallway and door, and dropping from the shadows above—until we're so far past outnumbered that it's almost laughable.

Voss orders us to lower our weapons, and the tightness in my throat grows worse. I can't swallow. I can't speak. I can't even move, until someone grabs my arm from behind and rips the gun from my hand. I draw back my fist, turn, and swing, but I'm met by two men twice my size; one of them easily catches my clenched hand and twists it—along with my other arm—behind my back, while the other one jabs a syringe filled with some sort of clear liquid into the side of my neck.

I hear Jaxon shout my name. My vision is starting to blur already, and my body feels strangely heavy—but I manage to fight my way to where I can meet his eyes.

And then he's throwing himself against the arms of the people holding him back, over and over, and he's desperately shouting my name again, shouting at them to let me go.

Somehow, he gets away.

He makes it all the way across the room before Voss fires the first shot. Jaxon trips, catches himself against the ground, and then pushes back to his feet. He stumbles the short distance left between us, grabs my arm with trembling fingers. That touch is all I feel. His labored, heavy breathing is all that I hear. His eyes are all I see, each one a calm blue oasis in all of the chaos around us. And then they close.

He falls at my feet, and I'm still screaming when they drag me away from him.

CHAPTER TWENTY

Experiments

When I open my eyes, I'm blinded by cold, white light. An alarm is sounding somewhere close by. A steady siren pulsing louder, softer, louder again. On and on and on.

The signal jammer on my left wrist is gone, and my right one has been wrapped up and properly splintered. There's a dry, cottony taste in my mouth. A strange pins-and-needles sensation in my fingers and toes. My head throbs along with the pulsing alarm, and I have to close my eyes to focus, to try and remember what happened.

How did I get here? Where *is* here?

And then, bit by bit, things start to come back to me. The CCA headquarters. The clones. The scientists. Voss. The gun in Voss's hand.

Jaxon.

I bolt upright. Too fast; the room sways, and my stomach churns. I grab the edge of the metal bed I'm lying on and lean over the side, thinking I'm going to throw up. My last conscious moment at the CCA headquarters keeps replaying itself over and over in my thoughts: Jaxon's face going pale, his body collapsing to the floor . . . and what happened then? And since then? How long have I been out for?

Calm. I have to stay calm.

I recite the first half of the lines from a monologue I performed last year—from *Dido, Queen of Carthage*—focusing on remembering each word to take my mind off the nausea I'm feeling. As it settles, I ease back upright, taking in the large room around me. It's obvious that I've ended up somewhere in Huxley's lab, because the intricate *H* of their logo is on almost everything in here—from the computers to the door to the glass vials and containers that line every shelf along the wall. That doesn't surprise me. What does surprise me is that I'm not alone.

In the opposite corner of the room is another bed, and Violet is lying on it. I look away quickly, as if I can somehow pretend she's not there.

Like if I'm fast enough, I can somehow get away from all of this.

But there's nowhere to go. The steel door looming in front of me is like most of the doors in the lab, and the only way through it is via a card key. A single horizontal window breaks up the drab gray walls, but I see no obvious way to open it; I can't even tell what's on the other side of it, because it's an observation window—similar to the one in our science classroom at school. The glass is tinted, its surface so dark that I hardly recognize myself in it. If there's anyone on the other side, they can see me, but I can't see them.

I hear mumbling behind me, and turn toward Violet's still body.

Why is she here? What happened to her grand plan to

run away and leave all of this—and me—behind? I wasn't expecting to see her again. Especially not this soon. And I don't know that I *wanted* to see her again, because her being here only complicates things even more, just like it always does. I should be focused on getting myself out of this place, on finding out what happened to Jaxon and Seth, on finding my parents, and figuring out what the hell is going on in the city.

But as I cross the room, my own thoughts betray me, slipping away from all the things I'm trying to focus on and fighting their way back to Violet. To all the things I want to be mad at, but can't. Not when I see her like this.

She's still mumbling when I reach her side. Her eyes are half-shut, and there are wires attached to several electric nodes on her scalp, a tangle of blue snakes twisting into the computer beside us. Metal cuffs arching up out of the bed bind her arms and legs to it. I can tell she's been struggling against the restraints, because the skin all around her wrists and ankles is covered in bruises of different colors, all at different stages of healing. I make the mistake of softly saying her name, which only makes her lunge wildly away.

Anger wells in my chest, and my gaze jerks toward that window. Are there people behind it? Just watching, waiting to see what I'll do about this?

I know what I *want* to do. I want to grab everything within arm's reach and throw it as hard as I can at the glass, to break it down and reveal the monsters inside. I want to know how long they've been watching, and what they've seen, and what they were doing to us while we slept—even though part of me is afraid to find out.

President Huxley is very, very *interested in the relationship between the two of you.* The memory of that woman's voice, of her words, sends an uneasy feeling creeping through me.

And they have both of us now. They went after her, caught her, and dragged her back here because they had a bunch of sick experiments in mind for the two of us. And those things attached to Violet's head . . . they must be part of them.

I follow the trail of wires to the computer, slide my fingers across the screen to wake it from sleep mode. As it slowly fades back to life, I find myself staring at an intricate three-dimensional model of a brain—Violet's, I'm guessing. The diagram is divided into six sections, one for each of the nodes stuck to her head. Curious, I start clicking around on the screen, trying to find notes, documents—anything to help me understand exactly what I'm seeing.

The clicking noise upsets Violet. She throws herself against her restraints again, shouting at me to stop. *They're mine,* she keeps saying, over and over and over, until the words lose their meaning and her voice eventually fades back to quiet mumblings. She stops struggling and sinks back down onto the bed. I leave the computer alone for the moment and just watch her lying there, her eyelids fluttering open and closed and her lips still moving, still muttering things I can't understand.

And then her eyes flash wide open so suddenly, it actually makes me jump. She stops muttering. She stares straight ahead, and in a voice that's perfectly clear, she says, "They're mine. And you can't take her from me."

I'm afraid to say anything, afraid to upset her again, though I desperately want to ask her what she's talking about. What's hers? What does she mean, they "can't take her"?

I turn the words over in my mind, until I finally remember the last time I heard her say things like this: in the hotel room. When we fought that night, when the cut on my cheek reminded her of one of the old Violet's memories of us. What was it she said? *No matter how many times they try taking it away, it keeps coming back.*

She was talking about Huxley then. She has to have been. And she's talking about them now, and those memories must have been what they were trying to take—the same ones they uploaded into her brain. The same ones that they control. And they would have to take them, wouldn't they? Because the old Violet would never have hurt me. Not after everything we'd been through together.

One by one, they've been transforming her into a monster, trying to leave her with only the things they want her to know and think.

So where does that leave the two of us?

I jerk the wires out of the computer, too angry to look at it anymore. Error messages flash and beep at me. I ignore them and crawl underneath Violet's bed, searching for the buttons to release the metal cuffs holding her down. Once

I release them, I slowly climb back up to her side, trying not to startle her.

Too late.

Her eyes are crazed and unfocused as she reaches up with her newly freed hands, rips the wires from her head, and flings them at me. I duck, but not fast enough; the sharp tip of one of the wires catches me in the eye. It stings like hell, and I instinctively throw my hands in front of my face to protect it from any more flying wires.

But just like before, Violet's fit of rage is over as quickly as it came. She slinks away from me and starts to ramble again, words that I can understand this time but that don't make any sense.

"Dust to death, today or to-morrow, to-morrow, to-morrow," she chants to herself as she sinks down into the corner, "to-morrow, to-morrow, to-morrow."

"Knock it off," I say, crossing the room and cautiously lowering myself down beside her.

She stops chanting. I brace myself for another outburst, but it doesn't come. Instead, she just glances silently around the room, eyes searching for rest but not finding it. We're close, so close, but somehow it feels like there's an infinite amount of space between us.

"Come on Violet," I say softly. "Please snap out of it. Look at me. Talk to me."

She doesn't do either of those things for a long time. I'm not sure she can anymore. Her rantings are becoming more and more incoherent.

I don't know what to do. I'm too angry, too tired, to

think. I have to get out of here, I know—we both do. And Violet could probably help me with that, but not as long as she's like this. I feel weak, so unbearably weak, with nothing to do but lean my head next to her on the wall and try to find the words to bring her back to me.

Eventually, I give up on words and just start to hum, first whatever random song comes to mind, and then finally what I remember of a song my grandmother taught me. Violet closes her eyes and falls completely silent then, focusing on the tune.

"It has words, Birdy," she interrupts after a few minutes. And I don't even care that she's using that stupid nickname again. She can call me whatever she likes, as long as she keeps talking to me. As long as she keeps making sense. "I remember words," she goes on, and it's startling how normal her voice suddenly sounds. "And I remember you singing as we fell asleep."

My stomach clenches at the memory. Because I can see it in painfully vivid detail: the first night after we found out the old Violet was sick, I'd heard her crying, slipped into her room, and curled up in the bed beside her. I hadn't known what to say then any more than I do now, and so I'd just sung her to sleep with that song Grandma sang whenever we had a cold or a stomach bug or something. Like that song was what healed us of those things and if I hit all the notes right, then maybe I could have healed Violet of whatever was killing her, too.

Obviously, it didn't work.

"I don't want to sing the words," I say.

She gives me a sideways glance but doesn't say anything to that. Her gaze seems more focused now. Her body, less tense.

I hold in my questions until I'm sure she's snapped completely out of her trance. When she starts to get up and wander away from me, though, I can't take it anymore. "What are they doing to you?" I ask. "Why would they try to take your memories? How can they get away with something like that?"

"Get away with it?" She laughs. "Easy. Huxley created me. They created my brain. And eventually, all things must return to their creators, yes? All these lingering feelings, these memories of you and me—in the end they're only in the way of their plans. So they want them gone. Erased. How else would they manage to build their army of complacent little slaves? I've been more resistant than most, but . . ."

I push off the wall and stagger forward. I don't want to stay another second in this room, surrounded by the evidence of all the terrible things Huxley is doing. And I'm not going to let them do those things to us.

My gaze finds the observation window on the far wall again. I know there's a room behind it; I don't know if we'll be able to get out of it any better than we can this one, but it's worth a try.

"We're getting out of here," I say, nodding to the window. "And we're going through there."

I rip the computer monitor from its place on the wall, hand it to Violet, and stand back as she hurls it at the glass. I half expected her to hit people on the other side of it in the process, but the room behind it turns out to be empty. There are signs of recent activity, though—a half-full coffee mug, a laptop that's still almost fully charged, with various programs open on the screen. It looks like whoever *was* here left in a hurry; the door is still slightly ajar, there's a chair toppled over on its side, and a stack of files that looks like it might have been knocked over in the midst of a scramble. And, fortunately for us, there's also a lab coat still draped over the counter—and it has a set of ID key cards clipped to its front pocket. I pick it up and shake off the bits and pieces of broken glass.

The thought of putting on a Huxley uniform disgusts me a little. But I figure it will help us draw less attention to ourselves, so I brush the last bits of glass dust off and slip it on.

The hallway is mostly empty, aside from a few people shuffling in and out of the doors lining it. Most of them are focused on computers in their hands, or on the conversations they're having with each other. Me and Violet walk side by side, my hand on her arm like I'm an employee of Huxley leading her purposely forward.

A few people nod in our direction as we move through the hall, but most of their gazes don't linger. Maybe it's just me, but it feels like there's a nervous energy in the air, like people are moving more quickly than normal, like their whispers are too urgent, their thoughts too far off to focus on us. I should be grateful for that last part, I guess. But it just makes me uneasy.

"Something is happening," Violet says, giving voice to my own thoughts. "Something has them in a panic. It must be happening somewhere else in the lab, though; this wing is normally much more crowded. At least, it was earlier."

"Those sirens that have been going on and off," I think aloud, "I wonder if they have anything to do with whatever's going on? With whatever made the person in that room abandon their observation in such a hurry?"

Less than ten steps later, we hear shouting. It's far off, little more than a vague echo by the time it reaches our hallway—but soon other voices join in, and then I hear what has to be gunfire. I slow almost to a stop. Violet keeps marching forward, and I have to hurry after her, afraid of pausing too long, of doing anything that might make us look suspicious. The hall seems to be getting emptier and emptier, though; so when I catch up with her I'm feeling confident enough to whisper, "Do you think the CCA is here?"

"Only one way to know for sure," Violet says. She turns down the next corridor and heads toward the noise, her step getting quicker with every shout. I cast a hasty glance around, making sure no one's watching us, then jerk her to a stop.

"What, by running straight toward the people with guns? I feel like we can come up with a better plan than that."

"Don't you want to help your CCA friends?"

I frown. "'Friends' might be pushing it." More than

pushing it, actually. If it wasn't for Jaxon and Seth, I'd find my way to the nearest exit and maybe just let the CCA and Huxley finish each other off.

But if there's a chance that Jaxon is still alive, then I know I'm going to need help finding him. And who better to ask for help than his mother? If she's here, I have to find her. I have to tell her what happened.

"Okay, fine," I say, moving past Violet and continuing down the hall. "If those are CCA people out there, then hopefully the president is with them. She'll be able to tell us what's going on."

I'm running by the time we reach the end of the hall. The lab coat flutters around me; it's too long, and it twists around my legs and almost trips me several times until I just shrug out of it midstride and carry it instead. Keeping up this disguise suddenly seems less important than being able to move as fast as possible. I don't know how many people it's actually fooling, anyway.

A door no more than twenty feet ahead flings open, and several men in Huxley uniforms step out. I grab Violet's arm and pull her against the door closest to us, pressing as far as possible into the recess around it, praying the men walk the other way.

They don't.

I fumble with the lab coat draped over my arm, desperately searching for the set of key cards. There are four of them altogether, and I swipe them all. Of course it's the fourth and final one that finally makes the door open. Violet and I stumble into the dimly lit room behind it.

It smells like almost every other one we've passed through—a combination of disinfectant and formaldehyde that's borderline nauseating—but other than that I don't pay much attention to my surroundings. I just keep moving, as far away from the door as I can, around desks and shelves and anything else in my path. The room stretches on and on, and the farther we get, the colder it becomes; the frigid air burns down my throat and grabs at my hands and feet until they're numb and every step starts to hurt.

We reach the foot of a massive staircase, and suddenly I can't run anymore. I collapse on the bottom step, head spinning, body shaking from cold and exhaustion. Violet reaches my side a second later. Her breathing is normal, relaxed. She wanders around me like someone who's lost and is trying too hard to convince anyone who sees her that she knows exactly where she is.

"Maybe we should find someplace to hide for a few minutes," she says. "Just until we're sure no one's followed us in here."

I don't like the idea of sitting around with only Violet and my thoughts for company, but it's better than being found and ending up locked in another room. I tilt my head back so I can see what's upstairs, hoping it might lead to another way out, or at least to a good hiding place.

I stare for a long time, trying to make sense of what I'm seeing.

The staircase spirals up, up, up—so high that I can't see the ceiling. And about ten feet above us, the glass boxes start. Hundreds—maybe thousands—of them, wrapped around the steps, each one emitting a soft blue glow from the rectangular computer displays across their tops. Most of the boxes are empty.

Some of them still have bodies in them.

Some are relaxed and still; others are moving in place. Walking, running, reaching blindly for whatever their origin is reaching for right now.

I rise slowly to my feet, mouth still hanging open and refusing to close. One by one, I climb the steps to the closest holding box with a body in it. It's floating, suspended in a thick, sea green liquid. Its eyes are closed, its skin a pale, ghastly white. There are tubes inserted in its throat and nose. Pumping oxygen, I assume, judging by the way its chest rises and falls with disturbingly normal-looking breaths. Its arms are stretched out in front of it, hands wide and opening toward me. It looks like it's sleeping. I press my own hand to the warm glass, splay my fingers across it and swallow hard to try to combat the sudden dryness in my throat.

I knew this was here—knew that they had to grow the clones somewhere, somehow; and I knew that they moved like this, thanks to the neural chip that links them with their origin's movements. But seeing it is different. All of this is a footnote in Huxley's propaganda videos. They never show it or dwell on the details, and now it's obvious why they wouldn't. Because this body floating in front of me looks completely human. All too human. And there is something beyond unsettling about the way it's confined in this little box. Something that makes me want to break the glass and set it free.

Would it live if I broke the glass?

Would death be so much worse than whatever Huxley has planned for it?

This is what Violet meant earlier. To be created, life emerging out of a glass box—given her very breath by Huxley. But seeing it in front of me is so much worse. How could our parents have agreed to something so sick?

How could *anybody* agree to this?

I turn to where I left Violet at the foot of the stairs and see her backing away, her eyes focused on me and me alone. She's not looking at the body next to me. She's not looking at any of the dozens of empty boxes—one of which might have been hers only a few years ago. How could she stand to look at that? How could anyone in her place?

My eyes drift back to the clone in front of me, and then to the computer display above his container: 0627. A number. No name.

My number is here too, I realize suddenly.

Without thinking I'm running up the stairs, the cold and exhaustion in my muscles forgotten. The ID numbers rush by, into the seven hundreds, the eight hundreds, the nine hundreds—the closer I get to one thousand, the more often the boxes have bodies in them, and the slower I get. Because what will I do, when I'm face to face with clone number 1001? What am I supposed to do? She's only my copy, right? A potentially dangerous copy that I don't want anywhere near my family, or anyone else I care about—but is she alive like 0627? Is she breathing, like he is? Can she see me, hear me? If I could reach in and take her hand, what would she do? If she replaces me, will she be like Violet, fighting the control Huxley has over her?

Fighting to be human?

The higher nine hundreds start at the top of the stairs, and from there the boxes branch off into a long hallway. I find number 1001 tucked in the corner of that hallway, right where it curves and splits into two separate paths. My eyes almost jump right over it, because the display above is flickering, and so faint it's barely readable.

And because the box itself is empty.

CHAPTER TWENTY-ONE

Complete

By the time we make it back to the hallway outside the cloneroom, I still haven't found the words to tell Violet what I saw.

Or what I didn't see, I guess.

I stared at that display for longer than I should have. I wasted too much time there, reading the number on it. Checking the boxes on either side of my clone's, searching for a break in the pattern, desperate to convince myself that I had the wrong place, that I was reading the wrong display.

I had to have been in the wrong place. I'm still alive. I'm still here. They can't replace me if I'm still here.

Maybe there's another explanation for why she's gone, though. Because who knows what really goes on in this place. They could have taken my clone anywhere, they could be doing anything with her. Maybe something went wrong with her. Maybe they thought she was a mistake too, just like Violet—but an even bigger mistake. One they've decided to just get rid of before she becomes a problem.

Maybe.

"Things seem to have calmed down," Violet says as we

step cautiously into the corridor. My thoughts are still in the room we left behind, and it takes me a couple tries to redirect them to the here, the now—and to realize that she's right: It's a lot quieter than before. It isn't a peaceful quiet, though. It's a quiet thick with unease and heavy with questions I'm afraid to ask.

"Does that mean somebody lost?" I wonder out loud. And was it the CCA? Were they really here? How many more are dead now? Is that the only reason they're silent?

"I think *we* may be about to lose," Violet says, in that airy, distant tone she uses when she's about to start musing about something. "Because we have company."

I turn back to her. She stopped several yards back, and now she's staring at the half-dozen people walking straight toward us. A tall woman with long, blond hair and eyes the color of gray-tinted glass is leading them. Her gaze is locked on me. I don't know her name, but I know I've seen her in the CCA crowd before. The CCA torch hangs around her neck—a shiny silver pendant flickering in the fluorescent lights. But that doesn't mean anything. It doesn't mean she's not working for Huxley. Voss had the same necklace. The ironic thing is, that symbol is supposed to stand for truth, for enlightenment—but truth is always a casualty of war, isn't it?

She leaves several feet between us when she and the rest of her group stop. "You're the origin that ran off with the president's son, aren't you?" she asks after a moment.

"He ran off with me, technically," I say. And the thought of that, the memory of that night in the warehouse—of the way he refused to let me leave without him—it makes my knees tremble. Something tells me he would have followed me anywhere that night.

Suddenly my mouth is a desert again, and I have to swallow several times before I can finish answering her. "But . . . yeah. I am. That doesn't matter right now, though. Where is the president? Is she here?"

She doesn't answer me at first; she's too busy studying Violet. "And you must be her sister's clone. The one who killed Voss's daughter."

For once, Violet is completely silent.

The woman goes back to watching me, and I see the familiar scorn in her eyes, that contempt for me and Violet that marks her as a member of the CCA more than that little torch around her neck ever could. It's different this time, though. There's a weariness about it, an uncertainty, almost; like maybe she's not sure she wants to waste her energy on hating me when there are so many other places that hatred could go. I'd like to think that's the case, anyway. That she could move past that stupid prejudice and we could both focus on stopping Huxley before their plans escalate any further. A common enemy, almost. I've always heard that nothing brings people together like that.

But then she draws the gun from her hip and fires.

The shot misses me by no more than an inch; I instinctively cover my head, brace myself for its inevitable follow-up. But then I hear a groan, a *thump* from somewhere behind me. I turn to see a man in a Huxley lab coat collapsing to the ground.

"Nice shot," says one of the CCA men.

"That makes lucky number seven for me," says the woman. "I'm not sure where all of them keep coming from. I thought they had all run away by this point."

The confusion must be evident on Violet's face and mine, because she smugly explains, "We managed to take them by surprise. Reinforcements from other CCA chapters—they had no clue what sort of numbers they were dealing with, or that we fully anticipated their attack against us. They thought they would manage to stamp us out so easily, but they made the mistake of sending far too many of their clones to our headquarters and leaving this place vulnerable in the process."

I open my mouth to speak, but she continues in a rush, "And to answer your question, origin, I'm afraid the president is in a very important meeting at the moment. I'll have to take a message."

"We don't have time for that," I say. "Her son . . . he . . ." It turns out to be even harder to say these things out loud than I thought it would be. "Something is wrong," I finally manage to whisper. "Something she should know about."

She smiles placidly, focusing on setting her gun to recharge. "What could an origin possibly have to say that would merit the president's attention?"

I clench the fist that isn't splinted and immobile, digging my nails into the palm of my hand so I can focus on the pain it causes instead of how angry I'm getting. "If she knew about her son, if she knew what had happened at your headquarters—"

"At headquarters?" The woman's gaze shifts abruptly back to me. "You've been there recently?"

She finally seems at least mildly interested in what I have to say, so I give her the quickest recap possible of everything that happened.

When I finish, she turns to the man on her right and says, "You were with the ones who took care of Voss's group, weren't you?"

My heart skips a beat when the man nods. "We took care of most of them, intercepted the ones who had the president's son when they were on their way back here. Both Jaxon and the other one—Seth, isn't it? They're both around here somewhere. Or they were earlier. Against the president's wishes, I believe, but . . ."

It's like mental whiplash, what those words do to my brain. Jaxon is alive. Jaxon is here. Or he was here, at least. He could still be here. He could be looking for me. That's probably why he was here in the first place, right?

At first I'm too dazed to speak, or to try to stop the CCA people when they make their way around us and continue down the hall. But soon my feet are moving automatically after them. I catch up to the blond woman, ignore the irritated glance she gives me, and cut directly into her path.

"Where is he now?" I demand. "Where are the rest of the CCA? Is that where you're going? Back to them?"

"You are annoyingly persistent, aren't you?"

"I just need to find Jaxon. I just need to see for myself that he's okay. Please. Let's just pretend we're all on the same side here for a second, and you just tell me where you saw him last, or just point me in the right direction, or something, *anything . . .*"

She raises both of her pencil-stroke eyebrows. "Fine. You can come with us if you can keep up." Without another word she starts to turn around, and me and Violet both move to follow—but the woman stops Violet with a single finger against her chest. Her nails are painted the same violent red shade as her lips. "I should have been more specific," she says with that calm smile from before. "When I said *you*, I meant her." She nods in my direction. "If I had any sense, clone, I'd kill you right now. It's going to come to that eventually anyway. But for now I'm willing to let you walk away—so long as you aren't going the same way as me."

"I'm not leaving her," I say.

"Then you are not coming with us," the woman says simply. And then she turns and continues walking away, the rest of her group falling silently in line beside her.

"Wait!"

"It's not really keeping up if I have to wait for you, is it?" she calls without looking back.

"Just go with them," Violet says under her breath. "Don't worry about me."

"Shut up," I say through clenched teeth. "I've spent my entire life worrying about you. You really think I can just stop now?"

"They'll take you to Jaxon. I know you want to see that he's all right, and he's probably worried about you, too." Her voice is quiet, and more detached than ever. I can tell by the look in her eyes that her mind is someplace far away; I'm a little afraid to think about where it's gone, exactly.

"What about you?" I ask, my gaze jumping back and forth, from Violet's empty eyes to the CCA group. They've almost made it to the end of the hall. Almost out of sight. My heart aches at the thought of staying behind, literal pain shooting through it every time the group takes a step. I should be going with them. It isn't a want. It's a need. I need to see Jaxon, because I don't trust their words; I won't believe he's okay until I see it for myself.

"There's something I need to do, anyway," she says. "And I'd rather not have to worry about you while I'm doing it."

"What are you talking about?"

She smiles slyly and in typical annoying big-sister fashion informs me that it's none of my business. "Look," she adds with a sigh, "I'll catch up with you when this is over with. I always do, don't I?"

She says it like this will all be over with tomorrow. Like somehow we'll wake up in the morning and everything will be different, and none of the things we've done or seen will still be there, weighing us down. Like we'll be normal and everyone will accept us and me and her and Mother and Father will all be one big, happy family. Complete again.

I wonder if we'll ever be complete again.

"Now get out of here before I make you," Violet says.

I still don't budge. "You take too long, I'm coming back for you. Whether you like it or not."

"I know you will," she says, and then she meets my

eyes—truly meets them—for what might be the very first time in her life.

She reaches for the key cards I'd clipped to the bottom of my shirt. Her focus grows hazy again. "I'll be needing these," she says. She looks over her shoulder, finds the door to the clone-holding room. Every second her eyes stay locked on it makes the uneasy feeling in my stomach creep a little farther up the back of my neck.

I know I can't make her come with me now any more than I could back at the graveyard, though. I've spent the past four years wishing I could control her, and letting her control my life because of that. But maybe sometimes you have to let go of people, and of all the things they do, and just hope that they'll find their way back to you if they're supposed to.

I catch up with the CCA group a few hallways down. At first they don't acknowledge me, but soon I guess they get tired of listening to all of my questions, and so they start answering. And they tell me why they're here: not simply to get even with Huxley for plotting against them, but also to initiate their own plot to stop the clones at their source. They tell me how successful they've been in destroying computer after computer full of vital information, in ruining the equipment responsible for transferring thoughts, images, orders—all of the things Huxley has been using to give life to their clones and their plans.

I can't help but wonder, though, what else they've destroyed in the process.

As we make our way through the halls, I see entire rooms that have been reduced to pieces of broken things: cracked computer screens, twisted, melted file cabinets, and shattered lights. The scene is almost a perfect reflection of the obliteration back at the CCA headquarters. So much destruction on both sides that it's hard to say which side won this round. Neither of them, from where I'm standing.

By the time we reach the north wing, where most of the fighting took place, I can't look anywhere without seeing signs of ruin and devastation. I was so angry with Huxley before, and so a part of me feels like I should be glad for this. But all I feel is that thick and pressing numbness of uncertainty, of a chaos so overwhelming that I don't know what to make of it.

We're almost to the entrance, to those same glass doors that I walked through four years ago, when another alarm starts to echo through the intercom system. It's different from the one before. It's higher pitched, and joined soon by a recorded voice repeating warning after warning in a stiffly urgent tone:

Security threat, holding room B13.

Contamination threat, holding room B13.

Bio threat, holding room B13.

All available personnel report.

B13. That was the number above the clone room. That's where Violet is.

Of course it is.

One by one, our group slows to a stop and looks back.

I think about saying something. About telling them what I saw in holding room B13. But for some reason I don't want to. What will happen if they all go rushing back there? Will they lose their patience with my sister this time? Will they kill her? What about the rest of the clones in there? Surely they'll kill them. While their eyes are still closed, their brains still without conscious thought.

Maybe that would be for the best, in the grand scheme of things. Because if the clones in that room wake up, how many people are they going to hurt? How many will they kill? If we can stop the possibility of Huxley turning them into monsters, shouldn't we?

If only it was that simple.

If only I could not think about how many in that room would be like my sister's clone. Maybe they wouldn't be monsters at all, despite what I know the CCA members think. Maybe they would fight for control. And even if they didn't win, how could I take away their chance? I should just keep quiet. Pretend I don't know anything about room B13 and just keep walking away.

We've started moving again, still heading for the main entrance, when another group of CCA people meet us. I don't want to talk to them. I don't want to look at any of them or have to answer any of their questions. But then I hear a familiar voice.

Seth.

"Cate? What the hell are you doing here?" He grabs my arm and pulls me away from the crowd. It's so quick, and I'm so overcome with emotion at seeing him alive, and without so much as a scratch on his tan skin, that the only thing I can think to do is throw my arms around him. Because yes, it's Seth—but maybe he's grown on me more than I'd cared to admit. Plus, if he's here, then Jaxon has to be close, as inseparable as the two of them are.

"Cut it out," he says, shoving me away.

He seems considerably less excited to see me than I am to see him.

"Sorry," I stammer, confused. "I was just . . . I'm just glad you're okay."

"As okay as I was twenty minutes ago—it's a miracle, isn't it?" There's definitely something wrong with that tone he's using. I've never heard him so angry. "Now answer my question—why the hell are you still here? And where is Jaxon?"

"Jaxon . . . ?"

"You two were in such a damn hurry to leave."

"I—"

The realization of what's happened hits me all at once, so hard and so fast that it's a miracle I manage to stay standing.

"Where did we say we were going?" I ask. My voice is shaking. I can't help it; all of my strength is being channeled into my effort to not pass out, leaving nothing to steady my words.

"Are you serious?" Seth snaps. "Your house? Your parents? Your hysterical insistence that you had to go make sure they were okay, right this second? That I was a terrible, terrible person who didn't care about anyone but himself? None of that ringing any bells?" His voice gets quieter toward the end, the edge of it softening as his gaze fully meets mine. The realization hits him more slowly, but when it does, the horror that spreads across his face is quick and merciless.

"I probably should have tried a little harder to stop him." His words aren't much steadier than mine. I nod, even though I know he isn't asking a question.

Because now we both uncerstand.

Jaxon didn't leave with me. He left with my clone.

CHAPTER TWENTY-TWO

Shattered

Jaxon's car is parked at the end of our driveway.

We're the first ones to make it here. Partly because Jaxon is the one who taught Seth how to drive, and partly because the rest of the CCA members were too busy arguing among themselves about who should go and who should stay, and who should investigate what was happening in room B13. It was easy enough to talk one of them into lending us his car, because so many seemed more eager to keep fighting at the lab, more interested in running back to that room and dealing with whatever pandemonium my sister created this time.

I'd worry about them dealing with her, too, but there's no need. Because she's waiting on the front porch steps for us.

"I told you I'd catch up."

"What did you do back there?" Seth demands. "What was going on in that room?"

Instead of answering him, Violet lifts her gaze and stares dreamily off toward the city's center. I follow it automatically, and just as quickly wish I hadn't. Because there's a plume of smoke rising in the distance, tendrils of it reaching like long, dark fingers out across the skyline.

"Is that coming from over the lab?" Seth asks.

"You know, I think it might be," Violet says. Then she smiles at him.

And it turns out that it actually *is* possible to render Seth Lancaster speechless.

"We're here for Jaxon," I remind them both. I jog up the steps and into the house before they have a chance to start arguing, and before my brain can get too caught up in thoughts of what's happening at Huxley.

Inside, the familiar scent of cleaning supplies and a busy top layer of lilac potpourri hits me harder than I expected. It's only been, what, three days? But somehow it feels like it's been years since the last time I stepped through these doors. Maybe because the Cate I left behind is years away from who I am now.

At least half a dozen people originally followed Jaxon and my clone, Seth told me; President Cross insisted on it the second she found out he'd left with who she thought was the actual me. We find the first of those people lying in a pool of blood at the foot of the stairs. There's a long, thin burn across his neck.

"Well that's not encouraging," Seth says, stepping between me and the body, shielding me from the sight in a way that's almost protective.

He's right. And it's not any more encouraging than the silence, or the burn marks along the walls, or the broken vases and picture frames littering the floor. Where is Jaxon? Where are my parents?

Maybe I should be used to destruction, since it's all

I've seen these past few days. I should be immune to it. But I don't think anything could have made me numb to what I see now: the huge family photo—the one that used to hang proudly over our fireplace—lying facedown on the living room floor. I crouch down beside it and flip it back over. It's heavier than I expected, especially since I'm lifting it one-handed. I don't manage to do it gracefully; it lands hard against the floor, and the spider-web cracks across its glass front spread even farther.

I'm still staring at it when Seth reaches my side.

"It's not a very good picture of you anyway," he says softly. "Your hair looks awful."

"That's true," I agree, trying to find the heart to smile, because I know that's what he's hoping for. I remember when my mother made me get that haircut. I remember how much I hated her for telling them to cut it so short, because I thought it made me look like a boy. So of course she just had to blow it up as big as she could and put it over the fireplace. Five years ago that picture was taken, and so it's the old Violet staring back at me.

And the new Violet is staring at me now too, watching me with one shoulder leaning against the door frame.

I don't know why I never thought about it before now, but I wonder if it was hard for her to look at that every day? I wonder if it was hard for my clone to look at that picture of me, too? Maybe that's why she knocked it down and did her best to shatter it.

"I'm going to go check the other rooms. For more bodies or something," Violet announces.

She's gone before I can say anything, before I can suggest that we stick together. I glance one last time at the family portrait before rising again. My parents' smiles are familiar, of course, because by that point they were practiced and so they were always the same. Staring at them, I almost want to shatter them further, stomp my foot across their faces until the glass breaks into enough tiny little pieces that it's impossible to make out what's underneath. Because I want someone to blame for all of this. And right now, all of the reasons I know they had for the choices they made don't really matter. Not when there's a dead body by the stairs and who knows how many more still left to find.

"Come on." Seth grabs my arm and pulls me back toward the hall. "Not important right now," he says. And he's right. Because the people in that picture might share my blood, but family isn't just about blood; it's about who comes to your side and who stays there without flinching even when everything goes to hell.

Jaxon isn't in that picture, but he still feels like family to me.

He has to be here somewhere, and I have to find him.

Outside the living room, Seth heads straight for the steps at the end of the hall. I'm not far behind him, until the door to the basement catches my eye. It's halfway open. I slow to a stop, staring at it. That door is never open. For most of the past two years it's been locked, even, ever since the basement flooded during a nasty summer storm; my mother keeps saying that she's going to go through everything down there, sort through the water-logged boxes of keepsakes, of damaged photos, of mine and Violet's old school projects and honor roll and perfect attendance certificates. But she hasn't yet. Maybe because she's afraid of how much is ruined, and how much she'd have to throw away. And I guess she was afraid of anyone else throwing any of it away too, because she even had a new door installed—a metal one with an electric control panel and everything.

That computer panel now has a gaping, jagged hole in the center of its screen, as if some blunt object was thrown against it.

"Hey, Seth?" I call. He's already disappeared upstairs, though, and he doesn't answer. I should follow him. We should stay together. But there's a bad feeling surrounding the basement door, a feeling that's pulling me toward it in a way I can't explain.

"Seth?" I call again. Still no answer. I'm already moving again, my body in a sort of trance; I squeeze through the half-open door, and on the other side I stop, taking a moment to let my eyes adjust to the darkness.

Even before my mother declared it off limits, I never spent much time down here, so my brain's layout of the place is a bit fuzzy. I know there's one high-set window on the far side. I see the pale wave of sunlight washing through it and stretching toward the foot of the stairs, and it soothes some of the uneasiness in my chest. I take the steps one by one, moving in the direction of that light, listening closely and trying to anticipate all of the different angles my clone could possibly attack me from. I see all of the places she could hide, and I pause and stare long and hard at each one, silently watching for any sort of movement.

But when I reach the bottom, I still haven't seen anything. I sweep another glance over my surroundings, and a sudden memory strikes me: a clear picture of one of the few times I actually was down here. It was early summer, the first week we had off from school, and me and Old-Violet were running from Mother because we'd accidently knocked over and broken one of her favorite vases while we were jumping around on the living room furniture. Back then, cowering underneath the steps with my sister holding my shaking hand while Mother shouted from upstairs, was the most scared I'd ever been.

It's nothing compared with the fear driving my heart now. But the memory of it, bidden by the earthy metallic scent of this room, leaves behind the same hollow terror in my chest. It makes it hard to tell where my past and my present converge and separate. There's at least one thing that sets them apart, though: This present moment belongs to me and me alone. Because the moment they took my clone from her cell, our link—my link to Huxley and everything they've done—was severed. And something about that gives me the courage to keep moving.

The last step creaks as I lift my foot from it. The noise bounces around the room, settling and ringing in my ears so loudly that I can't focus on anything else. So I don't hear Jaxon come up beside me. I only hear his ever-calm voice say, "Don't move."

But how can I not move? How can I not turn to look at him? I have to see him.

Even in the dim light, I see the blood shadowing the entire right side of his face. He steps directly into the weary path of sunlight, and I see that his eyes are hard and unyielding, his mouth drawn in a harsh, even line.

He has a gun raised and pointed at me. I can tell he's trying desperately to keep the arm holding it straight. The muscles in it twitch and jump beneath his skin, and every few seconds a terrible shudder rips through it, all the way up into his shoulder.

"I said don't move," he says. A weak but somehow still violent-sounding cough follows the words. He closes his eyes for a split second, trying to focus. How much blood has he lost?

"Jaxon," I say slowly, carefully, "it's me."

"Don't—," he begins. He coughs, wipes away the blood that trickles out of his mouth, and tries again. "Don't make me kill you," he says. "Please."

"You don't want to kill me." My breath hitches in my throat at the thought. I reach for the gun without taking my eyes off his, but he stumbles back, trying to get away from me, and falls against the stair railing. "I'm the real one. The real Cate," I say, even though my words feel thin and pointless. Because he's not hearing me. He's not seeing me—not for the person I really am. He's too far gone. As far as he's concerned now, I am my clone, and who knows what I've done to him.

And who knows what else my clone did. What if she

went after my parents, too? What if I never see them again? What if I never get the chance to ask them *why*, to try to understand how things came to this? To try to fix things, somehow?

Jaxon closes his eyes again, and I know I can't waste any more time thinking. I throw myself on his arm and jerk the gun from his grip. He lets it go easily; it takes only my one good hand to work it free. And like that gun was the last thing anchoring him to reality, as soon as I step away his eyes roll back and his body convulses in a terrible sort of way; his hand slips from the stair railing and he starts to fall. I drop the gun and catch him as best I can, collapsing back to the stone floor underneath his weight.

His skin is flushed and hot to the touch, his breath just an occasional shudder in his chest. I see where all of the blood is coming from now—from the gash across the side of his face, and another one in the hollow of his throat. My fingers shake as they trace around the edges, trying to feel how deep the wounds are, trying to figure out what might have caused them. It could have been anything, though. When you're talking about the strength of a clone, any random object can potentially become a weapon.

Most of the blood, at least, is cold and dried. Not fresh. The bruises all over his skin concern me more, anyway. Because I know they might be signs of worse damage below the surface.

"What are you doing?" he asks suddenly. His eyes flash open and, after a few seconds of trying, he manages to get them to focus on me. "Why are you here?"

My mouth is too dry for me to speak at first. When I finally manage to, the words that come out of my mouth aren't just mine. They're mostly his. "Because there's something about you," I say softly. "Something that's never let me go, ever since the first day we met."

His eyes close for what feels like a long time. Then the corners of his lips turn up into that familiar smile, and it tells me that, somehow, even now he remembers what he said the other night.

"That moment in the hotel," I say, "after we blocked the signal. You held me, and I felt safe. It was me and you, and Huxley will never, ever have that memory. Nobody else will. Nobody but us. And we're going to have so much more that they're never going to get, I know we are, but you just have to stay awake. You have to keep looking at me. Jaxon?"

He keeps trying to speak, but it's hard to make sense of most of what he's saying. He's trying to explain what happened, I think. How he was tricked, and how close my clone came to finishing him off, and how the only reason she left was because they heard something upstairs—me and Seth and Violet. I don't even want to think about what would have happened if we'd arrived a few minutes later.

Or about where my clone's disappeared to now.

"I'm sorry," Jaxon says suddenly, his voice a bit stronger as his hand finds mine.

"Don't waste your energy apologizing, all right?"

"I understand how you felt now," he says. "About your

sister, I mean. Because I couldn't shoot either. She looked too much like you." He tries to laugh but ends up just wincing from pain. "And god knows I could never hurt you. . . . I couldn't even get mad at her. I was stupid to follow her in the first place. Maybe . . . maybe I should have known better, but I . . . I just . . ."

"You didn't know it wasn't me."

"It's hard to know, isn't it?" That strength is already fading again, the words getting more slurred, more difficult to follow every second.

"Maybe you shouldn't talk right now," I say. I feel something warm against my cheek, and I reach up and realize I've started crying; my skin is already covered in dried, sticky tears. I hastily wipe away any fresh ones. Crying isn't going to do anybody any good right now.

The movement makes his eyes blink open again.

"Don't do that," he says, shaking his head. It's obvious how painful just that simple motion is for him. "Please don't cry."

But that only makes it worse, and soon there's a wall of water blurring his face. And that only upsets me more, because right now I just need to see him. I just need to see life in his eyes, to watch his lips part as he breathes in, breathes out.

Please keep breathing.

I don't know what else to say. I don't know what to do. I feel so helpless holding him like this, like I should be picking him up and carrying him to someplace safe instead, to someone who can save him. But I can't move. I'm afraid to move him, and I don't think I could lift him, anyway. I try shouting for Seth, but the words scatter soundlessly into the air, like sand swept from my desert mouth.

His fingers are getting cold. So cold. I try to warm them with my own, but it's no use.

I can't just sit here and watch him die.

"I'm going to be right back," I say, gently laying him on the floor. I pick his gun back up and get to my feet. My balance sways dangerously, and I have to grab the banister to steady myself. I take a deep breath.

"I'm going to get Seth," I tell Jaxon, even though the thought of leaving him behind now—even just for a minute—makes me sick in the worst possible way. "And the other CCA people . . . I . . . I bet they're here by now. I bet they're looking for us, and for you, and I'll bring them here, and then we'll take you to the hospital and you'll be fine. You're going to be fine." I push out the nasty voice in my mind that wonders how much of him is already damaged beyond repair, even if he's still alive when we get to that hospital.

"I won't be long," I say, my voice breaking. "And I swear you better still be breathing when I get back, or I'm going to be so pissed, it's not even funny."

I want to ask him if he understands what I'm saying. I want to make him tell me—make him promise me—that he'll still be here when I get back. But I'm afraid he won't answer. So I take one more deep breath, and I press my free hand to his cold, clammy cheek. It's probably my imagination at this point, but I could swear I feel him lean into my touch. The pressure on my wrist sends pain shooting up my arm. But it doesn't matter. Because in that moment, it literally feels like the weight of his whole life is in my hand, and no amount of pain could take my mind off that.

I choke down a breath, turn, and run as fast as I can up the stairs.

Seth. I have to find Seth. Or Violet, or the CCA members. Somebody. Anybody.

At the top of the steps, I don't even slow down; in one fluid motion I'm darting, squeezing my way back through the small space between the wall and the ajar door. I'm still going so fast when I reach the other side that I can't stop in time to avoid colliding with the person standing there. I take less than the span of a second to compose myself in their shadow before I look up. A gasp escapes my lips.

Because it's not Seth staring back at me. Or Violet.

It's myself.

CHAPTER TWENTY-THREE

The Way It Ends

She is my perfect copy.

Completely.

Perfect.

I wouldn't be so surprised, maybe, if they hadn't gone above and beyond to make her look exactly as I do now; she even has a fresh scar just below her eye, and her dark copper bangs are cut at the same angle, to the same length, as mine. Which just proves that this was completely planned by Huxley. While I was locked in that room for god knows how long, they put the final touches on her and then set her after Jaxon. For revenge, maybe, like Violet said, or maybe just to distract President Cross from her assault on their headquarters. Either way, I should have known they would use him—that they would use everything between us—to whatever advantage they could, no matter how low it meant they had to stoop.

The night I walked away from him, I think this is exactly what I was afraid of, even if I couldn't put it into words then. This is exactly why I wanted to do it. Because of course Jaxon couldn't tell the difference between us. And even if he had been able to, I don't think it would have mattered.

Because she's too fast.

Her hand catches me in the stomach, throws me back against the basement door. She's in my face an instant later.

"Hello, origin," she says, smiling sweetly. The reflection of my green eyes in hers gives her gaze an infinite, bottomless look. While I'm staring into them I can't think about the pain of her hand pressing up into my rib cage, or of my wrist throbbing from being slammed against the door; I can only think about the pain she's caused everyone else by stealing those eyes. By pretending to be someone she's not. Did she look at Jaxon the same way she's looking at me now? And my parents? Did she smile at all of them? I wonder if it was the last thing they saw before she hit them, bruised them, broke them.

It won't be the last thing I see.

Jaxon's gun is still in my hand.

I get it twisted around, aimed as well as I can in the small space between her hip and mine, and pull the trigger. Light and heat explode between us with more force than I was anticipating; the flash is similar to the one a distress disc gives off, and for several seconds afterward I'm blind. My surroundings come back to me in slow motion, white pinpricks of light still flitting in front of my eyes as my clone materializes in front of me. She's down on one knee and holding her side, her fingers pressed against her charred shirt and the bloody strip of skin showing through it.

I still haven't fully caught my breath after being thrown

into the door. But I can't miss this chance to escape, so I peel away from the support of it and half sprint, half stumble toward the living room. I need to get to someplace more open, to someplace where I have a better chance of getting behind her. Because I remember what Violet said when we fought Samantha: Aim for the back of the head. That's where the central processing unit is. That's the best—maybe the only—way to stop her.

I reach the living room just as I hear her footsteps thundering behind me, and I make the mistake of glancing over my shoulder. Her fist is right there to meet me. I twist violently to the side, and her swing ends up just grazing my cheekbone. I still lose my footing and fall over one of the side tables; I hit the floor on my hands and knees. My gun goes flying, and my head just barely misses the corner of my father's armchair. I kick up and back as hard as I can, catching the glass-topped table from underneath and knocking it into my clone's path so she ends up tripping too. While she stumbles, I scramble after the gun, grab it, and aim directly for her chest.

But when I pull the trigger, it doesn't fire.

I shake the gun, and a strange rattling sound echoes in the handle; something must have been knocked loose when I dropped it. Cursing under my breath, I switch the useless gun to my hand with the weak wrist and use my good hand to grab everything I can reach and fling it at my clone. The TV remote, the picture frames I knocked off the table, that ugly angel figurine my mother loves so much. I throw it all. The figurine's wing catches her just below the eye and reopens the cut there; while she wipes away the fresh blood, I jump to my feet and start to run. I'm not sure where I'm going—or what I'm going to do—exactly; if I don't have a functioning gun, how am I supposed to stop her?

Shouldn't I have backup by now? Where are the rest of the CCA people? Where is Seth? Violet? Maybe if I can just get to them, or just stay alive long enough to let them get to me . . .

Except meanwhile, Jaxon is dying in the basement, and I still don't know where my parents are. I need to put a stop to this, so I can focus on finding help.

I cut a sharp right into the kitchen, thinking I'll be able to find some sort of weapon in there. I dive behind the island and fling open the drawer above me, sift through the useless slotted spoons and tongs and other not exactly lethal weapons until my hand falls on the grip of the biggest knife we have.

The trick, of course, is going to be getting close enough to my clone to actually do any damage with it.

It's better than being unarmed, though. I set the malfunctioning gun, which is now making a pitiful buzzing noise, safely inside one of the cabinets. Then I gently shut the cabinet door and press back against it, holding my breath and listening to my clone's voice carrying down the hall.

"Come on now," she calls. "Let's be reasonable about this. We can't *both* live, now can we? That would just get confusing. There can only be one you, and I think we can both agree that I'm the more impressive one." She's silent for a minute, and the next words she speaks aren't softened by any walls between us; she sounds like she's standing in the doorway of the kitchen. "Huxley has done this country a favor, you know, by creating us. We're going to bring this country back from the edge, and it's going to be even better than before. It's going to be perfect."

She moves slowly into the kitchen, each unhurried step unbearably loud against the tile floor. Something slams on the counter above me—her fists, maybe—and I jump and scrape my back against the metal doorknob of the cabinet. The handle of the knife is slick and covered with sweat from my shaking hand gripping it too tightly.

"I have a lot of things to do, origin," she says. "An entire bright, new future to help build."

A future that doesn't belong to you, I want to shout. Just like all of the horrible things she's done don't belong to me, and the things I've done don't belong to her. She's an actress. The same way I used to put on all those costumes and memorize all those lines—that's all she's done. She has my mask. My costume. But those things don't make her anything more than a stolen life parading around in a stolen body.

And I'm going to take it back.

She's stopped talking. Stopped moving. I don't even hear her breathing; all I hear is the beating of my own heart as I edge my way along the island. I get to the corner and press even closer to the smooth wood, curving my neck in an awkward, uncomfortable angle so I can peer around.

She's gone.

This is not good.

It happens in a flurry of noise—a thump against the granite countertop, the clanking and clattering of pots and pans being knocked from the ceiling rack they hang from. And her breathing, calm and deep, as if she's savoring the moment, just waiting for me to look up and find her staring down at me.

She jumps.

I thrust the knife up and feel pressure—her tough, biologically enhanced skin resisting at first—and then finally it pierces, allowing the blade to sink in deep, just beneath her rib cage. Blood drips down over the knife, winding a hot, sticky trail down my arm. Her face is right in front of mine, our noses practically touching and her strangely sweet-smelling breath washing over me.

"Why would you do that to your own body?" she asks through clenched teeth. It's hard to tell if the look in her eyes is pain, or just insanity.

"You aren't me," I say, twisting the knife until she jerks away in obvious agony and I'm able to roll out from underneath her. She tries to grab me by the ankle, but I manage a well-placed kick to her face, right between her eyes. It slows her down just long enough for me to get to my feet.

I don't stay on them long.

She's lost her patience. That much is very obvious very quickly. With a blood-chilling scream she dives after me, and her arms wrap around my waist and drag me down. I hit the tile face-first and feel my lip split, taste the blood rising between my teeth. The knife slips out of my hand. By the time I manage to flip myself onto my back, my clone already has it in her hand. She looms over me, one impossibly strong hand pinning my chest down while the other traces the tip of its blade across my neck. My skin isn't like hers; it's not nearly as tough, and soon I feel little beads of blood bubbling up and spilling across it.

She pulls the blade away and leans her face closer to mine.

"Good-bye." It's the only thing she says, and there's no grand flourish to it—just a simple, whispered word without malice or pain or intent. It just is. And in the split second between the word and the action, I decide that this is how I would have wanted to go, anyway; no dramatic flourishes for once. I just am, and then I just won't be, and that's how it should go.

She raises the knife and stabs.

My eyes are closed before the knife comes all the way down. So I don't see the exact moment when she's hit; but I can feel her body being knocked off me, and I can sense the sudden emptiness above; I open my eyes just as Violet gets a solid grip on my clone's arm. She swings, sending her flying back into the kitchen island. I hear the wooden cabinets crack and split as she slams into them, and the soft groan she lets out as her body slumps against the floor. Then there's no sound except the beating of Violet's heart and mine, and the charging hum of the gun in her hand.

"How did you know which of us was the real me?" I ask, breathless.

"Lucky guess." Violet shrugs. "And I figured you'd be the one losing."

I make a face. "Thanks." Even now, she just can't help herself, can she?

"Welcome," she says, and then she lifts the gun and starts to turn toward my clone. To finish this.

But she's not fast enough.

Her face is still tilted toward mine when the shot hits her in the back of the head.

The moment unfolds the way I imagine the glass covering our family photo broke: a strike to the center, cracks slowly branching toward the edges. And then everything shatters.

Violet's eyes blink several times, rapid and twitching. Even when they close, I can still see them moving beneath her lids, darting frantically around. Then they open and widen slowly, her irises like dark ink bleeding into a perfect circle on the page. Her body crumples, falling sideways into my arms. I push her back, hold her out in front of me and try to get her to look at me, shake her and try to get her to say something.

"Violet? Violet!"

Her body goes limp, turns to dead weight that my tired, exhausted body can hold up for only so long. My broken wrist feels like it's on fire from the pressure. My knees start to buckle. When the gun drops from Violet's hand, I let myself drop with it.

But my clone is already back on her feet, and she's holding my weapon from earlier—the one I thought was broken. How did she get it to work? And how is she still standing, still walking toward me so easily? Violet couldn't even slow her down. How am I supposed to stop her?

"Why do you look so upset?" She smiles knowingly, stepping toward me. "This is what you wanted, isn't it?"

I shake my head, over and over, but I can't seem to get any words to come out of my mouth.

"You can't hide how you feel from me, you know. Your thoughts are mine. Every single hateful thought you had about her? I have it too, stored nice and safe in this brain of mine. So I know you were jealous of all the attention she drew. I know you were disgusted by the show she put on. I know she never took the first Violet's place."

"Shut up."

"We both know you never saw her as your real sister."

"I said shut up!" I carefully push Violet's body out of my lap, grab her gun, and jump to my feet, a mixture of rage and adrenaline fueling me.

"I know about this anger, too," my clone says, still smiling. "I expected it. Because I know you hate this life. You hate the things your parents have done. You hate your first sister for dying, and you hated this Violet for living. You hated it all so much that you hid in the shadows and wasted every second, every breath you had, trying to pretend to be somebody else. Just like a human, to waste the gift of life." Her smile becomes a smirk. "But don't worry. I'm going to make up for it. I have big plans for Catelyn Benson."

"I've got bigger plans," I say.

That smirk only widens.

Because she obviously doesn't know everything I do. She doesn't have the moments I blocked from her. She doesn't know about the way Jaxon held me, or about Seth's teasing, and she doesn't see what I've only just realized about Violet—that despite the storm that's always raged between us, she's never failed to fight her way back to my side. That she's all wrong in so many different ways, but she's still my sister in every way that counts.

My clone doesn't get that.

It's too late for her to see and understand everything I have to live for.

She lifts her gun.

I lift my sister's gun, and I fire first.

My shot hits her directly in the stomach, just above the cut I made with the knife. She stumbles back but manages to fire at me at the same time; the shot hits my own gun and sends it flying, leaving behind a nasty-looking burn on my hand.

She's still on the ground, which gives me enough time to run for the door. And I've never moved so desperately— because now I have an idea. I know exactly where and how to end this. I just have to get there first.

A red-hot bullet hits the door frame. Misses me. Barely. I've taken only one step into the hall, though, when the knife flies through the air and lodges deep into the back of my leg, cutting straight through my skin as easily as if it were made of air. I stumble, and my hand automatically reaches for the handle of the knife; I stop myself from pulling it out, though. I don't remember where I heard this, or why I know it, but I know that taking the blade out will only increase the amount of blood lost if you can't apply pressure right away—and I can't stop to apply pressure. I have to keep moving.

Because my clone is moving too. Slowly but surely; I can hear her stumbling through the kitchen, knocking utensils and dishes from the countertops, shouting threats in between gasps for air. She sounds like she's struggling too now, at least.

I stagger toward my room, the knife bouncing around and shooting searing pain in every direction, up and down my leg. *This is where it will end*, I keep telling myself. *I just have to keep going a little bit longer.* Because she thinks she knows everything about me. She's so sure that she has me all figured out—so she'll think I'm running to hide. Because that's what Catelyn Benson was always so good at, wasn't it? She knows all about my favorite safe, quiet place.

So that's where I'm running to.

But I'm not going there to hide.

When I reach my room, though, that's exactly what I try to stage. My desperate flight into hiding. I move to the closet, leaving a bloody trail in my wake, and I push my clothes in random directions to imitate my hurried attempt to get to that safe, hidden space. When I back away, I grab a long-sleeved shirt, because I know I'm going to need it when I have to pull this knife out, and I leave the door cracked just slightly.

Then I scramble into the tiny space between my bed and the wall.

And I wait.

It isn't long before I hear her footsteps coming up the hall. I wrap the shirt around my leg and get it ready to tie. I grab a wad of the quilt hanging off my bed and shove it in my mouth, bite down on it as hard as I can as I take the handle of the knife in my grip. My arm shakes, and the seared skin of my palm stings as I put pressure on it. My hold with this hand is unsteady and awkward, but with the other wrapped up and useless, and that wrist still burning with pain, I don't have any choice but to use it.

I close my eyes.

I think about Jaxon pressing against my hand. I think about Violet collapsing into my arms. I think about my parents, and our shattered family portrait, and the world outside falling to ruin at the hands of Huxley. At the hands of my own clone.

Then I pull the knife out.

I manage to bite down hard enough to stop the scream, but my eyes water so much that it takes me a minute to find the ends of the shirtsleeves and get them tied into a makeshift tourniquet. After that's done, the pain becomes a steady throb—not as bad as I was expecting, but I wonder if the true pain is only numbed from shock. Blood is already soaking through the thin cotton shirt, turning the light blue color to a dark navy.

I have a decent weapon now, though—one much

sharper than the butter knife under my bed that I would have had to use otherwise.

A second later, I hear my clone walk into the room.

"Hiding again?" she says. "Do you honestly think you can hide from me?"

She wanders close—too close—to the bed. I want to crawl farther underneath it, but I'm afraid moving will pull the quilt and she'll see it. So I just hold my breath and keep perfectly still until she finally turns around and walks back toward the closet.

"If I was Catelyn Benson, where would I hide?" she muses. "Oh, wait. I am Catelyn Benson, aren't I? So this should be easy."

I hear the closet door swing open. I take a deep breath. She's still talking, but I can't make out anything she's saying now because her voice is muffled—both from the closet walls as she slips farther inside and from the thrumming in my own ears as my brain tries to help me not dwell on what I'm about to do.

I don't remember moving. But suddenly I'm pressed against the wall outside the closet. And then I end up behind her the same way. Her hair—my hair—is pulled up, and I have a clear view of exactly where I need to stab. She begins to turn around.

This time, she's the one who's too late.

When my head stops pounding, when my eyes are able to make out distinct shapes again, I watch my clone only long enough to see that she's not moving anymore. Then I drop the knife from my trembling hand, and I stagger back out into the bright light of my room. Except it doesn't feel like my room anymore. Nothing feels like it's mine anymore.

I leave the room and pull myself along the wall, down the hallway, and back to the kitchen. The shirt-tourniquet is completely soaked with blood at this point. I've lost the feeling in that leg, and I'm starting to lose it in the other one and in the tips of my fingers as well. My vision is past blurry. The room is spinning, careening, crashing in around me.

Somehow I find Violet, and I drop to my knees and lie down beside her. She blinks once and reaches for me.

And so this is the way my world really ends. Side by side with my sister, her hand going cold in mine.

CHAPTER TWENTY-FOUR

Slipping

There's a strength inside you that exists, whether you want it to or not. It waits until you're ready to give up, until you want nothing more than to close your eyes and never have to face the pain of sunlight again. And then it shows up.

And it makes you get to your feet.

I go to the yard. I meet the CCA people when they pull into the driveway, and I tell them where Jaxon is, and I tell them where Violet is, and I tell them the last place I saw Seth. I don't know what to tell them about my parents.

Part of me knows it is too late for all of them. Far, far too late. I was asleep for too long. Jaxon and Violet were slipping already, and Seth . . . I never saw him after I left the basement, which makes me wonder if my clone ran into him first.

But still I tell the CCA—President Cross herself—to hurry. Maybe there's a chance.

Hurry, hurry, hurry. Please hurry.

I watch them run into the house.

And then I lie down in my father's perfectly manicured grass, and I stare at our perfect white house with its perfect porch and perfect windows and perfect outside everything, until my vision blurs and the darkness takes me back.

Answers

Life comes back to me slowly at first, and then all at once in an explosion of colors and sounds. When it all settles, I manage to focus on a single sensation—the feel of fingertips softly tracing my palm.

I lift my head from the pillow and see Jaxon sitting beside the bed, his eyes closed and his body leaned forward in almost-sleep. His head, his shoulder, his arm—his whole body, it seems—is covered in bandages. The skin that isn't covered is bruised, some of it swollen. I close my hand over his tracing fingers and he jumps, his gaze snapping to mine.

Neither of us speaks. The moment lives on a breath held collectively between us, until we exhale as a single, tired being; then he stands up so quick that his chair topples behind him, and next thing I know he's leaning over me and carefully, gently, pressing his lips to mine. He holds them there for a long time. Long enough for most of what we need to say to pass between us, so that when he finally pulls away we still don't speak for a long time.

The first words that I find are simple, obvious. "You're alive. You're okay." It's all I can think right away, and everything after that is just question after question about *how* he's alive. And how I'm alive. And I'm really alive, aren't I? This isn't pretend, this isn't something I'm making up inside my head, right?

Most of Jaxon's answers—about the CCA, about the doctors, about Huxley—he only gets halfway through before having to stop and take my face in his hands and kiss me again. It takes us a long time to make sense of everything. And even then I feel like we don't have all the answers. Maybe we never will.

After the destruction of most of their lab, thanks largely to the quickly spreading fire that started in room B13, most of Huxley's scientists have retreated to other divisions in other cities. They can regroup there, but Haven was their main headquarters—so running them away from here, slowing their plans . . . it should feel like a victory.

I guess I'm just not in the mood to celebrate.

I keep going back to my memory of that holding room, to the way I felt when I saw those bodies suspended there. . . . I'd thought about breaking the glass. Even if it might have killed them, I wondered if it would have been better. Is that why Violet started the fire there? To stop them from waking up, and to save them from everything she'd had to go through? Or did she wake them up and free them before she set anything on fire? Could she have managed something like that?

"And I thought that was it," Jaxon is saying. "When I watched you walk up the basement steps. I thought that was it."

"I didn't want to leave you," I say, after he's repeated

that for the fifth time, and I finally manage to stop wondering about the fate of the clones long enough to look him in the eyes. "I never wanted to leave. I went to find Seth, to find help . . ."

Seth.

"What happened to Seth?" I ask. "Is he okay?"

"Yeah. Thanks to your sister."

"My sister?"

He nods. "Apparently, she managed to barricade him in the attic before she went after your clone. He's pissed about missing all the action, of course, but to be honest, she . . . she probably saved his life." His voice trails off toward the end, and his cheeks flush a bit as he fidgets with one of the bandages on his arm. "Anyway, he was in here earlier. He was worried about you, too—don't tell him I said that—but you know how his attention span is. He went to find something to distract himself with, I think."

I try to smile, but now my mind is slowly getting back to a functioning calmness, and I find myself with still more questions, each one more painful, more terrifying to ask, than the last. What happened to Violet? My parents? Is anything left of my home now? Where am I supposed to go?

What am I supposed to do now?

None of the questions make it to my lips. I'll ask them soon enough, I know. I'll have to. But right now I want to keep them close to my heart, and instead I want to focus on just this—on the sound of Jaxon's voice, and his touch, and the way the bed sinks a little under his weight when he leans in to kiss me again.

His lips are still hovering close to mine when someone clears their throat from the doorway. Jaxon slowly leans back, and I see his mother standing in the doorway, watching us from beneath raised eyebrows.

"I see she's doing much better," she says. Not unkindly. She sounds relieved, almost—even if it is in a reluctant sort of way, and I'm guessing she's actually more relieved for her son's sake than for mine.

I sit the rest of the way up. I move as slowly as I can, but the motion still makes my head spin. Jaxon offers me his arm; I take it and he helps me to my feet and then across the room to his mother, who seems to be making a genuine attempt to smile at the two of us being so close to each other. She's not quite pulling it off, but at least she's making the effort. I'll take that as hope for the future.

"There are a couple of people who wish to speak with you, Catelyn," President Cross says.

"Who?"

"You'll see" is all she says, and then she turns and disappears into the hall. I follow slowly, my steps shaky and my head still swimming.

Once I'm in the hall, I start to see things I recognize, and I realize I'm back at the CCA's headquarters. Things look a lot different from the last time I was here, thankfully. No dead bodies this time.

The president leads me to a small room with mismatched furniture and a handful of generic paintings slapped onto the cream-colored walls. It looks like an uncomfortable family room, put together by someone who had no concept of family. I sit on the stiff couch. President Cross leaves and insists that Jaxon go with her.

And as they're walking out, my parents walk in.

Because I guess sometimes life has a way of forcing answers on you, even if you're too scared to ask the questions.

I'm glad to see them. I'm glad they're alive. Of course I'm glad, and I run straight to my mother—who's obviously been crying—and I throw my arms around her, and then I even start to cry too. And I don't flinch when my father kisses the top of my head, and I don't complain when my mother hugs me tighter and tighter still, until I can hardly breathe.

But there's an emptiness between us now, even if my mother leaves no space between our embrace. And I'm not sure what to fill it with. Anger is the simplest filling. So that's what hits me first. I'm angry about what I had to do, about all the blood that's ended up on my hands. About everything me and Violet had to go through. I'm angry and I don't understand, and so instead of *I love you* or *I'm so glad you're okay* or anything like that, when I find my voice this time the first word I think of is "Why?"

My parents stare at me for a long time after I ask the question.

It's my mother who finally moves first. She doesn't speak right away but instead takes off the jacket that hides those strange marks on her arms. She looks sadly at the bruised, mutated flesh, like I've seen her do so many times in the mirror. Then she takes a deep breath and says, "We never could have guessed that it would come to something like this."

She clears her throat and tries to force her expression back to unreadable, unbreakable stone. When she can't manage to do that, she focuses intently on pulling her jacket back on and buttoning every button, even though it has to be eighty degrees in here.

"Desperation," she finally continues, "can make a person do unthinkable things. And war can make you unbelievably desperate." She pauses, tugs on the hem of her jacket, and tries to flatten away wrinkles that are hardly there. "By the time you and Violet were born, we'd already seen too much. We'd watched too many people die. Too many children. Too many people we knew. Nothing felt certain about the future anymore—originally, we weren't even going to have children because of that, and we were told that we probably wouldn't be able to anyway"—she rolls up her right sleeve just enough to uncover one of the marks—"because of this."

She tries to keep going but chokes up. I feel like I should interrupt the silence in some way, but I don't know what to say or what to do with this new version of my mother who's suddenly talking and actually explaining herself. If I say the wrong thing, is she going to go away again? I want to just wait, to stay here a little longer and try to understand.

"But then we managed not one but two miracles," she

finally says. "And then Huxley came to us and told us they could guarantee that no one could take those miracles away. So what do you think we did?"

She meets my eyes then, and we're the only two in the room, and suddenly I don't want to be angry anymore.

My father puts an arm around her, but she twists away and goes to stand by the door. Her face stays tilted away from us. I can tell she regrets choking up like that and crying over the memory of Violet's sickness and everything else. A few days ago, I would have gotten mad all over again at the way she's gone silent and stone faced. I would have wished desperately for her to lower her defenses, for her to let the rest of the world in. To let me in. But now I see that it's never been about keeping everyone out. It's been about keeping herself together.

All she's ever tried to do was keep us all together.

The only problem is that sometimes, when you hold things too tightly, you end up crushing them and losing them anyway.

I feel my father's hand on my arm, and it gives me the strength to ask the question I've been the most afraid of since I woke up.

"How is my sister?"

He gives me a gentle squeeze. "I don't know if now is a good time for you to see her."

One day, I might tell him everything that's happened these past few days, in detail, and maybe it will convince him to stop trying to protect me from everything. Probably not. But maybe. For now, though, I just give him the most reassuring hug I can, and I head out to find the answer for myself.

I run into President Cross a few minutes later, and she takes me to the room where Violet is resting. Her eyes are closed, her breathing slow, her body completely unresponsive when I touch her arm. She has computers and IVs and an assortment of other equipment all hooked up to her.

"Physically, her body seems to be doing fine," the president says. "These clones really are something, biologically speaking."

"But mentally?"

"You were with her when she was shot, weren't you?"

I nod.

"Her CPU was fried, melted and destroyed beyond repair. We can replace it, I think, but most of the data on it isn't going to be recoverable. Huxley had backup copies, I'm sure, but in a bit of an ironic twist of fate, the stunt she pulled probably means they were reduced to ashes along with the majority of the rest of the lab. If there are any surviving copies, tracking them down won't be easy.

"So, if she manages to pull through, physically speaking, she will not be the same Violet. She won't even remember her name is Violet." She hesitates. "Nor will she remember you, or anything else about her past life. Or lives, as it were."

I sit down on the little bit of bed that isn't taken up by Violet, or any of the life-giving apparatuses attached to her. For a long time I watch her breathing, stare at her eyelids closed in what I assume must be dreamless sleep. "But will she be able to function?" I ask. The thought is bittersweet, I admit. I want her to live, of course. But what will it be like when she looks at me as if I'm a stranger? Somehow, I think that would be worse than all our fighting. Like indifference would be worse than any of the hate that existed between us.

"That's what we're working on," President Cross says, motioning to the computer monitors surrounding the bed. "We're not Huxley, but we do have a few brilliant scientists on our side too—including yours truly. And this is something we've been developing for years—we've been trying to create a fully functional brain module like the ones Huxley uses. But in our case, the brain is more or less a blank slate with only the more basic human functions programmed in."

"A blank slate?"

"To start with, yes. But our programming will allow more room for it to grow, for the clones to develop into something more human—something that Huxley was trying to prevent. We're embracing it, though, and in this way we hope to take back the lives that Huxley stole."

"Why?" I can't help but ask. "I thought you hated clones. Why are you helping Violet? Why are you worried about giving her any sort of life at all?"

"You simplify our ambitions," she says. "To let her—or any clone in our possession—die would be to lose a very powerful potential ally in the fight against Huxley. She's essentially a superhuman—a marvel of biology. You've witnessed that firsthand, haven't you?"

"So you want her to fight for you."

"If she chooses."

"You're honestly going to give her a choice?" I spit the words, poisoned with doubt, from my mouth.

"She attempted to burn Huxley's laboratory to the ground." She tilts her head toward me, looking almost amused. "It would seem she's already made her choice."

"She didn't do that for you." I may not ever know exactly why she *did* do it, but I know it wasn't for the CCA.

She smiles tactfully, pulls out a keyboard from beneath one of the monitors, and starts typing. "Nevertheless," she says offhandedly, "I feel like we have the potential for a mutually beneficial relationship. And you could be included in it if you like. Because, after all, I'd be lying if I said the scientist in me wasn't as interested as Huxley was in your relationship with your sister. You're what kept her human—I believe that was their hypothesis, and it's mine as well. And of course now I'm wondering; how will things work out between the two of you when she wakes up?"

She stops messing with the keyboard and slides it back into place. "Besides, I can't help feeling like my son would be glad to have you around more," she adds, turning to leave. "So think about it, won't you?"

And I do. For at least an hour I stay by Violet's side, thinking about it. I'm still thinking about it when I leave the headquarters and go back to the parking garage and find myself a spot to sit on a concrete wall overlooking the city.

It's unnaturally quiet. The lights are off, the cars are

parked, the sidewalks all but empty. People are scared, I guess. And confused. I wonder what's on the news, and how sensationalized the story of what happened between Huxley and the CCA has already become. I wonder what's happening to other families like ours. Jaxon told me that a lot of clones have been reported missing—retreated with Huxley, they think. But what about the ones who didn't? Maybe, with the destruction of so much of the lab's equipment and files, there's a chance that some of the already active clones will now be able to live without having to worry about Huxley interfering with their thoughts and memories.

They'll still be clones, though. And after everything that's happened, in the aftermath of all this violence and the fear it's sent through the city, it will only be worse for them.

So maybe they'll all stay inside forever, hiding. I wouldn't blame them if they did, because I'm only just getting used to this new skin myself, to the Catelyn Benson who doesn't want to hide from all this. And even as I'm sitting here, I think of getting up and going to find my parents, of telling them we should pack up and leave it all behind. To move out of the country, even. Away from the CCA, away from Huxley, away from everything that's happened here. Part of me keeps wishing I knew of a place where none of these things could find me.

But I'm still sitting on that wall when Jaxon shows up what might be minutes, or maybe hours, later, for all the attention I'm paying to time right then.

"I was afraid you'd already run off on me," he says.

"I'm trying out this new thing where I don't run and hide anymore."

"How's that working out for you?"

I meet his eyes as he sits down beside me. "It's going pretty good, now," I say. Now that he's here, staying doesn't seem all that bad.

"It's strange to see it so quiet," he says, turning his attention to the cityscape in front of us.

"Makes it easier to think, at least."

"What are you thinking about?"

"You really want to know?"

"Desperately."

So I tell him. Everything that my parents told me. Everything his mother said. All the parts that hurt, and all the parts that confuse, and even all the parts that I want to bury out of existence. He listens patiently, silently, and when I finish he stays quiet for a long time, a thoughtful look on his face.

"I'm not really sure how I'm supposed to feel about everything," I admit.

He's silent for another minute and then asks, "What are you going to do when Violet wakes up?"

"I don't know." I meet his gaze again. "Start over, I guess."

It wouldn't be so bad, maybe, to have a second chance. Especially knowing what I know now. If Violet wakes up again and she's not the same, it's not like I wouldn't have seen it coming. I've been there before. She was never the same. But maybe just because people don't turn out to be what you expect them to be, or follow the path you want them to . . . I don't know. Maybe that doesn't mean they've gotten lost. And maybe just because they don't love you the way you want them to, it doesn't mean they aren't doing the best they can. So it could still be okay in the end.

Jaxon doesn't say anything else for a long time. I lean against his shoulder and close my eyes. He wraps his arm around my waist, and I let my mind drift to safer places, back to the first day we met, back to the first time I got in his car. Before everything got so complicated.

"Speaking of starting over," he eventually says, "that whole date we went on the other day? In retrospect, it turned out to be pretty terrible, especially for our first one. We should probably start over too."

I laugh, then take his hand and give it a squeeze. "Okay. But we're getting my family's driver to chauffeur us this time."

His gaze meets mine, and that smile I've been in love with from the first time I saw him is suddenly there, brighter than I've seen it in a really long time.

"Deal," he agrees.

And then he laces his fingers through mine and leans in close again, and together we watch the shadow of night fall over the city.